It Comes Back to You

Amelia C Rose

Paperback ISBN: 979-8-9999317-0-2

First Paperback Edition January 2026

Edited by Emilie Ocean Editing Services

Cover art and design by LoveLitDesign

It Comes Back to You

To those who thought their past limited them, I hope you take that
leap into the beautiful unknown.

Dear reader,

Thank you for picking up *It Comes Back to You*. At its core, this story is about overcoming grief, learning to accept love, and learning to love others. There are strong familial relationships and plenty of happy moments that intertwine through grief and sadness.

Some of the mature themes mentioned include: explicit sexual scenes meant for adults only, death of a parent (mentioned but off-page), death of a sibling (described after the fact), vehicle accident that results in death (described), motorcycle accident that results in injury, hospital stay, grief, depression, and anxiety.

This is a romance and ends in a happily-ever-after. I hope you enjoy this story as much as I enjoyed writing it.

Love,

Amelia

Playlist

The following songs, in no particular order, helped inspire me as I wrote Kat and Sam's story.

Contents

Chapter 1

I t isn't until I glance up at the clock on the wall opposite my desk that I realize I'm late for lunch with Liv. "Shit," I mutter to myself as I quickly hit save on the draft I'm working on and rush out of my office building.

I practically ran down the street to the restaurant where we were supposed to meet 10 minutes ago. I know she'll understand, but I still hate being late to our lunches.

Olivia and I have been friends since we were kids, and I was over-the-moon excited when she moved to Columbia with me. Her office, where she works as an interior designer, is a couple of blocks from mine. Even though we live together, we meet for lunch whenever we can.

I remind myself to slow down as I approach the restaurant. Walking in, I immediately spot Liv at a table and see she's already ordered drinks for us—her long, blonde hair glistens in the sun shining through the window. I used to wish my light brown hair looked more like hers. But I've learned to love my uniqueness.

Liv is wearing a funky, burnt orange, boho-style shirt with long sleeves shaped like bells. Her outfit starkly contrasts with my simple black A-line dress and gray suit jacket. I laugh at myself as I think about how perfectly our respective outfits match our personalities.

"Liv," I say, a little out of breath.

"You went into hyperfocus mode again, didn't you, Katherine?" Her vivid blue eyes gleam with laughter I know she's trying to hold back. Ugh, I know I'm in trouble when she uses my full first name.

"I'm so sorry! I've been working on this motion all morning, and I was just in the groove and lost track of time." The words come out too fast as I sit down across from her.

"No biggie. I get it." She shrugs, eyes still gleaming. "But that's why I ordered you unsweetened tea, ya bitch!" A grin spreads across her face as she gestures at the drink on the table in front of me. I groan internally. I hate unsweetened anything.

"I deserve that. I would say it won't happen again, but you and I both know that would be a lie." I give her a contrite expression and stare at the offending unsweetened tea.

"So," I begin slowly, "how did dinner go last night? You got home late." I take a sip of my tea and grimace. Placing the glass back on the table, I search for a packet of sugar and sigh, resigned, when I don't find any. I settle for putting my hands in my lap.

Liv blows out a breath. "Fuck, dinner was rough. I swear, Talia's dad hates me. Or maybe not *me*, but the concept of me. I'm the first girlfriend she's brought home, and I think her dad was... I don't know... shocked? That I'm a woman." Liv audibly breathes and spins her glass on the table. "I know she talked to her family beforehand, but I think her dad seeing me made everything more real to him. I don't think he's handling the fact that his *baby girl* is gay very well."

"Yikes. I'm so sorry."

"Yeah, well, we both knew going into this that there would be challenges." She sips on her drink, "I really like her. I want this to work, but sometimes I worry about our families accepting us. Because... fuck everyone else that judges us for who we are. But not having our families on our side? I think that would crush us both."

The server takes this moment to ask us if we know what we want to order. We've been here more times than I can count, so I don't have to look at the menu. Once we place our orders, the server leaves us to our conversation.

"Do you think your parents wouldn't accept Talia?"

She shakes her head, her hair swaying with the movement. "No. They've known for a while who I like. It's really about her family accepting her, and then accepting me. She's kept that side hidden from her family for a long time, even though she's dated other women."

"I guess the bright side is that she obviously cares about you since she's ready to share this part of herself with her family. If you have strong feelings for her, just give them time to accept her *and* you."

"Yeah, you're right." She spins her glass on the table again. "You know, Sam called me yesterday afternoon." Liv's voice is tentative. The last thing I want to do is talk about Sam. But she continues before I can stop her. "Do you think you'll ever let him back in?"

Frowning at her words, I fiddle with my hands under the table, nervous and a little upset with the turn of conversation. "Liv, please."

Samuel Harris is my brother Ethan's best friend. We all grew up together. Ethan and Sam are the same age, two years older than me. When we were kids, Ethan, Sam, Liv, and I were inseparable. We would frequently come up with wild schemes. When we weren't scheming, we were out riding our bikes through the neighborhood.

"Come on, Kat. It's been years," she scolds me, making me feel like a berated child.

"Yeah," I lean back in my chair, "and I still don't know how to have a relationship with him when I still—I don't know how—I don't want to talk about this." I glare at the glass of unsweetened tea again, avoiding Liv's attention.

"I'm sorry, I just—"

"I know." It comes out softer than before. I know she means well. This isn't the first time we've had this conversation.

I'm saved from talking about Sam when our food comes, matching grilled chicken, spinach, and strawberry salads with balsamic vinaigrette dressing. We quickly eat our food, partly because I was late for lunch and partly because she has a client meeting to get to, and I have a document I need to finish writing.

***

I'm back at the office and deep into the draft again when my phone starts ringing, interrupting the music playing through my earbuds.

Looking around my desk, I realize that, distracted, I left my phone in my purse after lunch. Sam... I shove the thought into the recesses of my mind, just as I open the drawer in my desk and pull out my phone.

Glancing at my phone's screen, I see that Dad is calling. He doesn't usually call during working hours. He's an attorney, too, and understands the grind.

Declining the call, I start typing a quick message that I'll call him later. But before I can hit send, he's calling again. "Ok. Something must be up." Answering the call, I greet, "Hey, Dad, what's shakin'?" As I lean back into my office chair, my attention fixes on the photos of outdoor scenery I've hung up across from my desk. The images are mostly of pictures I took while hiking in Seattle... with Sam.

Sam went to college in Seattle, and I followed him shortly after. These photos inevitably remind me of him—even when I don't want them to.

"Kat." Dad's hoarse voice interrupts my wayward thoughts. His tone sets my nerves on edge. "It's Ethan." He pauses, and I hear him take a ragged breath. "He was in a car accident." His words are slow, like he's choking on them.

"Is he ok?" Still leaning back in my chair, I try to stop my mind from reeling. I don't know anything yet.

"He's in rough shape. He's in surgery now, but it doesn't look good." Tears stream down my face, and I choke back a sob.

I immediately shoot up from my chair, unable to sit as I process Dad's words. I just talked to Ethan this morning and asked for his advice on a case I'm working on.

I can't speak yet, and there is only silence on the other side—like Dad knows I need a minute.

I force myself to look at the potted plants I keep on my windowsill. Anything to try to ground myself so I don't spiral.

Standing still isn't working, so I start pacing back and forth in my small office. My heart thumps too loudly in my ears as the world turns too quiet.

"Kat?" Dad's voice breaks.

"An accident?" It comes out wobbly. I lean over the front of my desk and place my hands on the surface, feeling the grooves of the dark oak beneath my fingertips.

Just breathe.

I look at the neat piles of documents scattered across the flat surface of my desk, not really seeing anything.

"You should come home," Dad says softly.

I clear my throat, "I'll be there as soon as I can." My voice sounds like I'm sucking down molasses.

"Drive safe." I can hear the tears in his voice now. "I love you, baby girl."

"I love you, too, Dad."

We hang up, and I stay leaning over my desk, my hands planted in place. After a few moments, I stand up and wipe the tears from my cheeks as I walk around my desk. Thankfully, I don't wear much makeup and don't have to worry about it smearing.

Like most junior attorneys, my office is small. Truthfully, I'm just grateful to have a spot where I can shut the door and tune out the noise of the bustling law firm I work at. I'm even more thankful for this space right now; I don't want anyone to see me crying at work.

Sitting back in my chair, I quickly send the draft I've been working on with a quick overview to my boss before walking to his office. As calmly as I can, I begin to explain the situation.

I don't get past saying my brother was in an accident before my boss cuts me off. "Go home, Katherine, we have everything handled here."

I don't hesitate at his words; I walk back to my office, gather my purse and phone, and leave.

I stop at my apartment long enough to change into leggings and a T-shirt and fill a bag with some necessities for the trip. Mostly clothes and my toothbrush.

Throwing my bag into the trunk of my car, I send a quick text message to Liv:

> Ethan was in an accident, and I'm headed to Charleston. I don't know much but it sounds bad. I'll call you when I know more.

> Shit, girl

> Ok. Please keep me posted and drive safe!

Briefly, I contemplate sending a message to Sam. The thought of messaging him makes my stomach churn. I know he would want to know. He deserves to know. I wish someone else could tell him. But I can't put this on my parents.

I can't remember the last time I texted him outside of responding to his holiday or birthday greetings—usually with something vague and noncommittal. I type and retype the message several times before I bite the bullet and hit send.

> Hi Sam. I'm not sure if you've heard. Ethan was in a car accident and is in surgery. I don't know much but it sounds bad.

I don't wait for a reply before shoving my phone into my purse and tossing my bag on the passenger seat of my car. Right now, all I can think about is Ethan.

Chapter 2

I spent the entire two-hour drive from Columbia to Charleston trying not to catastrophize. But my brain wasn't having any of that. Each time I tried to think of something positive or nothing at all, my brain forced me to think about the worst.

When I called Ethan this morning, I asked him for advice on this case I'm working on—something I do more often than I'd like to admit. I can't remember if I said I love you before hanging up.

I must have. Right?

We spoke for only a few minutes before we both had to get back to work.

Will that be the last time I talk to him?

I try to shake the thought from my head.

I'll never see him again. Did I say I love you? Does he know?

By the time I make it to the hospital, my hands are sore from how tightly I gripped the steering wheel. I'm feeling disoriented. I don't even remember what played on the radio or if it was even on. My mind was bouncing from one topic to the next, trying to latch onto something. Anything.

I knew my mind was spinning out, bordering on an anxiety attack. But I couldn't do anything to stop it. I was just the passenger in my brain, forced to go where it led me.

I make my way to the waiting room, where I find my parents. Glancing around the space, I notice a few other people.

My parents look exhausted—like they carry the weight of the world on their shoulders; I suppose in many ways, they do. They're both staring at the wall; neither of them is speaking. Worry is plastered on their faces, and I'm positive my expression mirrors theirs. I feel the anxiety rolling off my body, my heart won't slow down, and my palms feel sweaty. It's like I can't catch a full breath.

I look down to see Mom clutching Dad's hand with both of hers; the sight is jolting. He's her lifeline, and I'm glad he's been here, so she isn't dealing with this on her own.

Dad notices me first and pats Mom on her leg with his free hand to get her attention, then gestures to me.

I've always known Dad to be confident, always speaking with authority. Growing up, I knew I could always rely on him for anything. He always listened to Ethan and me, offering advice when we needed it. He's still that rock for me.

They must have come straight from work. Dad is still wearing a dark gray suit, but he's taken the jacket and tie off—which are now on the empty seat next to him—and rolled up the sleeves of his white button-down shirt. Mom is wearing jeans, a T-shirt with her bakery logo on it, and a cardigan.

Dad is the stereotypical tall, dark, and handsome. He's just over six feet tall, with dark brown hair peppered with gray. He gives me a small smile as I make my way over to them. He seems so small right now. His shoulders are slightly hunched forward, and his usually vivid blue eyes, a little darker than Ethan's, are dull and lifeless.

I've always thought Mom was the most beautiful woman I've ever seen. She's the same height as me—five feet, five inches. Her blonde hair is sprinkled with silver-gray threads. It's currently twisted in a bun held in place with a black clip. Her usually vibrant green-with-gold flecks eyes—the same color as mine—are watery, and I know she's trying to hold back tears.

She doesn't live for the trends or care what others think about her. She knows what she wants and has never been afraid to demand it. I've always loved that about her.

They're both fit and have stayed active, even though they are in their early sixties now. They've always loved to go on hikes, ride their bikes through the neighborhood, and go boating on the weekends.

Now? They look so broken, and it's startling to see them this way. It makes me more worried for Ethan.

"Hey, baby girl, how was the drive?" Dad's usually smooth voice is shaky as he approaches me, giving me a quick hug.

"It was fine, Dad. I stopped at my apartment to grab a few clothes." I don't want to tell them how chaotic the drive felt. That I couldn't stop thinking about Ethan. That I'm terrified.

Mom kisses me on the cheek before wrapping me in her arms. "Hi, pretty girl." Her voice is fragile—it cracks my heart open. The use of the nickname she gave me as a child always warms my heart. But it feels off right now.

"Hey, Ma." I hug her back. Once we step away from our embrace, I ask the question burning through me: "What happened?"

Mom's face crumples as her body racks with sobs.

Oh God!

I can count the number of times I've seen Mom cry on one hand. My mind immediately goes to the worst, but I remain silent as Dad and I pull her into an embrace, one of us on each side of her.

We stand there until Mom's body calms and her tears stop. My world is at a standstill until I know what's going on.

When we finally sit down, my parents share what they know.

"Ethan was on his way to meet one of his clients," Dad explains, his voice quiet. "About an hour after he left the office, I got a call from one of the people here. I'm his emergency contact." He shrugs at the last part. "So, anyway, the man told me Ethan was being admitted to the hospital and needed emergency surgery."

He pauses, taking a deep breath and blowing it out before continuing. I remind myself to breathe as Dad quietly speaks.

"He said Ethan was in a car accident and they suspected internal bleeding and a possible brain injury."

Shit. That… that can't be right. I furiously brush away the silent, hot tears streaming down my face.

"I dropped everything at work—practically ran to my car." Dad lets out a choked sob as he looks down at his hands in his lap. I just stare at him—stunned. I don't know how to process Dad crying.

I've never seen him like this. He's always stoic, even when his parents died a few years back. I've always thought of Dad as being strong. But now? Right now, he looks—it terrifies me.

Putting her hand on his knee, Mom picks up where he left off. "Dad picked me up, and we came straight here." She squeezes his knee and gives him a small smile.

The one thing I've always loved about my parents is how they support each other, always picking up where the other one falters. They care deeply for each other and aren't afraid to show it. I only hope I can have the kind of love they have.

"There were police officers here when we arrived. They told us someone who saw the accident called 911. Ethan was driving on the interstate when his tire blew. His car hit the median." Mom can't hold back the tears anymore; mine haven't stopped despite my best efforts to wipe them away.

"His car bounced off the median and rolled a few times." Dad's voice is all business now, as if he has to put on his work persona so he can finish telling me what happened. "He had to be extricated from his car," he says that last part so quietly, I almost didn't hear it.

Stunned into silence, I just sit here, my hands gripping the strap of my purse. I'm trying to wrap my head around what they're telling me, but it doesn't seem right.

Nothing seems right.

"Have you talked to the doctors?" I finally croak out.

"No," Dad responds. "No one has been out to see us. I asked someone at the nurse's station, but they didn't have any updates."

I don't know what else to say as my mind reels from the news. Ethan's been in surgery for a few hours already.

My parents' words play on a continuous loop in my mind as I try to make sense of them. But nothing does.

I can't understand what happened. How did his car hit the median and then flip? How did he lose control? Why did his tire blow like that?

Did I tell him I love him when we spoke this morning?

Did I say I love you?

Did I say I love you?

Did I say I love you?

We sit in silence as I stare at a spot on the wall—a stain left from who knows how long ago. I'm not even sure how much time passes, but I start to feel my legs cramp.

My parents snap their attention to me when I stand suddenly. "I just need to stretch my legs. I'm going to take a walk; maybe find the cafeteria and see if they have anything to eat." I wave Dad off when he starts reaching for his wallet.

I wander the hospital halls, following the signs that point me in the direction of the cafeteria. After purchasing pre-made salads and bottles of water for each of us, I head back. My parents are the only ones left in the waiting room when I return. Handing them their food and drinks, I sit back down in one of the uncomfortable chairs.

The worry twisting my gut makes it impossible to eat, but I push the salad around the plastic bowl it came in with my fork.

The silence of the hospital waiting room is deafening.

Finally, a doctor walks in, breaking the quiet. "Oaks?" he calls from the doorway. It's weird since we're the only ones sitting here. But we all raise our heads at the name and watch with bated breath as he sits in a chair across from my parents.

The doctor's expression is guarded. *This can't be good, then.* "I'm Dr. Ford. I'm the emergency-room doctor today and have been helping your son." He takes a breath, composing himself.

"Is my brother ok?" I blurt out.

Dr. Ford shifts his focus to me. "We did everything we could, but his injuries were too extensive. I'm afraid to tell you that Ethan died on the operating table."

The waiting room is too bright, and all I hear is buzzing. I can't make out the words Dr. Ford is saying.

Did I say I love you?

Chapter 3

*E**leven years old*

There are only a couple more people in front of us before it's our turn to ride Space Mountain.

My feet hurt from standing at Disneyland the last couple of days, but I won't let that slow me down.

The flight from Charleston to Anaheim was loooong. I made sure to have Treasure Island, *my headphones, and my iPod loaded with music to help pass the time.*

We finally got to Anaheim and spent the evening eating pizza and playing in the hotel pool. I had a hard time sleeping that first night because I was too excited to get to Disneyland.

One more group and then it's our turn!

I didn't expect it, but Disneyland is so different from Disney World. When Mom first told Ethan and me that we were going on this trip, I couldn't understand why we weren't just going to Disney World—it's much closer.

"Where is your sense of adventure, Kat?" I could practically feel the excitement rolling off Mom.

We were hesitant at first since we wouldn't be able to see our friends. But once we got to Disneyland, nothing could hold us back.

Ethan and I practically ran to every ride, Mom yelling after us, "Ethan, stay with Kat!"

But I was always right next to him. I think it's because I'm getting faster, but more likely, it's because he's slowing down for me.

At each ride, we waited impatiently in line until it was our turn. I can tell my parents hate the lines; I get more excited the closer we get.

This trip was part of a surprise for Mom's 45th birthday. Not a surprise for her. My parents had planned this for months. But it was a surprise for Ethan and me. And since we're celebrating, we each get to choose two souvenirs to take home.

I picked out a Minnie Mouse sweatshirt on the first day, and I've been wearing it when I get cold. I've been looking at all the stores to figure out what else I want. I keep looking at the pretty, tall, pointed princess hats with fuzzy trim on the bottom and ribbons and lace that trail from the highest point down past the bottom. I'm definitely going to get one of the pink ones.

Ethan chose his souvenirs on the first day. He picked out some trading cards and a vest from one of the adventure stores; he immediately put the vest on and didn't stop talking about the tools he was going to put in the pockets when we got home. He's worn that vest every day we've been here.

We've spent four amazing days at Disneyland. On the first day, we scouted the area and rode some of the roller coasters. The rest of the time, we've been re-riding our favorite rides as many times as we could.

But the best part? Ethan's been sitting next to me on all of the rollercoasters, and we've been screaming our heads off as we plunge back to the ground from the tallest heights.

***

Present Day

I turn off my car's engine and stare up at my parents' house. I don't remember getting into my car or even driving from the hospital.

But here I am. My car parked at the curb.

This house has seen me grow up, have my heart broken, and be put back together again. I always knew I had a home here, no matter what. If I ever needed anything, I could go home.

Looking at it now, I can't help but wonder how things will change knowing Ethan won't ever walk through that door again.

Every memory I have of Ethan will be in the past.

My heart sinks at the thought.

This house has been in my family for generations. My granddad owned it before passing it on to Mom, and his dad owned it before him. Located in Charleston's South of Broad neighborhood, the house is a classic three-story, red-brick, narrow house called a Charleston Single House, built in the mid-1800s.

The upscale neighborhood is filled with these historic homes. The lawns are perfectly manicured, and the houses are well-maintained. Growing up here, there were always plenty of kids to play with and a couple of parks nearby.

I stare out the windshield, hands still gripping the steering wheel, and look down the narrow road, admiring the old trees that line the street. I've always loved these trees. The branches and leaves form a canopy over the road, providing shade during the hot summer days.

I fix my attention back on the house. Each level features three sets of windows facing the street, all equipped with black shutters. When I was a kid, I would always ask Mom why we never closed the shutters. *"Do they even work?"* I would ask. *"Yes, pretty girl, but I like feeling the sunshine that comes through those windows."*

As I exit my car, my mind drifts to when I last visited. It was only two weeks ago. I like to visit every other month. The drive is far enough that I can't visit as frequently as my parents would like, but close enough that I can make a quick weekend trip when I'm feeling homesick.

That was the reason for my trip two weeks ago. I just needed to feel the comfort of being home.

I broke up with my boyfriend, Philip. We had dated for over a year, and I couldn't picture him in my life anymore. I drove over after work on Friday and spent the entire weekend playing cards with my parents and Ethan, walking on the beach, and drinking lots of wine.

I grab my bag out of the trunk of the car and begin my walk up to the house. On the southern side of the house sit three white piazzas—one for each level. These outdoor covered porches stretch the full length of the house and offer some much-needed respite from the summer heat.

Growing up, that third-level piazza was my sanctuary. While Ethan and Sam played video games, I could often be found in one of the lounge chairs, reading a book, sipping sweet tea, or playing Barbies with my friends.

I walk up the few short steps to the black door that faces the street, tucked under a small alcove. My parents always keep this door unlocked since it isn't the real front door. This street door leads directly onto the first-level piazza.

Even though it's October, it's still warm in Charleston. Making my way to the front door, the decor on the piazza hasn't changed much. There are two wooden Adirondack chairs on the far end. White pots with red flowers sit on each side of the front door.

Walking to the midway point, I stop and stare at the black front door. I know I should walk in, but my legs won't move yet.

I take a deep breath before testing the handle and find it locked. Pulling my keys out of my bag and inserting the correct one, I open the door and step inside. The house feels different; the air has been sucked out of it. Or maybe it's just me?

Glancing at my watch, I see it's 9:00 p.m. My parents are still at the hospital, wrapping things up there. This never-ending day is finally catching up to me, and suddenly I feel exhausted.

I carefully step over the fifth step—avoiding the creak it makes—as I make my way up to the third floor, where Ethan and my childhood rooms are. My steps are slow, like I'm trudging through mud.

Chapter 4

*T**wenty Years Old*

"Come on, Kitty Kat." Sam and I are quickly making our way through the mall. He's basically tugging me behind him.

"Why are you walking so fast, Sammy? I thought we were just window shopping?" Sam just smirks down at me, his brown eyes twinkle, his light brown hair is slightly wet from the drizzle outside, but doesn't answer my question. He tugs on my hand slightly, urging me forward.

By the time he slows his pace, I see we are heading straight to a jewelry store. I look up at him, trying to figure out what he's doing, but he ignores my gaze.

He drops my hand as he walks straight to an area of the store like he knows exactly where he's going. Slowly, I follow him but stop in my tracks when I see the section he's standing in front of is full of engagement rings and wedding bands.

"Sam," I say his name slowly, "what are we doing here?"

Finally, he looks at me, and I can't place his expression. "I need you to help me pick out a ring for Claire."

A ring.

For Claire.

The noise of the busy mall goes quiet, and I know Sam is saying something to me because his mouth is moving, but the words don't register. I knew he was dating Claire, but I didn't realize it was serious.

I mean, Sam was just holding my hand less than a minute ago.

He brushed my hair out of my face as I was getting ready to leave my dorm. He has dinner with me almost every night. It felt like Sam spent nearly every waking hour with me when we weren't in our respective classes.

When has he even had the time to spend with Claire?

My mind is reeling, and I feel my body go rigid when Sam places his hand on my arm. I try to focus on him again when I hear him, "Kat, are you ok?" *Sam's confident smirk from before is nowhere in sight. Instead, his expression is tight.*

"Sam, I don't—" *understand? I don't want you to marry her. What am I trying to say here? I can't live without you.*

Fuck.

"Please don't marry her." *The words are out before I can think them over, and now that I'm speaking, I can't stop, even when Sam drops his hand from my shoulder and shoves both into his pockets.* "I love you. I've been in love with you for so long. Please, don't marry Claire. Be with me. I... I want you to choose me."

I drop my gaze from him when I see him look around us. I forgot we were standing in the middle of this stupid jewelry store, and now? All I want to do is leave, curl up in my bed, and forget this ever happened.

I take a step back, ready to bolt. I can't believe what's happening. I can't believe Sam brought me here to help him choose a ring for someone else. I can't believe I just confessed my feelings for him. But I had been so sure he felt the same way.

At least, until now.

Sam clears his throat, and I look back up at him. His expression is... pained when he finally speaks, "I love you, but—" *he clears his throat again and briefly looks down at the floor before squaring his shoulders.* "Not in that way. You're Ethan's sister and my friend. I'm sorry."

My heart feels like it's clawing its way out of my chest. How could I have gotten this so wrong? Of course, he only saw me as a friend.

"I, um," I look around the store, "I have to go." Before I lose my nerve, I turn around and quickly walk through the wide opening of the jewelry store.

I hear Sam say something behind me, but my ears are ringing so loudly that I can't make out his words. I don't dare stop to talk to him, I don't dare turn around to see his beautiful face again.

I feel my phone buzz in my back pocket. Pulling it out, I decline Sam's call. I make it halfway down one corridor of the mall before I stop to order an Uber to pick me up.

My chest feels tight, and I can't seem to catch a breath as I wait at the curb for my ride; my mind drifts to memories of the last two years.

Sam and I were close when we were kids, not as close as he was with Ethan, but we had gotten even closer during college. When I heard Sam talk about how much he loved going to school in Seattle, I knew that was where my path would lead.

Sam was starting his junior year at the University of Washington when I was a freshman. Far from home, he took me under his wing. I'm sure it was at my brother's insistence to "take care of my little sister." But I was grateful all the same.

My first year, I struggled with balancing classes and feeling homesick. It was my first time being away from my parents. I was having a hard time not seeing them regularly. I spoke to them on the phone every day, but it wasn't the same.

During the second quarter of my freshman year, my boyfriend, Kevin, broke up with me. We had been dating since the middle of our sophomore year in high school.

Kevin was still in Charleston, and the long distance was taking its toll on our relationship. When I left for Seattle, I thought Kevin and I were endgame. I thought we would be one of those cute couples that were high school sweethearts. I was naive.

A few weeks into my first semester, I felt things shifting. Kevin didn't answer my calls as much, and his text messages were slow and inconsistent. When he responded, it was usually with one or two-word responses. I knew our relationship was creeping toward a natural end. Even though I was expecting it, I was still devastated when Kevin called to break up with me.

Sam showed up at my dorm room one day and nearly dragged me to the library to study with him. He finished his homework before I did and then helped me with mine—math was never my strong suit. Once we were finished, we ate dinner in the food court, and I told him what was wrong.

From that day forward, Sam and I studied together nearly every day. We met for coffee and often ate lunch together whenever our schedules aligned. We adventured around Seattle and hiked on the nearby trails.

Having him there made me feel less lonely.

I don't think I would have gotten through that first year if it hadn't been for Sam.

One day during my second year, I realized I couldn't stop thinking about Sam. He was all I thought about when we weren't together. When we were together? Well, I thought about him then, too. I couldn't stop thinking about his laugh and the way his eyes crinkle at the corners, or his small touches: brushing my hand, or putting his hand on the small of my back.

I went on dates with other guys but couldn't stop imagining it was Sam's lips on mine, his hands around my waist. So, naturally, those relationships never went anywhere.

There was no doubt in my mind that I had fallen for my brother's best friend. For my friend. Thinking about it now, I just feel like a walking cliché.

Sam just rejected me.

I don't know how I've managed to hold back the tears fighting to spill down my cheeks, but once I'm safely in the back of the car, they won't stop. The driver doesn't say anything, just lets me cry. Twenty minutes later, I stumble into my dorm room and fall onto my bed, burying my head into my pillow as the sobs wrack my body.

***

P resent Day

As I reach the third-floor landing, despite my exhaustion from the day, I discard my bags in the hall and turn toward Ethan's bedroom instead of mine.

Slowly, I open the door and step inside. I'm not even really sure why I'm here, but I feel nervous. I stop myself from glancing over my shoulder just to be sure no one is behind me.

As if Ethan might be lurking in the shadows, waiting to catch me sneaking in here.

But of course, no one is there. Ethan won't ever catch me in his room again. The thought makes my stomach plummet as I hold back my tears.

Once fully inside, I shut the door behind me. Closing my eyes, I take a deep breath, trying to calm my nerves.

This day is nothing like what I expected. I wanted to spend the day finishing my work. I wanted to spend the evening eating Chinese takeout with Liv and her girlfriend, Talia, while we watched reruns of Gilmore Girls—something we do every fall.

I think back to my call with Ethan this morning. *God, that seems like a lifetime ago.* I can't wrap my head around the idea that I won't be able to pick up the phone and call him. That he won't ever see the memes and reels I send him that I think he will laugh at. Or that I won't get similar messages from him.

Did I say I love you?

I shake my head, trying to coax the thoughts away, and look around his room.

It hasn't changed much since we were in high school. Mom always wanted us to feel like we had a place to stay if we needed it, so she never changed our rooms. They are both exactly how we left them when we moved out to go to college.

It's almost funny looking at Ethan's room now because it could be one of those fake room setups in a museum with a plaque that says: "Typical Teenage Boy Bedroom Circa 2010." I chuckle softly at the thought.

The walls are still stark white. Ethan and I begged Mom for years to let us paint our bedrooms. Ethan insisted that green walls would make him smarter.

I wanted pink. I'm not even sure why, because I've never been a girly-girl. If I had to wear a dress or a skirt, it was a bad day. It's funny that now I wear mostly dresses to work. Despite Liv's very vocal distaste for my wardrobe choices, it's easier than having to coordinate patterns and styles.

My attention focuses on Ethan's letterman's jacket hanging on a hook by the door. I glide my fingers along it, feeling the soft leather. I run my hand along the OAKS patch on the back.

He was so proud the day he lettered in track. He begged Mom all summer to get him a letterman's jacket so he could *show off his accomplishment.* She caved, and he never stopped wearing it.

He even took it with him when he left for the University of South Carolina. Over Christmas break, he brought it back and hung it here. He was so worried that people would view him as *"peaking in high school,"* and he *"didn't want that reputation."*

Looking at Ethan's jacket, I wonder if it's moved from this spot since that Christmas. I lift it off the hook and slip it on, wanting to feel its weight. It's a little big on me, but it's worn in all the right places and feels warm over my chilled skin.

It's strange to think how far we've both come. Ethan wanted to walk in Dad's footsteps. He attended the same school as Dad and worked at the firm Dad founded with his law school buddies a couple of years after they graduated.

I couldn't stand the idea of becoming another Oaks at Wilde, Oaks, and Harris PLLC, so I set off on my own adventure. After graduating from high school, I moved across the country and attended school in Seattle, Washington. I had a job waiting for me in Columbia when I graduated. Actually, I never intended to go to law school. But when it came time to decide on a career path after completing my undergraduate degree, I realized that law school made sense.

Keeping his jacket on, I slowly walk further into his room and sit down on his queen-size bed. Ethan was tall, 6'3, and his bed got bigger as he did.

I feel the tears sting my eyes again as I look around the room, taking it all in but not actually seeing anything.

My gaze lands on a photo in a simple black picture frame on Ethan's nightstand. I recognize the image from the summer when Liv and I graduated from high school.

Ethan and Sam were home from college for the summer. Liv and I wanted to celebrate by being pulled on the tube behind my parents' boat. The four of us used to beg my parents every weekend to take us out on the boat.

I remember Mom took this photo at the end of the day. The four of us all lined up, Liv and me in our swimsuits and the guys in board shorts. We all had huge smiles on our faces, and our skin was sun kissed. The exhaustion from a long day on the lake settled into our eyes. It was one of the best days I've had.

Little did I know that things would change so drastically between Sam and me just a couple of years later.

I can't take my eyes off the photo. Off Sam.

He's standing next to me, his arm around my shoulders. His light brown hair is cut short and appears spiky from the salt water. His chocolate-brown eyes stare straight into the camera. He's smiling so big I can see the dimple on his left cheek.

Clutching the picture to my chest, my mind drifts to how we left things when Sam graduated from college. Me, standing in the jewelry store begging him to love me, and him saying no.

I felt pathetic even now. The way I reacted, and, if I'm being honest, still acting.

Sam tried to reach out several times after that horrible afternoon. He called and sent several text messages each day asking me to call him.

I never responded. I was too embarrassed. After a week, he showed up at my dorm room. I didn't answer the door. I tried to stay quiet so he would think I wasn't there.

At the end of the month, I watched him walk across the stage and get his diploma. It took everything in me not to break down in front of everyone—my heart had been shattered.

After the ceremony, he started making his way over to us, but before he could reach us, I made up some excuse and took off.

His messages continued despite my lack of response. A month after graduation, his messages stopped cold turkey. I kept checking my phone, hoping he would message me. I'm not even really sure why, because I probably wouldn't have responded anyway. But it felt like I wasn't drowning as much, while I knew he was still trying.

I finished my last two years and then went on to law school. Without him.

I heard from my parents that Claire said yes when he proposed to her—I cried for days after. About a year later, the wedding was off. I never learned why. I never asked, and my family didn't tell me. I think they knew something happened between Sam and me.

Whenever Ethan brought Sam up, I quickly changed the subject or left the room. Whenever we were in Charleston at the same time, I made myself scarce.

Pathetic, I know.

I acted like a child.

Even now, knowing I should have reacted differently, should have been excited for Sam, I still can't get the crushing weight of his rejection and embarrassment off my chest. I can't stop his words from repeating in my mind: I was just his friend's kid sister. He didn't want more. He didn't want *me*.

I groan slightly as I run my fingers along the picture frame in my hands. I take a deep breath and blow it back out as I set the frame back on Ethan's nightstand, willing Sam from my mind.

Slowly, I stand up and walk toward the bookcase. It still has the track trophies and awards he won, and so many Stephen King books. Ethan went through a phase where he read everything Stephen King wrote that he could get his hands on, including *IT* and *Children of the Corn*. After he read *IT*, he made me watch the movie with him. I still have nightmares about that shower scene, even after all these years.

Continuing my perusal, I notice some we both have—the ones Mom insisted we read and love as much as she does—Harper Lee's *To Kill a Mockingbird* and S.E. Hinton's *The Outsiders*. To her credit, these are my favorite books, too.

"Stay gold, Ponyboy" is a line that lives in my head rent-free. I pick up To *Kill a Mockingbird* and flip through the pages, noticing some underlined passages.

Walking back to Ethan's bed, I read through some of his notes and highlights. "Greasers will still be greasers and Socs will still be Socs," and "Nothing gold can stay," are among the highlights in *The Outsiders*.

Skipping ahead, I read the small passage of Johnny Cade's death and his dying wish for Pony, that he "Stay gold." I can't stop the tears that I've been holding back. Once they start, it's like a dam has broken because they won't stop now.

Chapter 5

Nine years old.

"Should we watch Beauty and the Beast *or* Cinderella?" I ask my friends.

"Definitely Beauty and the Beast." Sophie's voice is sure and confident in her decision. "I love Belle!"

Everyone says, "Yes!" in unison.

It's my birthday, and I really wanted to have a sleepover and movie night with my closest friends.

We started the evening off by eating pizza and drinking chocolate milk. Once we finished eating, we played Uno, and then Mom brought out the cake.

Mom owns a bakery and bakes the best cakes! The chocolate with strawberry filled cake had pink frosting with purple and blue pansy flowers decorated on it. Pansies are my favorite flowers because they have cute little faces on them.

Next, I opened up presents from my friends. Liv gave me some barrettes and a makeup kit; Sophie and Kristen gave me Barbies; and Sam gave me this cool keychain with a cat on it. He's called me Kitty Kat for as long as I can remember. Ethan gave me some X-Men comic books, and my parents gave me a new bike that I can't wait to try out.

After we finished our cake, we all helped my parents clean up and then went up to the third floor to watch movies.

Sam and Ethan went to Ethan's room and stayed there the rest of the night. I guess they are too cool to hang out with "a bunch of girls." Whatever, it's better this way.

Settling into the loft between Ethan's and my rooms, I see that Mom made each of us a movie tray with a bowl of popcorn and a box of our favorite candy. Liv and I both have red licorice; Sophie has Skittles; and Kristen has M&Ms.

I grab the disk and pop it into the machine. Then, grabbing my tray off the coffee table, I snuggle into my blanket between Sophie and Liv.

"This is the best birthday ever!" I squeal to my friends.

"I know. I'm so excited for all this popcorn and licorice!" Liv beams back at me.

"Especially after we already had pizza and cake!" Sophie snuggles into the couch more.

Glancing over at Kristen, I see she's already digging into her popcorn with the biggest smile.

We've all seen Beauty and the Beast *before, so we sing along to all the songs. Once the movie is over, we start* Cinderella.

The last thing I remember is Cinderella dancing with Prince Charming in her blue dress before I fell asleep, surrounded by my best friends.

***

P resent Day

I'm startled awake when I hear my bedroom door open. Rubbing my eyes to wipe away the sleep, I find that I'm still in Ethan's room. *I must have fallen asleep here.*

The sun shining through the windows is brighter than it has any right to be, and I groan internally.

Looking towards the door to see who has opened it, I'm shocked to see Sam standing there, surprise showing in his chocolate-brown eyes.

I jolt upright, and my stomach clenches with anxiety. I'm not ready to see him, and certainly not like this.

I knew it was inevitable that I would see him this week. I just thought I'd be fresh and wearing clean clothes. Not startled awake, probably with drool dripping down my face. I quickly wipe my mouth only to find it dry. *Thank God!*

I look down at myself to see I'm still wearing Ethan's letterman's jacket. Running my hands through my hair, I find it's a tangled mess. My face feels flushed, and my eyes are sore. I can only imagine they're puffy from crying all night.

Why did he have to find me like this? Of course, he looks like the god I know he is. Perfectly put together and sexy as sin.

Sam's light brown hair is shorter than when I last saw him, but still long enough to brush along his forehead. It looks a little mussed, like he's been running his hands through it.

Sam has a short beard, making me think he hasn't shaved in a couple of weeks. I want to rub my hands through his beard.

Woman! Stop. Right. Now.

I shake my head slightly as if that will help clear my thoughts. These kinds of thoughts are one of the main reasons I avoid him when he's around.

God, it's ridiculous that after seven years, I'm still overwhelmingly attracted to Sam. I still want him and still want him to want me. I can't seem to stop myself from thinking about how good he looks. About how much I want to...

Nope!

He's wearing dark jeans and a fitted cobalt blue T-shirt that shows off his muscular arms and tattoos. Sam was always fit, but this version? He looks like he's spent some serious time at the gym. Sam's hands are by his sides, flexing.

I've never seen him with tattoos, and I take a moment to admire them now. Black and white pine trees are inked down the length of his left arm, stopping just before his wrist. I can't see the entire thing, but I'm positive he has a full sleeve. It reminds me of the forests in Seattle.

His right arm also has tattoos that stop just below his shirt sleeve, but I can't tell what they are. The sight of Sam with tattoos does something to my stomach. I bite my bottom lip as I contemplate this version of him.

Neither of us has spoken yet, and I've been staring at him for what feels like several minutes.

Well, this is awkward.

Looking away from him to break the weird connection, I shift my focus to the blanket partially covering me. I wonder which of my parents found me here last night. The thought makes my heart ache. They probably came in here for the same reason I did, to feel closer to Ethan and lessen the pain, only to find me here instead.

Remembering I still haven't said anything to him, I look back up at Sam, my voice cracks when I finally speak, "What are you doing here?" My throat feels like sandpaper. It's only now that I see his eyes look heavy and red with exhaustion.

I don't know if I'll ever be over this constant ache to be near him.

To have his arms around me.

To be loved by him.

Because no matter how much time passes, whenever I see Sam, I can't stop thinking about how much I want him and how much I wish he would choose me.

And then I think about standing in that jewelry store confessing my love for a man who didn't want me back. It's a vicious cycle, really.

"Sorry for waking you, Kitty Kat," he smirks, but it isn't the one I'm used to seeing on his gorgeous face. This is half-hearted, as if it's all he can muster.

I want to be mad at him for using the nickname he gave me when we were kids, but my heart obviously has a mind of its own since it's galloping at the endearment. The way he says it makes my stomach do somersaults as if it's getting ready to try out for the Olympics.

"I didn't expect you would be in here." Sam continues. Is he upset that I'm in Ethan's room? All I know is that I don't have the mental or emotional energy to find out.

"I didn't expect to see you here either." He flinches at my defensive tone and averts his gaze. *Shit.* I would do anything to remove that look from his face.

Why is it that even after seven years, my body grovels at his feet, begging him to give me attention? At some point, I'll be able to move past this man, right?

Standing up from the bed, I try again. "I didn't mean to fall asleep in here." My voice is distant but not sharp. *That's better.*

He looks at me again, and I can see his eyes rake up my body. I can't place his expression, but when his gaze meets mine, I can tell he knows I caught him assessing me. He almost seems smug about it.

I hate him.

Except, I don't think I could ever actually hate Sam.

Sam's eyes drop to my lips before he slowly licks his own. Butterflies are having a field day in my stomach. I avert my gaze before my body steps towards him of its own accord.

"I booked a flight as soon as I got your text. I messaged you back, telling you I was on my way." He says it matter-of-factly and without emotion. He crosses his arms across his chest, his forearms flex slightly in the process; I'm back to staring at his muscular arms.

It takes me a moment to remember the text I sent him before I drove to Charleston.

Yesterday seems like a lifetime ago.

"I'm so sorry, Kat." I finally look at his face again. He takes a step forward but stops when I take a step back.

It isn't that I don't want him to be near me—quite the opposite. No matter how much time has passed, I can't stop thinking about Sam. I can't seem to stop pining after him.

It's better that I just stay away.

"I... I forgot I messaged you." I rub my eyes in an attempt to stop the tears I feel prickling at the corners.

He runs a hand across his face like he's trying to wipe away this situation. I wish it worked that easily. "My flight landed a couple of hours ago, and my dad asked if I could help out here. He's helping your parents with..." Sam clears his throat, "the arrangements."

I wince at his words. We aren't all here to set up another one of my parents' parties. I follow the movement of his hand as he drags it through his hair. He used to do this when he was nervous, and I briefly wonder if the gesture still means the same thing to him now.

Sam clears his throat again and looks around the room. "I saw your mom downstairs, and she asked if I would check on you. I went to your room first. You weren't there." He looks a little sheepish. "I haven't been in Ethan's room in a while and thought I would take a look before heading back downstairs." He shrugs, like that explains it.

Turning toward the bed, I fold the gray fuzzy blanket someone covered me with and place it at the foot of the bed. "How long are you in town for?" I try to speak evenly, but even I can tell my voice is shaky. I hate asking this, but I need to know the answer. *How long do I have to navigate him?*

"I'm not sure yet. A week, probably." Turning back toward him, I look at him; his gaze burns into me.

All of a sudden, the emotions coursing through me are too much, and I feel my heart breaking. Not just for the loss of my brother, but also the loss of this man I've loved almost my entire life, standing in front of me.

"I can't believe he's gone." My voice is no louder than a whisper.

Sam drops his arms to his sides and steps toward me again, hesitant at first. I don't move and don't remove my gaze from him, hoping he comes closer but trying to will him to stay where he is. As much as I know I need to keep my distance from Sam, I don't think I have the strength to deny his comfort right now.

When I don't move away from him again, he quickly closes the gap and wraps me in his arms.

Sam is several inches taller than me, the same height as Ethan. I feel him trying to take the pain away with his contact alone, and I can't stop my body from melting into his embrace. He feels warm, strong, and comfortable.

"Me too, Kat. Me too." His tone is choked with emotion.

I want to stay with him like this forever.

The smell of his cologne hits me; it's the same one he always wore, a little like pines and the salty sea air. It takes all my strength not to bury my face in his chest so I can soak up his scent.

But I can't stay here. I can't let myself fall back into his orbit, pining after someone I can't have. It would crush me. Again. And this time, I don't think I would survive it.

Slowly, I pull away and wipe the remaining tears from my cheeks. Glancing at his shirt, I see I've left it wet with tear stains. "Sorry for ruining your shirt." I offer a small smile, embarrassed, before stepping away fully. He looks down, smiles, and responds with a shrug.

"He used to love that jacket." Sam reaches out and pulls lightly on one edge of the jacket I'm still wearing. "I never told you this, but I was always grateful that you and your parents were there to support Ethan and me at our track meets. Dad couldn't always be there, but I knew I would find you in the crowd and knew you would be cheering me on." He shifts his focus down to his hands, "Thanks for that."

God, I used to love watching Ethan glide over the hurdles. Given his height, I never understood how he looked so graceful. But there he was, always at the front of the pack.

They made it to Districts in their freshman year and went on to State every year after that. Track was the only sport Ethan participated in, and he loved every minute of it. He would work out during the off-season so he could *"have the best season ever!"*

When I started high school, Ethan tried to convince me to participate in track with him. He never stopped trying to persuade me, even after he graduated. Unlike Ethan, I didn't play sports in high school—a decision I've never regretted. I'm just not coordinated that way. I joined the high school choir instead.

Did I say I love you?

"I loved watching you both compete. I was sad when you decided to stop pole vaulting after freshman year. You were so good at it. I never understood why you hated it so much."

A shrug is his only response. I don't push him to say more. Sam and Ethan both tried each event out that first year. After that, they both chose to participate in a couple of events. Sam chose the long-distance running events. Ethan decided to continue hurdling and sprints, leaving behind the field events altogether.

I'm feeling awkward and don't want to be in this room with Sam anymore. It feels too small with him in it. Like I can't breathe unless I am breathing him in. I don't want to reminisce with him. I need to get away. "I'd better go get cleaned up. I guess I'll see you downstairs."

"Ok. I'll see you down there." He looks like he wants to say more, but I avert my gaze and move towards the door before he can.

I can't stop myself from looking over my shoulder at him. He's watching me with an expression that I can't place. His eyes have darkened—with longing?

Before I go down that rabbit hole with no return, I take off Ethan's jacket, hang it on the hook by the door, and walk out of the room.

My legs feel like Jello but somehow, I keep myself upright as I make my way over to my room, quickly grabbing the bags I left at the top of the stairs last night.

Once in my room, I quietly shut my bedroom door behind me and lean against it, staring at the pink princess hat I got at Disneyland when I was a kid.

I stand there for several moments, just breathing.

Chapter 6

I stay in my room until I hear the floors creak. Sam is going back downstairs. Only when he is gone do I gather my clothes and make my way to the shared bathroom.

I take my time in the shower, allowing myself several moments to wallow in everything I'm feeling—the water washing away the evidence of my tears.

I can't resist thinking of Ethan and our call yesterday morning. It feels like it was so much longer than that.

Did I say I love you?

I try to remember each word we exchanged, but I can't remember if I said I loved him before we hung up. This detail haunts me. I try to force my brain to remember but finally give up and finish my shower.

I dress in comfortable jeans and a T-shirt. Remembering I forgot to call Liv last night, I grab my phone and headphones out of my purse. Putting in the headphones, I unlock my phone and see the messages from Sam.

Fuck! Is he ok?

I'm booking a flight now and will be in Charleston as soon as I can.

Leaving my Messages app, I click on Liv's name in my Favorites list. The phone rings only a couple of times before she answers.

"How is Ethan?" Three words, and I feel my world shatter again.

"He's not... he didn't..." I sink to the floor against my door, pull my knees to my chest, and drop my head. I can't speak past the sobs racking my body.

Liv is quiet on the line as I try to regain my composure. Once I can speak again, I tell her what happened.

"Fuck." Her voice is strained, and I know she's crying too. "I'm so sorry. I can't believe this. I'm just... I'm so sorry."

Liv wasn't particularly close to Ethan, but she still thought of him as family. I know this is hard for her, too.

"I don't know if I can be there until Friday evening, but I will be there as soon as I can," she croaks out.

"Thanks. I need you." I choke out the words. Blowing out a breath and leaning my head back against the door, I try to stop the tears from coming again before I continue. "Liv, Sam is here too. I don't know if I can handle my feelings for him with everything else. I don't know what to do."

"Oh shit!" Her voice jumps several octaves. "Well, it makes sense that you would see him. What are you going to do?" Liv knows my history with Sam. I've told her everything, including the fact that I've never gotten over him.

"I don't know. Avoid him as much as I can?" That doesn't feel right. Sam was Ethan's best friend. Running my hands across my cheeks, I wipe away the stray tears. "No, I'm not going to avoid him. But I don't know how to act around him. We haven't exactly talked other than the required, 'hi, how are you,' in so many years." I groan audibly. "The other issue is that he is as gorgeous as ever. I feel like that pathetic twenty-year-old begging him to love me." I blow out my breath.

"I know things have been strained between you two for a long time. But, you know, I think you should talk to him even if you don't feel like you can be completely honest with him about what happened. Sam and Ethan were, well, they were like brothers. I know losing Ethan is going to be really hard for him." While I know he didn't fully show it, I know she is right, this is devastating for Sam, too.

"I know." Standing up from the floor, I make my way over to my bed and sit on the edge.

"Kat, you know I would never place the burden of helping him through this on you. He needs to grieve on his terms. But I think it will help you both to have each other to talk to."

She's right. Of course, she is. I've always known that I couldn't avoid Sam forever, even though I've tried. I've kept my distance from him for the last seven years, but even I can admit that my resolve has slowly been cracking.

I know Liv has kept in contact with Sam all these years, and she continues to encourage me to reach out to him—like she was attempting at lunch yesterday. *God, how was that just yesterday?* I just never felt like I could put myself out there with him again, even if it were just as friends. "I don't know," I finally say. "I'll try, but I don't know that I can fully put myself out there with him."

"I know you care for him still. I know all of this is hard. It isn't something you should have to deal with. Just think about it, ok?"

"I'll try with him. I don't know what will happen. But I'll try."

"How are you doing with... everything else?"

"I don't know—" I suck in a breath through my teeth as Liv waits for me to continue. "I don't know how I'm supposed to go on without my older brother. I don't know how I can say goodbye," and I feel the need to beat myself up about whether I told him I love him or not. I don't say the last part out loud. I'm not ready to admit that to Liv yet.

"You don't have to have all of your feelings sorted out right now. I'm just worried you won't take the time you need to grieve. I know you want to stuff your feelings down and not show them. But Kat, and I say this with all of the love I can give, you have to let yourself feel this." I can't stop the flow of tears streaming down my cheeks again as I listen to her, "You have to process this. Losing Ethan—" she chokes on the words and clears her throat, "losing Ethan is never going to feel right. It's never going to be the same. It's ok to take your time. Please take that time."

I understand what she's telling me, and I know she's right. I've never lost anyone close to me before. Sure, my grandparents, but no one as close to me as my brother. "Ethan is—" *was*. I can't hold back the sob that escapes at the thought.

"I know. I know what he means to you. I'm so sorry. I wish I were there with you right now so I could give you the biggest hug and help you navigate the next few days. It might take me a couple of days because I have this huge project with a bunch of things hanging on my work.

"Fuck, I wish I could pass it off to someone else, but I can't. I'll be there as soon as I can. I love you, Kat. I'm so sorry about Ethan, and having to navigate Sam on top of it? Call me anytime. I'm here for you. I love you so much."

"Love you too. Let me know when you're on your way?"

"Definitely. Bye, babe."

We hang up, and I sit on the bed while I try to compose myself before going downstairs. I quickly check my reflection in the floor-length mirror by my bedroom door. My chestnut hair is long, reaching just past my shoulder blades. It's still wet from my shower. Knowing I can't deal with it today, I put my hair in a side braid. My green eyes are red-rimmed and a little puffy. *Not much I can do about that.* Shrugging at my reflection, I walk out of my bedroom and make my way downstairs.

I'm not even halfway down when I start to smell eggs and bacon. My stomach chooses this moment to remind me that it needs to be fed.

I hurry the rest of the way to the dining room, but halt as soon as I see Sam and his dad, Dan, eating breakfast with my parents. My gut clenches at the thought of having breakfast with Sam. Usually, when I know Sam is over, I walk slowly, listening for him and avoiding the spaces he's in. But I can't do that this time.

My parents are laughing at something Dan said. The sound is sincere and makes my heart happy, knowing they can find some joy in this terrible situation.

Noticing I've entered the room, Sam winks at me. It's too late to pretend I wasn't here, so I force my limbs to move. Dan stands up and embraces me. "Hey, Kat. It's nice to see you." Dan gives firm hugs—the kind of hug you know is genuine. He pulls you in and wraps you up.

"It's nice to see you, too." Dan is an older version of Sam. He's handsome with light brown eyes and gray hair. He's the same height as Sam, with a similar build, but with fewer muscles than Sam has.

I never understood why Dan didn't remarry after his wife died. He's a total catch—smart, attractive, and successful.

He sits back down, and I walk around the table to hug my parents from behind, wrapping an arm around each of them. I avoid Sam's gaze, taking as much time as I can before I'm forced to interact with him again. I tell myself it has nothing to do with the butterflies that invade my stomach when I look at him.

Hesitantly, I walk to the kitchen island, where the food is ready, and scoop scrambled eggs, hashbrowns, and a slice of bacon onto my plate. Everything looks and smells delicious.

I've spent more time in this kitchen than I can even remember. We ate meals together here. Ethan and I would work on homework at the small breakfast table while my parents cooked dinner and talked about their days. The kitchen is cozy but spacious enough that several people can be in here without feeling like they are step-ping on each other. The large windows allow natural light in.

"Thanks for making breakfast, Sam." Mom's voice stops my reminiscing. *Sam cooked breakfast?* I didn't know he cooked. Turn-ing around, I mumble my thanks to him.

It's only now, as I'm walking back to the table, that I realize the only open space is the one right next to Sam. I groan inwardly. *Why is this my life?!*

"Feeling better?" Sam asks quietly, giving me his traditional smirk before taking a bite of one of his pieces of bacon.

God, he's going to be the death of me. Why can't he be ugly?

Even in my currently deteriorated mental and emotional state, I know Sam is the opposite of ugly. He's all strong jaw line, soft brown eyes, and his lips are plump in all the right places. He lifts his eyebrow, making me realize I'm staring at him and haven't answered him yet.

"Well, I showered." I give a slight chuckle. I know he can tell it isn't genuine. It's all the energy I have for this conversation right now. I look at my parents, who both give me a curious look. I'm grateful when they both turn back to their conversation with Dan. I know I told Liv I would try, but sitting here with Sam, it just feels impossible to untangle my broken heart and be the friend I should be to him.

Ethan would be disappointed in me right now. I feel the sting of tears at the corner of my eyes and try to shift my mind away from Ethan and the realization that he isn't going to eat breakfast with us this morning. My mind was waiting for him to show up.

I turn to my breakfast to distract me. While I eat—mostly pushing the food around my plate—the rest of the group discusses floral arrangements and funeral plans. I provide my feedback when asked but otherwise keep my focus on the food on my plate.

By the time I finish eating, the group is split into three. My parents will go to the funeral home and get everything sorted there.

Dan will return to the law firm to begin the probate and review Ethan's life insurance policy.

Which leaves Sam and me to go to the florist. I don't have any idea why the group was split this way because, truthfully, I heard the words, but they just wouldn't register in my brain.

We all stand from the table and clear our dishes. I say goodbye to my parents and head out to the street where Dan's SUV is parked. We decided to drop Dan off at the office, and Sam would drive his dad's SUV to the florist.

I would have offered to drive my car, but the thought of driving is the last thing I want to do. I know Dan could tell when he suggested this arrangement.

I get in the back seat and look around, noticing how clean it is. There doesn't seem to be a speck of dirt anywhere.

"Hey, Dad, would you mind stopping at the coffee shop down the street before we drop you off?"

He couldn't be asking this for me. Could he?

Sam was never a big coffee person, but I am. When we were in college, we had a running joke that I would go anywhere as long as coffee or food was involved.

"Yeah, sure, kid." I grin at Dan's use of the word "kid" because not only is Sam 29 and not a kid by age, but he's also clearly adult-sized—at six feet, three inches, he's taller than a lot of adult men.

Dan starts up his SUV and pulls away from my parents' house. His favorite country music station plays through the speakers. The music is quiet but still loud enough that I recognize the song I can't name: "whiskey for my men and beer for my horses."

I see Dan looking at me from the rearview mirror, inquiring, before I realize I just snorted. Sam turns around in the front seat, waiting for me to speak.

"This song." I shake my head. "I never understood why someone would give beer to horses. It almost seems like animal abuse."

Dan chuckles softly, his gaze returning to the road. Sam's face cracks with a big smile that shows off the dimple in his left cheek.

"Beer can actually calm horses down, but I don't think the song is about the beer." Sam's voice is filled with humor—he's holding back a laugh. "The song is about taking justice into their own hands, and I think the reference to beer just means they are taking care of their traveling companions, including the horses."

"Hmm," is my only response as I stare out the window, not really seeing anything.

Once we have our drinks from the coffee shop drive-thru, the car fills with silence as we make our way to the law firm. It's about a fifteen-minute drive, and I lean back, resigned to the quiet, slowly sipping on my vanilla latte.

Just as I close my eyes, I hear Dan speak up, "How are you doing, Kat?" His voice is gentle, but I sense a small amount of hesitation.

Dan has never really done well when people cry. When I was a pre-teen, he teased me about something I can't even remember, but it made me cry. I remember Dan getting this look of sheer panic as he shouted for my parents. "Shit, I made her cry. What do I do?"

I look at him for a moment trying to unravel my thoughts. I'm at a loss for words to explain how I'm doing, and I certainly don't want to open the can of worms that is my relationship with his son.

"I'm not sure," I finally say. "None of this feels real." I stare out the window again. "It still feels like Ethan will call me at any moment." I close my eyes and breathe. "It doesn't feel real." My voice is too quiet. "I just talked to him yesterday morning. We talked about work and a case I needed help with. Did I even say I loved him before we hung up? I can't stop thinking about that." I didn't mean to say the last part out loud, but talking to Dan always feels comfortable.

I don't even realize tears are streaming down my face until Sam reaches back, handing me a tissue. Leave it to Dan to be prepared and carry tissues in his car.

I expect Sam to pull his hand back after I take the tissue. But he surprises me by taking my hand in his. I have to lean forward a little for us to reach, but his hand is comforting.

"Ethan knew how much you loved him. While I am sure you told him, even if you didn't, there was no doubt in his mind." Dan's voice is strong and assured, and it somehow makes me feel better. Sam rubs his thumb along the back of my hand. "You two have always been inseparable," Dan continues. "Even during those awkward teenage years when you were both trying to figure out your individuality, he would have done anything for you."

"Thanks." That's all I can get out as I sniffle and try to compose myself again.

Sam squeezes my hand gently, reminding me he's there. I don't know how long this will last, but I can't imagine being without him. I can't imagine having to do this without Sam. Maybe Liv is right. Maybe I need to try to be friends with him again.

"When Sam's mom died, I remember feeling the same way. Like it wasn't real, I mean." Dan looks sad whenever he talks about Carrie. "Even at the funeral, it felt like we were just pretending."

I was eight when Sam's mom died. Sam and Ethan were ten. All I know about Carrie is what I hear from others. But she seemed like a great woman. She grew up a couple of houses down from Mom. They were instant best friends. Carrie and Mom did every-thing together. They attended college together, went to law school with Dad and Dan, and started working at the same law firm. They even discussed opening a bakery together, which they eventually did, leaving the law firm they disliked. Their friendship reminds me of how Liv and I are—besties from the first moment our eyes connected. Ride or die.

To this day, Mom celebrates Carrie's birthday and donates clothes, shoes, and toiletries to the local women's shelter in her honor. I think briefly that I want to do something for Ethan, too.

"It wasn't until a couple of weeks later, when the mailbox was overflowing, that it hit me that she wasn't coming back." Dan chuckles softly, but it isn't a real laugh. It's the one he makes when he's feeling uncomfortable.

"I never thought about the bills. They just got paid." His voice lowers, "Your mom always paid them." He looks at Sam, and I know Dan is embarrassed by this confession.

"Hell, I rarely even got the mail out of the box unless I was waiting on a package." He chuckles his awkward chuckle again. I just watch him waiting for him to continue the story.

"There was so much mail that the postal worker knocked on the door to hand it to me instead of leaving it in the box. I sat down at the table that evening and started going through everything."

He glances in the rearview mirror again and then looks over at Sam. Dan's eyes glisten with unshed tears. He focuses back on the road and continues, "Do you know how dumb I felt at that moment? I'm a lawyer and a damn good one. But I had a stack of bills I didn't know how to pay and another heap of mail I couldn't figure out what to do with." He shrugs, resigned. "All I'm saying is, it takes time."

Dan parks at the curb in front of his office. It's only when Sam releases my hand to get out of the SUV that I realize he never let go. His hand felt like an extension of my own. The loss feels devastating.

Sam gets out of the SUV, opens my door, and closes it once I've gotten out of the backseat before he walks around and gets into the driver's seat. Before I can get into the front seat, Dan reaches for my hand and gives it a light squeeze. "It's going to take time, but the one thing you need to remember is how much Ethan knew you loved him. No matter what. He knew."

"Thanks," I choke out. Dan offers me a grimace smile before walking into the building.

Sam and I are quiet as he drives us to the florist. I silently wish he would reach for my hand again. I know I won't do it myself. I couldn't handle his rejection.

We spend the next hour choosing flowers. I never knew how many different arrangements were needed, one for on top of the casket, one for the entrance, one or two on stands by the casket. There were so many options that it felt like my head was swimming.

What would Ethan like? Does it matter if he would have liked them? Will my parents like them? Is that more important than what Ethan would like?

I'm feeling overwhelmed, as though I'm slowly spinning out.

I keep getting stuck trying to decide, only for Sam to provide his thoughts on what Ethan would like. Sam's constant help reminds me of all the times that he helped me while we were in Seattle.

No matter what, he was always there, always present, always offering advice or just simply listening.

Now that we've chosen everything, I fill out the necessary paperwork and provide the date of the funeral—this Saturday.

When we get back to my parents' house, Sam walks me to the door.

"I need to help my dad with some things tomorrow, but—" he hesitates, his expression is tight. "I'd like to spend some time with you this week, if you'd be up for it."

My heart doesn't hesitate in thumping its approval because this man has built a permanent home there. I'm nervous to let him back in. My heart wins out. "Ok. I would like that."

The smile he gives me makes my knees feel weak, and it takes everything in me to keep standing.

"Good. I'll call you?"

"Yeah. OK."

He steps forward, pulls me into a brief hug—so brief I don't have the chance to wrap my arms around his waist—and kisses the top of my head before walking away. I stand there stunned that he just kissed me and watch him walk back to his dad's SUV.

Chapter 7

The next morning, after breakfast, my parents left the house quickly. They wanted to get a jump start on figuring out what to do with Ethan's things. Ethan has a safe at his condo that Dad thinks holds his life insurance, 401(k), and investment policies.

I don't understand why they want to deal with all this right now when all I want to do is wallow. They asked if I wanted to tag along, but the idea of going to his place without him felt too overwhelming.

Liv won't be here for two more days, and Sam is helping his dad with something. Looking around my parents' living room, I notice the dust collecting on the bookcase.

Cleaning it is.

I pull up the notes app on my phone and make a quick list of the tasks I want to complete. Wash the bedding. I list out each bedroom separately. Deep clean the bathrooms and kitchen. Vacuum, sweep, and mop the floors. For each major category, I list the smaller tasks, including emptying and restocking the fridge.

Checklists are a great way of tricking my brain into actually completing the task. Otherwise, I get bored and distracted, and it doesn't hurt to have the little dopamine bursts as I cross items off the list.

When Ethan and I were kids, we would wake up every Saturday morning, watch an hour of cartoons, eat breakfast together, and then help my parents clean the house. Mom would blast music in the background for us. I loved listening to her sing along to the Mama's & the Papa's or Creedence Clearwater Revival.

As we got older, she would let Ethan and me choose some of our favorite music. We had a great variety of the classics Mom adored, the rock my brother couldn't get enough of, and pop hits that I loved. Dad wasn't really into music, but he jammed along with whatever was playing. Sometimes we would stop cleaning and break out in a dance until the next song came on.

I know chores are the bane of everyone's existence, but to this day, every Saturday morning, I pump up the music and get that shit done—even doing my own little dance routine when one of my favorite songs comes on.

So, with my headphones blasting one of my favorite playlists, I get to work. I clean all the bathrooms and the kitchen, reorganize the pantry, and wash all of the bedding. All except for Ethan's, because I can't seem to make myself go into his room again.

Every time I look at his closed door, I think about our last conversation. *Did. I. Say. I. Love. You?*

I'm disappointed when I look at the clock and realize it's 5:00 p.m. and my parents haven't returned yet. Quickly pulling out my phone, I send them a group text message.

> Hey are you guys getting dinner while you're out, or should I make something for us?

Mom responds almost immediately.

> We'll be home in just a few minutes and dinner would be great.

With that, I pull out some food from the fridge and make chicken fajita quesadillas—a family favorite. My parents walk in as I'm assembling the quesadillas and putting them onto the flat skillet.

After dinner, we watch *Jurassic Park* together, and I head to bed early. I'm climbing into bed when I realize I haven't heard from Sam all day. He didn't say he would call or text today specifically, but I guess I expected it since he said he wanted to spend time together tomorrow.

Not hearing from him is a relief but leaves me feeling empty.

Why do I feel like there's a massive crater in my heart just because I went a single day without him?

I'm not ready to mull over and obsess these feelings. So, I shove them down and do my best to fall asleep.

***

The next day, my parents leave the house early again. I'm resigned to staying in the house again. With all the cleaning done, I pull out my work laptop and start drafting a business contract for one of my clients. Within a few minutes, I see an email from my boss.

Katherine,

Why are you working? You are on leave. We have everything handled. Spend time with your family. Work will be here when you get back.

I don't want to see your name pop up in the system this week. I mean it. Take the time off.

Cliff

I know he's just trying to look out for me, but I feel frustrated that I can't work this week. *Well, now what am I going to do?* Sitting down on the couch, I decide to watch a movie to fill the time.

Maybe an old favorite like Ever After *would keep my mind busy.* Before I even turn on the TV, Sam walks into the living room. He's wearing dark jeans and a fitted hunter green shirt, and I can't seem to stop gaping at how amazing he looks. *Is he trying out for GQ?*

"Hey, Kitty Kat," he says as he walks towards me. He sounds too upbeat for my dark mood. "Your mom mentioned you stressed cleaned all day yesterday, and," he looks around the space, "by the looks of things, I would say she was right." He smiles his full smile, showing the dimple on his left cheek. I'm left breathless.

It's all I can do not to fall on my knees before him. *God, I've missed that smile.*

I shrug, trying to cover the reaction my body has in his presence. "I tried to do some work today, buuuut my boss basically threatened to fire me if he caught me online again," I grumble, standing up from the couch.

"What a mean boss you have." His tone is full of sarcasm as he chuckles.

"The worst. Well, I was going to watch a movie, if you want to join?"

"I have a better idea." I can't read his expression, but something about it makes me worried. "Let's go for a walk to the park. You need to get out of this house, and I need some Charleston sun." He raises an eyebrow in challenge.

This isn't what I expected. A walk sounds... innocent. I look at him, contemplating his offer. *Some sunshine and the great outdoors are probably a good idea.*

"Can we get coffee first?" My voice perks up, and I'm reminded of our drive to the florist. *Did he ask his dad to get coffee because of me?* I want to ask him. But I don't.

He chuckles—the sound is like the air, and I can't breathe without it.

"I would never dare to ask you to leave the house without ensuring coffee was involved, Kitty Kat. Go change and we'll go."

Looking down at myself, I remember I never changed out of my pajamas. I run upstairs, leaving Sam standing in the living room, and quickly change into black leggings and a loose blue knit sweater.

My parents' house is within walking distance to a popular park we used to frequent as kids. We walk in relative silence until we get to one of my favorite coffee stands where I order a vanilla latte for myself and a chai tea latte for Sam. Once our order is ready, we continue to the park.

I sigh as I take my first sip of my coffee. The air is warm and comfortable. The sun is bright and feels good as it soaks into me, lifting my mood the longer I'm under its rays.

"Thanks for getting me out of the house." The wind blows my hair slightly, and I tuck a loose strand behind my ear.

"You're awfully quiet." Sam's voice is hypnotic, and I've missed hearing it. His chocolate eyes twinkle in the sunlight.

"I don't know what to say." I look at the ground as I speak, avoiding his gaze. "I feel like I don't know you anymore." It isn't the whole truth. But I can't exactly tell him I've avoided him the last several years because I'm a scared little girl who would rather hide than face him. I refuse to tell him that I've never stopped loving him, even if only from a distance. That I can't seem to be in the same room as him without wanting to beg him to pick me again.

"For what it's worth, I haven't changed, Kat." His lips turn down slightly, and his brow furrows. His sad tone makes me feel the cavernous distance that's grown between us. "I'm still the same guy who played Barbies with you, danced with you at the homecoming dance, and the same guy who helped you study in college. I'm still the same guy that—" he abruptly stops speaking, looks away from me, and runs his hand through his hair.

"That what?" I need to know what he was going to say.

"Nothing." His answer is too quick. It sets me on edge. "Just, I'm still me." He blows out a breath and sips on his tea.

I don't push him for an answer and instead, feel an uncomfortable silence settle over us. He's holding back. So am I.

As I take a deeper look at Sam, I notice he's aged, but in the best of ways. He has these cute crinkles at the corners of his eyes and laugh lines around his mouth when he smiles. He seems to fill out his clothes more, like he's gained more muscle. He always enjoyed working out, but he typically went for a run on the treadmill and avoided using weights.

I can't help but wonder when he started lifting. The thought makes me realize how much of his life I've missed out on.

I don't know him anymore. At least not where it matters.

My gaze trails down his tattooed arm and I hold back the urge to run my fingers along the lines of the pine trees.

Shifting back to his face, he's watching me. His eyes are soft. Caring. He smiles gently, but big enough I see his cute dimple. *Why are dimples so delicious?*

All of the reasons I fell for him all those years ago are so obvious as I continue looking at him. I avert my gaze from him and drink more of my coffee, embarrassed that he caught me staring at him.

"I never should have stopped reaching out to you. I should have kept banging on your dorm room door until you let me in." His words surprise me and I stop walking, trying to absorb them.

I search his eyes, not sure what I'm looking for, but he seems sincere.

"I shouldn't have let you avoid me every time we were in the same room together. I should have forced you to talk to me when we were both home for the holidays." He pulls his hand out of his pocket; I trace his movement as he slowly reaches for me before stopping and letting his hand fall to his side.

His expression is torn. I know he's holding something back from me. I just don't know what it is. I don't respond because I'm unsure of what to say.

If he had kept pushing for me to talk to him, would things have been different between us? Would I have gotten over him?

Would I have been able to see him with Claire and not have my heart splinter with each breath? Claire is a lame excuse at this point since they were engaged for less than a year.

"There are a lot of things I regret, Kat. But I'm still your friend. I'm here when you're ready to have me back."

Friend... the word strikes me like a punch to the gut. I feel like I can't breathe.

I start walking again to put some distance between us. Seeing a nearby trashcan, I throw my empty coffee cup away and continue walking.

Sam catches up too quickly, and I feel his gaze on me. I refuse to look at him and instead look at the houses we pass without seeing them. I know I told Liv I would try to be Sam's friend again. But God, this is so hard. How do I set my broken heart aside and let him in again?

Feeling like I need something to do with my hands, I pull my hair back and loop it into a bun before releasing it and letting it cascade down my back again.

Once I know I can speak without my voice shaking, I try to break the tension. "Tell me what you've been up to over the last few years. I know you live in Chicago and that you're an architect. I know you didn't marry Claire..." My gaze snaps up to him, and I grimace. I didn't mean to say that last part out loud.

Rather than acknowledge my embarrassment, Sam tells me about his life in Chicago. "It's very different from Charleston. Different than even Seattle. I like it." His voice is almost hesitant.

"But?" I ask, sensing he's holding something back again.

"But..." He gives me a knowing look. "It isn't home. I miss being in Charleston. I moved to Chicago because of... well, because of Claire." He looks over at me. I school my expression at his mention of *her*.

As he searches my features for the answer to whatever question he's looking for, he continues. "I love my job, and Chicago is probably the best place for my career. It's…" He pauses like he's contemplating what to say next. "Chicago has this rich architectural history." His voice is laced with enthusiasm.

When we were kids, Sam would stop and just stare at different houses or businesses and admire the structure. Hearing him speak about his career like he enjoys it makes me happy for him.

"It's one of the major birthplaces of so many incredible architectural styles and designs. I couldn't be in a better place career-wise." He perks up a bit, but I can tell something is missing in his words.

"Tell me about your office. Is it fancy?"

He chuckles at my question but obliges. "It's on the 95th floor and the view is incredible. I wish you could see it." He peeks over at me before continuing, "I have a wall of windows that overlooks the city. There's something so calming about looking out at the buildings." He fully looks at me now—his expression is guarded.

"That sounds amazing, Sam."

"It is. You know, I had a few of the pictures we took hiking in Seattle blown up, and they're hanging on one of the walls in my office."

I look up at him in surprise. "Really?" I wonder if any of the photos we keep in our offices match.

"Of course! Those were some of the best days of my life. I loved spending time with you." I'm not sure what to think about this confession. *Best days of his life?*

"Mine too." It comes out little more than a whisper. I look at the ground as I take his words in.

When we get to the park, we walk over to a bench and sit in companionable silence, letting the weight of our conversation settle.

Looking around the park, I see the pineapple-shaped fountain, a popular tourist attraction in Charleston. The grass is green and looks lush. I want to take off my shoes and sink my feet into it. The park isn't crowded, but there is a steady stream of people. During the summer, this park is always packed.

I look over at Sam and realize he's watching me. I can't stop the flush that creeps into my cheeks and look down at my hands.

The wind blows again, causing some of my long hair to drift towards him. I pull my hair back and mutter an apology. He just smiles back at me.

"I worry about leaving Chicago," Sam breaks the silence, "and being able to keep my career moving forward like it has." I study his face as he speaks. He almost looks sad.

"You want to move back to Charleston." It's a statement, not a question. I cross one leg over the other and stare at my hands.

"Yes. Chicago is... lonely, I guess. Don't get me wrong, I have friends." He shifts his position, propping a knee onto the bench, filling the space between us. My breath catches as his knee brushes my thigh. I'm glad he doesn't seem to notice my reaction. "My dad is getting older, and I don't want to miss out on spending time with him while I still can. I've thought about it for a while."

I completely understand what he's saying because I've been thinking the same thing. I want to move back to Charleston. And now that Ethan is gone? I let the thought drift off before it takes hold.

He clears his throat. "Enough of that. Your turn. I have to admit I never thought you would go to law school."

Going to law school was always Ethan's dream. It wasn't mine. I wanted to follow in Mom's footsteps and open a bakery or a bookstore—maybe both. Mom was much happier after she opened the bakery with Sam's mom. Once the bakery took off, they were able to hire full-time employees and focus on new recipes and raising us kids.

"I know," I sigh. "I didn't know what to do. Law just seemed like the easy choice."

He laughs. "Law and easy are not words I imagine go together."

I smile. "Yeah, you're right about that. I just mean, my dad did it, Ethan did it, hell, Mom did it too. So, I figured I would have the support I needed to go through with it and people who understood the process."

It seemed inevitable that Ethan would follow in our dad's footsteps. He always had that analytical brain. School came easily to him.

I'm not like Ethan. I always had to work hard to get good grades, and learning how to read and interpret cases didn't come easily to me. I felt lost in my first year and heavily relied on my family to help me get by with just Bs throughout school. By my second year, I was in a good swing and understood what I needed to do to succeed.

Sam and I are both quiet for a moment, and I look up at him. He looks contemplative, as if something isn't adding up for him. Instead of asking, I barrel on about my career.

"My clients love me, and my colleagues respect me. I'm on the fast track to becoming a partner in five years. I've worked so fucking hard for this."

"So why do you sound miserable?" I look at him, searching his gaze, trying to place what made him think I'm miserable.

"I wouldn't say I'm miserable, exactly." *Am I miserable?*

He looks at me. Questioning. He doesn't push when I don't answer his silent question.

I don't know what to say, so I shrug and give him a small smile. I'm not miserable, but I never thought I'd end up living so far from my family and missing out on so much with them. I never imagined I would have a closet full of plain suits and boring work clothes. I feel like somewhere between going to college and now, I've become a person I never imagined for myself. I don't know that it's a bad thing. Just... different.

We sit in silence for several minutes, watching the other people in the park. My mind drifts to the times we spent here when we were kids. Riding our bikes, playing hide and seek, not a care in the world. Here we are now, adults, barely talking to each other, and Ethan—I miss him already.

"I've missed you, Kat. More than you know." Sam's quiet and tender words startle me, breaking into my internal thoughts. I look up at him and search his eyes. His expression is somber but sincere and vulnerable.

"I've missed you, too, Sam." My voice is too quiet. I've never really stopped thinking about Sam. Never stopped wanting him.

If I were being honest with myself, I've compared all of my partners to him, and they've never stacked up.

I've spent the last several years thinking back to our time at UW, wishing he hadn't been dating Claire. Wishing he wasn't ready to propose to her. Wishing I hadn't blurted out that I was in love with him.

I should have responded to his messages. I should have opened the door each time he came to my dorm room. I shouldn't have avoided him all these years. I should have done so many different things.

But I can't change the past. All I can do is move forward. Maybe Liv was right, and I need Sam to get through all of this.

As we made our way around the park and eventually returned to my parents' house, we continued chatting about everything: what we do in our free time, friends we've made in our respective cities, and how we thought our lives would be different.

Chapter 8

*N*ine years old.

"What are you doing, Kitty Kat? Hey, Livie." Sam spent the night at our house again last night. He spends a lot of time here.

During the school year, his dad drops him off in the morning, and Mom takes us all to school. Then she picks us up, and we do our homework or play games until after dinner.

During the summer, Sam stays over all the time and usually spends the night. He's basically like a second older brother. He tries to include me in things, and when Ethan isn't feeling well or is still sleeping, Sam will hang out with me. Sometimes we just read books outside. Other times, he will play Barbies with me, or we build Legos; sometimes, we play Mario Kart or watch movies.

"Liv and I are planning on hanging out and reading outside. Want to come?"

Liv's house is just a couple of houses away. I wish she could spend as much time here as Sam does, but her parents won't let her. She's still here almost every day during the summer, though.

"Nah, I'm just waiting for Ethan to put on his shoes, and then we're gonna ride our bikes to the park."

"Wait, I want to go to the park. Liv, wanna go, too?" She nods excitedly at me.

"Can we come, too, Sammy?"

"Yeah, but hurry up and get dressed. I'll go tell your mom."

Liv and I run off to change our clothes. The four of us spent the afternoon riding our bikes, swinging, playing tag, and eating snow cones.

We're riding our bikes back to my house, and I'm in front with Liv.

Suddenly, I see a car run a stop sign, and I have to slam on the brakes—my bike skids and then crashes to the ground.

Tears well in my eyes as I feel the sting of pain in my knee, leg, and the palm of my hand on the side I landed on.

"Oh my God, Kat!" Sam shouts as he and Ethan slide to a stop next to me.

"Let me have a look." Ethan's voice is calm, soothing. He's fuzzy as I look up at him through the tears blurring my vision. "Shhh. It'll be ok. Let me look at you to make sure it isn't anything too serious." I nod at him as Liv takes hold of my uninjured hand.

I hiss a little when Ethan helps me move over so he can examine my leg. "It isn't too bad. But we need to get you home and clean these out, so they don't get worse."

I wipe the tears from my cheeks with the back of my good hand and look up at Ethan. "I don't think I can ride home."

"I'll walk both of our bikes back, Kitty Kat." Sam looks at me with concern.

"Thanks, Sammy." I look at him, grateful for his help. Ethan helps me stand up and then picks up his and Liv's bikes from the ground. Sam already has his and mine, and the four of us slowly walk home.

When we get home, I can't hold back the tears any longer as Mom cleans and bandages the gashes.

Sam, Liv, Ethan, and I spend the rest of the day eating ice cream sundaes and watching Disney movies together.

***

P resent Day

Sam and I walk into my parents' house, and I pause the moment we step inside. "What's wrong, Kitty Kat?" Sam stops walking, too, and looks back at me. Worry etched across his expression.

I think I hear Philip's voice, but that doesn't make any sense. "I... I think I hear Philip."

"Who's Philip?"

I ignore his question and walk towards the voices I hear.

Philip and I work for the same law firm in Columbia. We met when I was a first-year associate, and he was a third-year associate. Philip was handsome in a traditional way: tall, broad shoulders, blue eyes, and blonde hair. Many of the women at the firm had crushes on him.

I thought he was an asshole. He walked around the firm like he owned the place. Arrogance wafted from every pore of his body. I knew he was going to be the death of me. Probably because I wouldn't be able to hold back stabbing him with my pen, or calling him an asshole to his face.

A few months after I joined the firm, he and I were put on the same case, which required us to spend almost every waking hour together. That's the thing about being a new associate: you were always assigned the grunt work that required you to be in the office for twelve or more hours each day. Some people enjoy document review. I'm not one of them.

So, there we were, confined to the law firm library with stacks of documents surrounding us, waiting to be reviewed and categorized. To maximize our time, we frequently ordered lunch and dinner and ate while we worked.

When you spend this much time with someone, it's inevitable to talk and actually get to know them. And that is exactly what we did over the next several months.

Philip's grandfather was a prominent judge in town. *"I feel like everyone expects me to follow in his footsteps. Like, I have to be the best lawyer, better than everyone else. Honestly, Katherine, it's exhausting."*

After a while, I realized my initial impression of Philip was wrong. He was kind and generous. Slowly, we became friends.

When our document review was finally over, he asked me on a date, and I was ecstatic.

But no matter how much I tried, things never really clicked for me with Philip. I continued our relationship because it was comfortable. And after a year, I knew his feelings ran deeper than mine. I couldn't let it go on any longer.

I never fell in love with Philip because I was too busy loving someone else. So, I broke things off. It's been a little over two weeks, and we haven't really talked since.

I walk into the kitchen, where I see my parents and Philip sitting at the table, chatting and drinking tea. They look like they've been buddies for a long time, which is weird because I never introduced him to my family. Sam is right on my heels and stops right behind me, blocking the exit.

"Philip, what are you doing here?" It comes out accusatory as I cross my arms.

Philip stands up and starts to make his way over to me. Before he reaches me, I step back, knocking into Sam's chest. The heat radiating into my back from Sam is distracting, and I feel my body slightly relax into him.

Philip's expression flashes with anger, but he quickly schools his features and halts his approach. "Olivia told me what happened. I'm so sorry, baby. I came as quickly as I could."

What the fuck, Liv?

I hear Sam mutter "baby?" under his breath. I ignore him. It takes everything in me not to look at Philip and correct the endearment he just gave me.

Still leaning against Sam, I straighten up and take the smallest step forward. Not enough to give Philip ideas, but enough to create some distance between Sam's body pressed against mine.

"Maybe we should talk in the other room." He looks at me like I've wounded him. *I do NOT want to have this conversation with an audience—and especially not in front of Sam.*

Sam steps aside so we can pass, and I motion for Philip to follow me. Avoiding Sam's gaze as I walk out of the kitchen, I lead Philip through the formal dining room to the living room on the other side of the house. I sit down in one of the armchairs and point him to the one across from me.

Sitting down, he looks at me tentatively, "You don't seem happy to see me, baby."

I sigh heavily, trying to calm my breathing, and just stare at Philip for a moment. "We broke up. Over two weeks ago, we haven't spoken since. So, I guess I'm just really confused as to why you are in my parents' home talking to them like you're besties."

He has the audacity to appear wounded again. "I honestly just thought you needed a little space. I didn't think you meant it. I figured I would give you some time to cool off, and then things would go back to normal. I miss you."

His hopeful expression lights a flame in me. It takes all of my self-control not to lash out at him.

I don't even know what to say to this revelation. *How could he think I didn't mean it?*

Before I can protest, Sam interrupts us. "Hey, Kat, your mom was wondering if your... *friend* is staying for dinner." Sam says "friend" like it pains him. He walks fully into the living room and looks at Philip, assessing, finding him wanting.

"Who the fuck is this?" Philip snaps and waves his hand in Sam's direction.

"Excuse me?" Sam takes a step forward. I quickly raise my hand to stop him and stand up from my seat. Sam's reaction is both infuriating and delicious. He has never been afraid of standing up for himself; it's incredibly attractive. I have to force myself to tear my gaze from him.

"Philip, you are in *my* parents' home, and you don't have the right to speak to anyone in this house that way." I'm all business now—no more beating around the bush with this guy. "I don't know why you came, but I don't want you here." I just want him to leave before Sam and Philip can get further into whatever is going on with them. Or better yet, before Philip tries to become friends with my parents.

"Baby, I came all this way to see you." I roll my eyes at Philip. As if he has any right to be upset that I'm not reacting the way he expected I would. As if we hadn't broken up and haven't spoken in two weeks. As if I'm not going through hell right now and need to console *him*.

Sam mutters something under his breath that sounds a lot like "what a douche," but I can't be sure.

"He is not staying for dinner." Sam doesn't leave the room like I expected him to. When I shift my attention to him, he's glaring at Philip. *If looks could kill...*

I clear my throat, grabbing Sam's attention. "Will you please give us a moment?" Sam eyes Philip suspiciously, as if he doesn't trust him to leave me alone with him. But he nods once and walks out back towards the kitchen. I watch him briefly; his movements are stiff, his muscular back looks tense, and his hands are balled into fists at his sides.

I wait a moment to make sure Sam is far enough away before I speak again. "I didn't break up with you because I needed a break." I blow out my breath. "I broke up with you because this," I gesture between us, "wasn't working for me. You're a good guy, but you aren't *my* guy."

He looks as if I've slapped him, but he doesn't speak.

"You deserve to be with someone who is head over heels for you. I'm not that person. I'm sorry you drove all this way to check on me. That was kind of you. But you need to leave." I can tell he's about to protest, so I quickly add, "Philip, please. Don't make this harder than it needs to be."

Giving him no room to argue, I walk towards the front of the house. He follows me, pausing before the front door I've opened. "I'm here if you change your mind," and with that, Philip walks out of the house.

I text Liv as I walk back into the kitchen.

You won't believe who just showed up at my parents' house…

???

Philip. Sam and I just got back from a walk and there he was, chatting with my parents like they were old friends.

He. Did. NOT! Is he still there?

He did. And no. I had to ask him to leave. Fuck, he told me he didn't believe I actually wanted to break up with him.

Wait. Walk? With Sam?! Ok. I need ALL the deets, girl!

LOL. I'll call you later.

And you need to explain why you were talking to Philip.

Slipping my phone into my back pocket, I join my parents and Sam back in the kitchen. Sam eyes me like he's trying to piece together my dynamic with Philip, and my parents just look at me questioningly. I slump down into one of the chairs and stare at the stove across the room, not seeing anything.

This fucking day. I can't believe *Olivia* is talking to Philip behind my back. I want to give her the benefit of the doubt, but this is too much. There's a reason I never invited Philip to meet my parents or visit my hometown, and I hate that he violated this part of my life without thinking how it would make me feel.

I want to know what he said to my parents. But I don't have the energy to navigate that—and especially not while Sam is sitting next to me.

I feel the tension radiating off Sam and don't dare look at him. I don't think I've ever seen Sam possessive over me like that before. Just thinking about it has me feeling flustered.

And the feel of his solid chest against my back?

God.

"Where's Philip?" Dad asks, breaking my stream of thoughts. Mom nudges him with her elbow.

"He left. I assume he's on his way back to Columbia." Sam shifts next to me, placing his arm on the back of my chair. He isn't touching me, but it still feels possessive. I want to lean into him to feel his warmth again, but I don't move closer.

Sensing I don't want to talk about this anymore, Mom speaks up, "Should we order takeout from that Chinese restaurant you love? I'll order while you two tell us about your day."

I couldn't be more grateful to Mom at this moment. She's always been great at knowing when to change the subject.

Chapter 9

I hear arguing coming from downstairs. Rushing down, I halt about halfway when I hear Philip's voice.

Why is Philip here again? I groan audibly.

And who is he yelling at? What the fuck?

I thought I was pretty clear yesterday. But apparently, not clear enough. Groaning again, I continue making my way down.

Once I'm far enough down the stairs, I see Sam punch Philip. *Oh my god!*

Philip stumbles back a little before catching himself.

Rushing the rest of the way down the stairs, the volume of my voice rises as I shout at these idiots. "What the fuck are you guys doing? You know what? Don't tell me. I don't care. Philip. Leave. Now. Sam, maybe you should go home, too. Why are you even here this early? You guys are acting like fucking children."

Philip turns around, making his way to the door, muttering an apology. I watch him as he shuts the door behind him.

"That's the guy you want to be with?" Sam waves a hand behind him in the direction of the front door; his words are dripping in distaste.

"Not that it's any of your business," I clench my hands in fists at my sides, "but I broke up with him. So, no. He isn't the guy I want to be with. It shouldn't matter to you anyway!" I'm still shouting.

I'm furious because this is the last thing I need right now when I've just lost my brother. I just need to get away from Sam, who obviously isn't leaving.

Quickly turning around, I start up the stairs and hear Sam call after me.

"Wait. Let's talk."

"Stop following me," I shout down to him, not caring where my parents are, or if they are even awake.

"Come on, just talk to me." Sam's voice is sincere, worried.

I practically run the rest of the way up the stairs to the third floor and ignore Sam's continued pleas.

He's right behind me and catches the door. Before I can close it, he slowly prowls into my room.

"Get out," I snarl at him and shove my hand against his solid chest.

"No." His tone is flat as he grabs onto my hand, keeping it against him. I feel his thunderous heart beneath his gray T-shirt.

He closes the door softly behind him. He's calm. Too calm. Which enrages me further. Yanking my hand away from his chest and crossing my arms in front of me, I step slightly closer to him and raise my chin in defiance.

"Get. Out."

Sam's eyes flicker, and before I can process what that was, he pulls me into him, spins us around, and pins me to the door. His lips are on mine in an instant.

This isn't a slow, sensual kiss. This is desperate, a little angry, even.

It takes only a heartbeat before I kiss him back, nipping at his bottom lip. My arms wrap around his waist, and I'm pulling him closer into me. Sam groans into my mouth and pulls away long enough to catch his breath.

"I've wanted to do that for a long time, Kitty Kat," he whispers in my ear, causing shivers to run down my spine. He plunges his tongue back into my mouth and the feel of him against me quickly brushes away any thoughts I might have on what he just said.

God, this man.

My body melts into his as he softly nips my ear and trails kisses along my neck. I shiver from the contact, my stomach tightens, and my core heats.

Sam's hands are still pinning me to the door.

I should stop this. But it feels so good.

Feels... right.

I've thought about his mouth on me more times than I'd like to admit.

I can't think straight, but my mind quickly stops arguing with me when he moves down further and trails kisses along my throat, down to my collarbone.

Sam grabs my hips with both hands and lifts me. I wrap my legs around him and grip his shoulders. His mouth is back on mine.

I want him. "Sam, please," I gasp in between breaths.

He grabs the hem of the oversized T-shirt I slept in and pauses, looking at me. I nod, and that's all the confirmation Sam needs. He pulls my T-shirt up just enough to give him access and pushes my panties to the side.

He pushes one finger inside me, and I moan at the contact. His other hand is still holding me up against the door.

"Fuck, you're soaked for me," Sam growls as he continues placing kisses along my neck.

I start to protest when he removes his fingers. He gives me a delicious wink as he lines up his length with my entrance. I didn't even realize he had unzipped his pants.

He pauses again, giving me time to say no. When I raise my eyebrow in challenge, he slowly pushes his cock into me, and my legs tighten slightly around him. Sam feels incredible inside me.

"Please, Sam," I beg. He's moving too slowly.

"I don't want to hurt you," he whispers, like it's taking all his strength not to slam into me.

I look up at him and hiss, "This isn't my first time. I'm not going to break."

At that, Sam grabs my hips with both of his hands and pushes the rest of the way into me. I gasp and dig my fingers into his shoulders.

He pulls out almost all the way and slams back into me.

An embarrassingly loud moan escapes my lips. "That better, Kitty Kat?" Sam chuckles.

"Yes. God, yes. Please don't stop, Sam." I'm barely able to form words as he continues to move inside of me.

"You don't have to beg me. Touch yourself, Kitty Kat." Sam's tone is desperate. A plea. His mouth is on mine again as he continues to drive into me, my back hitting against the door as he moves.

I do as he demands, my fingers go straight to my clit, and I begin to rub in circles. The tension inside of me builds until I'm panting. I'm so close.

God, he feels so amazing.

I jolt awake.

"Fuuuuck." I groan into my pillow.

***

Slowly, I get out of bed and head to the shower to get ready for the day. I can't stop thinking about that dream.

I can't stop thinking about Sam. About how much my body wishes that dream were reality. By the time I calm myself down, the water is starting to turn cold. *Oops. Hopefully, no one else needed to shower.*

Once I'm back in my bedroom, I get dressed in leggings, an old AC/DC shirt, and sandals.

Before I leave, I feel my phone buzz in my pocket. *Shit, I meant to call Liv last night.*

"Hey, Liv." My voice is more chipper than I feel.

"First of all, I swear I wasn't talking to Philip. He was worried when you didn't go to work, and he showed up at our place demanding that I tell him where you were." The words tumble out in a single breath.

"God, he is such a tool. I'm sorry he put you in that position."

"Fuck, I'm so sorry he showed up at your parents' house. What a creep! So... inquiring minds are *dying* to know about a certain walk with a certain hottie by the name of Samuel Harris." She's overly dramatic this morning, and I hear Liv's girlfriend, Talia, chuckle in the background.

Liv and Talia have been dating for about six months. Talia is five feet, six inches with gorgeous, dark skin and dark, curly hair. Talia's calm demeanor is a perfect balance to Liv's fire. I adore her.

I quickly go back into my room and close the door. *I don't want anyone to hear this conversation.* I tell Liv the details of my walk and about finding Philip at my house when we got back. I even tell her about my dream, including all the more unsavory details. She is my ride or die after all.

"I don't know how I'm going to look him in the face the next time I see him."

"Girl, that dream sounds hot as fuck! And by fuck, I mean, why not get a little action from that man? No. Not yet. Bad timing. But maybe soon?" She's mostly talking to herself at this point. I want to pull my hair out.

"Oh my *God*, Liv! Why are you this way?" I can't stop the borderline hysterical laugh that spills out. It feels good to laugh when everything feels so heavy.

"You fucking love me this way. Don't try to deny it." Liv is all sass. I run my hand down my face.

"I do love you. But my God." I lie down on my bed and stare at the ceiling. "In all seriousness, I just don't think I can put myself out there with him again. You know what happened last time."

"I was serious. You know I'm a big advocate of engaging in certain activities to relieve stress." She laughs out. I can almost see the wink she would inevitably give me if I were with her. "I know you were really hurt, and I understand why you both might be hesitant with everything going on." Her voice is serious now, but still gentle. "I'm just saying, it's been a long time. That man is still single. Kat, he never got married. And, I know we haven't talked about him much, but he asks about you every time he and I talk."

I've always suspected this, but she's never confirmed it before.

"He asks me when I think you'll be ready to talk to him again," Liv continues. "Maybe don't close the door on him yet. See how things go and be open to the possibilities."

I sigh audibly and run my fingers through my loose hair. "I just want to get through this week." Deciding it's best not to dwell on Sam, I change the subject. "When are you going to be here?"

"Tomorrow morning, babe!" She's trying to sound cheerful, but I know it's a mixture of excitement and grief.

"I can't wait to see you. God, I need you here to keep me sane. Is Talia coming with you?"

I hear the hesitance in her voice, "I'm not sure yet. Maybe?"

"How is everything going with her family?"

"It's... going." She groans, "It's going to be a long process, I think. We're trying to go slow with them. Even if I want to be anything but slow with her."

"I'm sorry this isn't easier, Liv."

"Hey, I was thinking. Maybe we could have a sleepover the first couple of nights I'm there? Watch some movies and eat our weight in popcorn and licorice like we used to do?"

I don't hesitate to respond, "yes! That would be great! We can share my bed!" I know she's stressed about her situation with Talia's family, and we could both use some girl time with sappy movies and good snacks.

"Well, I don't want to inhibit a little Kat and Sam action." She laughs out. "But seriously, it would be nice to veg out a bit and just be goofy."

I roll my eyes, even though she can't see me, and ignore her comment about Sam. "It means everything to me that you'll be here. I don't think I could go through all of this without you."

"You know, he was like a brother to me, too. I wouldn't miss this for anything. I'm just so sad and so sorry that this is the reason for us being back home."

We wrap up our call, and I finally make my way downstairs to embrace the day. I'm secretly hoping Sam isn't here. I don't know how I'm going to face him after that dream.

I'm grateful when I spend the entire day with Mom and Dad playing cards, drinking wine, and watching old western movies on the couch. I'm even more thankful that Sam doesn't make an appearance.

Chapter 10

Sixteen years old

I'm standing in front of the full-length mirror next to my bedroom door, staring at my reflection. I couldn't believe it when Kevin asked me to the Homecoming dance, but here I am. And I look so pretty!

I chose a strapless, rose-pink A-line dress that falls a few inches above my knees. The lace bodice and the small lace flowers that appear to be falling from the bodice down the length of the dress are my favorite.

Mom helped me with my hair—an intricate braid twisted into a bun. I put the finishing touches on my light makeup and step into my ballerina-style slip-on shoes, which match the color of my dress.

I grab my cell phone from the charger and see a message from Kevin.

> I'm so sorry Kat, but I must have eaten something bad and I'm not going to make it. I hope you still go and have a great time with your friends.

My heart sinks. I'm all dressed up and ready to go, and... and he's not coming. I send him the only response I can muster.

Ok. I hope you feel better.

I'm so sorry, Kat. I really wanted to go with
you.

I don't respond to his last message. Instead, I walk to my bed and sit down trying to figure out what to do. I feel bad that he got sick, but I'm also really disappointed.

I try to hold back the tears that are starting to blur my vision when I hear a knock on my door. Mom walks in before I can answer.

"Kat, are you almost rea—" She stops when she sees me, her brow furrows in concern. "What's wrong, pretty girl?"

"Kevin just messaged, and I guess he isn't feeling well. So, we aren't going." My voice is shaky, and I can't stop the slow trickle of tears that are now falling down my cheeks.

"Oh, Kat. I'm so sorry." She sits next to me and wraps her arm around my shoulders.

Once I've stopped crying, Mom asks me what I want to do about the dance.

"I don't know, Ma. My friends all have dates, and I'll feel weird about going with them." I shrug. "I don't want to be a third wheel."

She doesn't speak for a moment, and then, slowly, "Ethan and Sam are going with a few friends. They don't have dates. Why don't you go with them?"

My eyes widen in disbelief at her suggestion. "I don't want to tag along with my brother, Mom." My words come out half groan and half whine.

"It wouldn't be tagging along, and you know Ethan wouldn't mind. I would hate for your night to be ruined, and I bet you would have so much fun!" She tightens her arm around me encouragingly.

Her eyes are bright and optimistic. She's trying to make the most out of this situation.

After I think it over for a moment, I agree to go with them. I don't want to seem like an annoying little sister who never wants to leave her brother's side, but I also don't want to disappoint Mom. And she's right, I'll probably still have fun.

We stand from my bed at the same time, and I quickly work to fix my makeup, so it isn't so obvious that I've been crying.

We make our way downstairs, where Ethan and Sam are standing in the foyer. Both are wearing black suits with white shirts and no ties. Ethan's hair is in his standard messy style—it looks like it should have only taken him five minutes, but he actually spent an hour on it. Sam's hair is neat and just barely brushes across his forehead. My gaze lingers on Sam. He looks incredible.

"Dang, Kat. I'd better have a talk with Kevin about how to treat my little sister," Ethan teases me.

Sam looks at me. "Hey, Kitty Kat, you look—" he clears his throat and runs his hand through his hair, slightly messing up the neat style, "you look really nice." Briefly, Sam licks his bottom lip, and I track the movement.

"Thanks, Sammy." I feel the blush heating my cheeks at his compliment.

Ethan pointedly raises his eyebrow at Sam, and I look back at Mom to avoid whatever that silent conversation was.

"Um, is it ok if I ride with you guys?" I wring my hands together in front of me and look at the floor. Part of me hopes they say no.

"Where's Kevin?" Ethan quickly asks. I flinch at his irritated tone.

"He's sick and not coming."

Ethan's expression immediately softens. "Hell yeah, you can come with us!" Ethan wraps his arm around me and pulls me into a hug. "Let's go have some fuuuuun."

"Will you save a couple of dances for me, Kitty Kat?" Sam's genuine tone catches me off guard, and I quickly look to see Ethan raise his eyebrow at Sam again.

Ignoring Ethan, I turn my attention back to Sam. "I'd like that a lot. Thanks for letting me go with you."

***

P resent Day

Saturday morning comes too soon. I roll over to my side and see that Liv is still sleeping; she's on her stomach, her hands are under her pillow.

I've always dreamed we would live a couple of houses away from each other. Eating Sunday dinners, raising our kids, and growing old together.

Liv starts to stir, as I stretch.

"Hey." Her voice is flat as she rubs her eyes. "Do you want to shower or have breakfast first?"

I turn onto my back and stare at the ceiling. My stomach is in knots. While I know I need to eat, I'm not sure if I can. "I'm not sure I can eat yet, so... shower first, I guess."

Slowly, I crawl out of bed and head towards the bathroom in the hall. I'm grateful for the warm water as it cascades down my face and hides the tears that won't stop flowing.

Even with Liv here, I'm not sure how to handle this day. I don't know how to say goodbye to Ethan.

I can't imagine what life will be like without him. I've had all week to sort through all of this, but none of it feels real. I still think he's just on a trip and will walk in the door at any moment.

Did I say I love you?

I let my mind drift to Sam. I'm not sure how to act around him. Being around him feels comfortable. It's as if no time has passed at all. I could easily slip back into a friendship with him. But I don't want to be his friend. I want more. I just don't think I can face him rejecting me again if I make the first move. I think I need him to show me he wants more, too.

When I'm finally ready, I exit the shower and head to my room to get dressed while Liv showers. I chose a simple black dress that cinches just under my chest and flows out a little from there. It's modest but isn't uptight like most of my work wardrobe. I slip on my simple black ballet flats.

I'm almost finished blow-drying my hair when Liv comes back into the room, dressed similarly to me. It's a little jolting seeing her in simple clothes. Her usually vibrant style is nowhere in sight and only makes this day more real. I frown at her black shoes.

She walks over to me once I'm done with my hair and wraps her arms around me. "You look beautiful." I know she's only trying to give me a small beacon of light in the dark storm of my feelings.

"You do, too." I force my shoulders to relax and drag my fingers through my hair. "Should we go?"

Chapter 11

Liv and I slowly walk into the church. Everything feels surreal.

This can't actually be happening.

Liv squeezes my hand and tells me she's going to say hello to her parents.

I spot mine speaking with Sam, Dan and someone else I don't recognize. Dad's back is to me, but I can see Mom clearly. She gives me a slight smile in acknowledgement. Mom looks like she's aged 10 years just this morning. I don't want to think of her this way, so I shift my attention away.

My gaze snags on Sam. He looks nice in a black suit and white button-down shirt. His collar is open with a couple of buttons undone at the neck. I lift my gaze to his face and see that he's looking at me. His expression is tight, his eyes are sad. I can tell he's trying to remain stoic. My face crumples, and I watch as Sam immediately makes his way to me.

I'm sobbing, my face in my hands, by the time he gets to me. Sam gently pulls my hands from my face and wraps my shaking body in his arms. He holds me while tears stream down my cheeks.

"I'm so glad you're here." I croak out once I regain some semblance of composure.

"Me too," he says as he kisses the top of my head. I lean back just enough to look up at him. His arms remain firmly planted around my waist.

The way he immediately came to me and the way he's looking at me now? I've missed everything about him. He's kind, compassionate, and even after all of this time, it's evident that he cares for me. Even if it is just as a friend. Despite my feelings for him being in turmoil, I'm glad he's here with me. I offer him a small smile, which he returns. He reaches up and tucks my hair behind my ear before gently wiping at the tears remaining on my cheeks.

I overhear Liv talking to someone, so I turn to see who it is. Talia's here. They walk over to us, and Sam releases me from his embrace but doesn't leave my side. He stands close enough that I can feel the heat coming off his body. I take comfort in his proximity and warmth.

"Hey, Talia." My voice is rough.

She pulls me into a hug and whispers, "I'm so sorry." My tears start anew, and I just know they aren't going to stop today.

"Apparently, I should have brought a supersized box of tissues with me." I joke, trying to break some of the tension I'm feeling.

Sam briefly touches the small of my back and steps away. His absence is jolting. I watch him walk over to a box of tissues on a side table. He picks up the container and brings it over to me. *Why do I feel like I can't breathe without him being near me?*

I shouldn't be feeling like this. Not when we haven't spoken or seen each other in so long. Sam feels like home. It feels like we've never skipped a beat, even with the distance I forced on us.

Trying to avoid the feelings Sam is stirring in me today, I look at Talia. "When did you get into town?"

She looks a little embarrassed as her cheeks flush slightly. "Actually, last night." I cock my head to the side, about to protest when she hurries on to explain, "I wanted to be here for you and Livie, but I also knew how important it was for you both to have some time together."

Talia has always been incredibly thoughtful of everyone. It's as if she has a crystal-clear understanding of what people need and when they need it. She reminds me of Mom in all the best ways. This is probably why I like her so much.

"Thanks. You're right, I did need that. But I wish you didn't feel like you had to stay away."

Just then, an usher walks out into the hall and quietly invites everyone into the room where the service will take place.

I look up at Sam, and he gestures for me to walk with him. We make our way to the front, where the family and close friends are supposed to sit. My parents are already there, next to Dan, in the front row.

As we get past some of the people standing in the aisle, I notice the casket at the front of the room.

My heart drops and my body freezes.

I can't take another step forward.

Mom always thought it was strange to have an open casket because the person never really looks quite like they were supposed to.

So, it isn't a surprise that Ethan's casket is closed. It's just devastating to see it here and know that Ethan's body is in there. I don't notice I am crying again until Sam hands me another tissue from the box he still carries.

He steps towards me, places his hand on my arm, and whispers in my ear, "We can go back out, if you want." Looking up at his soft, chocolate brown eyes, I shake my head no.

"Will you—" It comes out gravelly. I clear my throat and try again, "will you sit with me?" I feel too vulnerable right now. Too raw. I'm not sure I can move forward if he says no.

Thankfully, Sam doesn't hesitate before he grabs my hand. "Always," he says as he looks into my eyes and brings my hand to his lips. He places a small kiss on the back.

Gently, Sam leads me to the row opposite my parents, which is now full, and guides me to take the seat next to him. Liv sits on my other side, Talia next to her.

I can't stop staring at that damn casket, knowing my big brother isn't coming back. Knowing I can't stop my mind from replaying that last phone call. *Did I say I love you?*

I try to listen to everyone who speaks at the service, but everything sounds garbled, like the adults on the Peanuts cartoons. I'm vaguely aware of the priest finishing his sermon and other people standing up and speaking, but it isn't until Sam squeezes my hand that I pull my gaze from the casket.

I look up at him and furrow my brows.

Answering my silent question, he leans in and whispers in my ear. "Your mom asked if I would say a few words, so I'm going to let go of your hand and go up there." I feel my panic rising, which he must notice in my expression, because he quickly adds, "I won't be gone long, and Livie is going to hold your hand for me until I get back."

He looks over my shoulder at Liv sitting on my other side. Sam nods once before I feel her arm come around me, pulling me into her side. Sam lets go of my hand and walks to the front. Liv takes my now free hand with her opposite one.

I stare at Sam as he walks away—this man who used to be the boy who was always at my house. This man, who used to tease me about how many books I read each summer. This man, who meant everything to my brother. Who meant everything to me. Who *means* everything to me. I can't stop looking at him.

He clears his throat, and when he starts speaking, his voice is husky but confident.

"Ethan was more than my best friend. He was my brother in so many ways. His absence will be a hole I don't think I'll ever be able to fill." He pauses, and I can see he's taking a breath—composing himself. He glances down. Only then do I see he's holding paper, his notes.

Sam looks back up when he speaks again, "I know he'd be mad at me if I spent this time being sad about him and talking to you all about how much I'm going to miss him." He gives the room a timid smile.

"So instead," he continues, "I want to share some stories about my friend that you probably haven't heard. We're going to celebrate who he was instead of being sad." He speaks slowly but with confidence.

"Most of you know that Ethan and I were inseparable as kids. We did everything together, from learning to surf, figuring out how to flirt with girls, to participating in track. We got into a lot of trouble, too. I'm not sure which of us was the bad influence. Probably both of us. We *definitely* encouraged each other a lot.

"Like that time that we collected a bunch of road hazard cones and left them in Sarah and George's front yard." He looks over at my parents, looking remorseful. I hear Dad mutter something, but I can't make out what it is. He's shaking his head like a huge puzzle piece just clicked into place for him. Sam chuckles lightly.

"I can't remember why we decided it would be a good idea. But I can tell you that we laughed so hard when we saw you come home trying to figure out why you had thirty cones in the yard." He chuckles again, and several people in the crowd join in the laughter. I feel Liv's body shake with her silent laugh, too. A small smile is all I can muster.

"Sorry about that." He shrugs before continuing, "Even as adults, we would spend as much time together as we could. Every summer, we'd take a couple of weeks off from our responsibilities and spend the time fishing and drinking beers."

He pauses and looks at me before shifting his gaze back to the crowd. I'm mesmerized by him.

"A couple of years ago, we took one of these trips. But instead of fishing, we decided to take a cross-country tour on our motorcycles. We'd talked about taking this trip for several years and finally decided to just do it. We packed up some saddle bags and backpacks and planned out our trip—making sure we knew where we were going to stop each night."

Another glance towards me. I can't quite place his expression. Almost, scared? Remorseful? But I have no idea why that would be. I heard about this trip. It seemed like they had a great time.

Sam is wringing his notes in front of him. "Only, we didn't make it very far into the trip," he continues.

Didn't make it far?

I sit up a little straighter in my seat, my eyes glued to Sam as he continues. Liv squeezes my hand.

"We were riding on a highway when my bike slid out from under me. I didn't see the debris on the road until it was too late." My knee starts bouncing on its own. "I slammed into a metal pipe off to the side of the road and was rushed to the hospital."

I feel my mouth open in shock, my leg still shaking. I glance over at Liv, and she squeezes my hand reassuringly. She subtly shakes her head. I don't know if she's telling me she didn't know or if she's telling me not now.

Why didn't I know about this? Why didn't Sam tell me? Why didn't *Ethan* tell me? I feel the anger rush into my senses. But more than anger, I'm embarrassed. Embarrassed that I let my feelings get in the way of my friendship with Sam, enough that no one told me about this.

I look back at Sam as he continues speaking. "I had surgery to repair some extensive damage to my shoulder and had too many stitches to count." I can tell he's avoiding my gaze now. "I went through rehab. Thankfully, everything worked out." He shrugs.

My body stiffens with his words, my knee finally stills. Liv's arm tightens around my shoulders. I dare a glance at my parents, but they don't seem to notice my reaction. No, they seem unfazed. They knew.

"But when I was going through the hard days. The ones when I just wanted to give up because the pain was too much, Ethan was there, encouraging me. Reminding me to be strong. Reminding me that we don't give up. That was the thing about Ethan, he was always there when people needed him.

"I'm going to miss that solid reassurance from him. But I'm so grateful I was able to share in the light and warmth he gave to everyone he met. I only hope that I can be half as kind as Ethan was to me and others. Half as protective. And half the man he was and was becoming."

Sam makes his way back to the seat next to me. Liv removes her arm from around my shoulders as Sam sits down. He finally looks at me. His eyes are full of apprehension, he's rigid, and I feel the tension radiating off his body.

I don't know why he didn't tell me, or why my family kept this from me. But it probably has a lot to do with how I've treated him the last few years. I give him a small smile before I take his hand in mine again. I lean into him slightly and feel Sam's body relax.

The service continues with a few more people sharing stories about my brother. Sam's hand doesn't leave mine. I'm grateful for his steady presence, but I can't shake the shock and sadness that he went through that experience.

After the formal service, a few of us, close friends and family, make our way to the cemetery. A couple more people speak, and once the graveside service is over, we're all invited to pay our last respects.

I'm one of the last people to leave my seat when I walk over to the casket to join my parents. My heart feels like it's shattered into a million pieces as I place my hand on top of the smooth, dark, stained wood.

I don't know how to put those pieces back together, or if they ever *will* go back together.

"I don't know how I'm supposed to go on without you," I croak through my sobs. "I'll miss you every day, big brother. Thank you for always being there for me. I... I love you." I feel the hot tears fall down my cheeks as I say those final words to him. Hoping he can hear them.

I'm not sure how long I stay rooted to my spot. It could have been seconds or hours. At some point, my parents hug me and tell me they're heading home.

I feel warmth at my back and watch as Sam places his hand on mine, still on my brother's casket. He gently picks my hand up, bringing it to his lips to place a soft kiss on the back before pulling my hand to his heart. Using his other arm, he pulls me into him.

I nuzzle my face into his chest and breathe him in. I shouldn't be doing this. Not now. Not ever. But I can't stop myself. Sam drops my hand pinned to his chest and wraps his arm around me, pulling me in tighter. He runs soothing patterns up and down my back.

I feel the pressure of his kiss on the top of my head and slowly extricate myself from him. Wiping the remaining tears from my cheeks, I look around. Most of the people have left.

"Can I take you back to the house?" Sam's eyes are soft as he looks at me.

"I'd like that."

I feel numb as we drive back to my parents' house, and I'm glad when neither of us speaks. Sam's hand stays firmly, but gently, wrapped around mine.

Chapter 12

S everal people are bustling around my parents' house by the time we get there. People are setting up food, plates, and utensils. Talking over drinks or looking awkwardly around like they don't know what to do. *I understand the feeling.*

It's weird having so many people in the house. Especially when the last thing I want to do right now is socialize.

We barely step inside when Sam's dad asks him to help with something. Sam squeezes my hand and then walks off with his dad.

I'm left there standing alone and feeling empty. I glance down at my empty hand Sam was holding just a moment ago, before looking around the room again. I don't see my parents or Liv and Talia.

Deciding I need a break before socializing, I slowly make my way upstairs.

I avoid glancing towards Ethan's room as I make it up to the third floor. Once in my room, I kick off my shoes and lie face down on my bed.

***

I must have fallen asleep because the next thing I know, the sun is starting to set. I turn from my stomach to my side and find Liv and Talia sitting on the floor of my room, quietly watching a show on Talia's laptop, both with headphones in.

I watch them for a moment. They are sitting cross-legged on the floor. Talia is leaning toward Liv, with her arm behind Liv's back, hand on the floor. Liv's hand is on Talia's thigh. They look so happy. They look like they're in love. I love this for them.

"How long have I been out?" my voice croaks as I slowly sit up in bed.

"A couple of hours, babe," Liv answers as she looks over at me, and Talia pauses whatever they're watching.

"Where's Sam? Where are my parents? What time is it?" Talia's lips turn up softly. I fight the urge to rub the sleep from my eyes, not wanting to smear more of my makeup.

"It's just after 5:30," Liv answers. "Sam went to his dad's house about 30 minutes ago."

I frown before Talia adds, "Sam was worried when he couldn't find you and came up here to see you fast asleep. He didn't want to disturb you. Your parents are downstairs on the porch drinking wine."

I'm still in my dress, and I feel uncomfortable. I arch my back in a stretch and slowly climb out of bed, making my way over to my closet. I pull out some pajama pants and a black tank top to relax in.

"I'm going to go get some food and check on my parents. Are you staying here tonight?" I look at Liv and Talia as I speak.

"Yes. We plan to be obnoxious and force you to watch The Princess Bride with us." Liv winks, and I smile at her. She knows her way into my heart.

I unlock my phone, about to message Same, when I see a message from him.

My dad and I will meet you at Ethan's place tomorrow. I wondered if you would get lunch with me Monday before you leave?

I'm sad I missed you. I'm sorry I fell asleep before you left. I would love to get lunch with you.

Please don't apologize. I know you needed the sleep. Let's make plans tomorrow.

See you tomorrow.

Thanks for today.

Always. See you tomorrow.

When I get downstairs, I see the food has all been cleared away, and Mom is cleaning some dishes. She's changed into sweatpants and a sweatshirt, and her hair is twisted into a neat bun.

"Hey, Ma. Why don't you go sit down, and I'll finish these."

"I've got these, but you should heat some food from the fridge. I know you didn't eat."

"That was a nice service," I say as I rummage through the containers in the fridge, looking for something that sounds appetizing.

"It was lovely. I think Ethan would have liked it." She sounds assured, but I can tell she's getting choked up.

"Ma?" My voice is quiet as I contemplate how to ask the question burning through me.

"Yes, pretty girl?" Mom sets a dish into the dishwasher before turning around, giving me her attention.

"Did you know about Sam's accident?" I force myself to continue meeting her gaze, even though I want to hide away from the truth that everyone knew but me.

She briefly looks down at her hands before returning her attention to me. I already know what she's going to say before she opens her mouth to speak. "Yes. I knew. Not the full extent, but we knew he was in rough shape." Mom gives me a small smile. "It wasn't our place to share that news—that was his story to tell," she answers my question before I can voice it.

I wish my parents had told me. But I know she's right. Same with Ethan, I guess.

Her voice is small when she speaks again, "I'm sorry you had to learn this way."

With my food heated up, I sit at the table, gripping the fork like it's my lifeline. "I'm not upset that you didn't tell me, Ma. I just felt a little dumb sitting there feeling like the only person who didn't know."

My heart aches knowing I can't ask Ethan about it. I resign myself to asking Sam when we get lunch on Monday.

"We've been hoping, waiting, for you and Sam to start talking again. I never thought it would take—" She chokes on a sob, and swallows hard. She's gripping the counter behind her with both hands. "I don't know what happened between you two; I'm just glad you seem to be getting along again." Mom turns around and continues working on the dishes.

"Yeah," I say it slowly. I'm relieved when she drops the subject.

Once I'm finished eating and she's finished with the dishes, she pulls out the bottle of wine she was drinking with Dad and offers me a glass. Liv and Talia make their way into the kitchen, and Mom grabs a couple of decks of cards for us to play.

We stay up late into the night, drinking wine, playing cards, and reminiscing about Ethan. We didn't watch The Princess Bride, but this was better.

We laugh at some of the ways Ethan would try to cheat when we played cards with him. It was so common that anyone sitting next to him was responsible for watching him closely and stopping him from slipping cards onto his lap or trying to discard two cards instead of one.

With each bottle of wine opened, we laughed more. It was refreshing and the perfect way to end this day.

***

The next morning, I wake up feeling groggy and very hungover. I haven't drunk that much in a long time. "Fuck." I groan as I sit up; the room is spinning. The first thing I need to do is get some water, food, and aspirin. I don't see Talia and Liv—they must already be downstairs. Slowly, I make my way down and into the kitchen.

I grimace when I see that Liv and Talia are already eating; they look as miserable as I feel. Dad is cooking omelets with bacon, onions, and bell peppers. A smile spreads across my face at the sight. This might be the only thing he knows how to cook.

"Where's Ma?"

"She's still sleeping off all that wine you let her drink last night." He chuckles and raises his eyebrows accusingly; I know he's teasing me. "I couldn't even tell you the last time I saw your mom that drunk. I was worried I might have to carry her up to our room." Dad flashes a huge smile at us. "Thank God she made it because this old back probably would have broken if I had to carry her." He laughs again and turns around, grabs a mug from the cupboard, and pours coffee into it.

I can't hold back the laugh that builds at the vision Dad plants in my mind of his over sixty-year-old body carrying Mom up the stairs because she was too drunk to make it herself.

Dad hands me the cup of coffee and I walk over to the table, sitting next to Liv; she slides the aspirin bottle towards me. I give her a grateful smile and add a generous amount of cream to my coffee. I've never been able to drink black coffee, and Liv loves to tease me about it. "Like a little coffee with that cream?"

"Yes. It's the only palatable way to drink it." We all laugh.

A few minutes later, Dad gives me an omelet. "Dad, you are a gentleman and a scholar." I beam up at him before quickly devouring the delicious breakfast.

Mom finally joins us when I've polished off my omelet and am working on my second cup of coffee. "I am not in my 20s anymore." She groans as she plops into the seat next to me. "I don't know why I thought I could keep up with you gals." She grimaces.

I try to hold back my laugh, but it comes out when I tease her: "Sorry, Ma. Next time, I'll send you to bed and tuck you in."

"Thanks," she grumbles. "Do you want to meet Dan and Sam at Ethan's apartment while I get some food and try to feel a little more sociable?"

"Sure." I kiss her on the cheek and wink at Dad. "Good luck with this one." I point my thumb at Mom as Talia, Liv, and I make our way out of the kitchen.

Liv and Talia plan to spend the day with Liv's parents today. Once we're all ready, I drive over to Ethan's condo.

I get there before Dan and Sam, and I'm grateful for the chance to walk through his place without feeling rushed.

I've been here more times than I can count, but never without him. It feels strange to be here, looking at his stuff. His decor is minimalist. He has dark furniture that contrasts with the white walls. For a bachelor, he's incredibly clean.

Making my way through each room, I mentally take in the things that we might want to look at today. The goal isn't to completely empty the place; instead, it's to categorize the items here and create a plan. But I also know the more we accomplish today, the less my parents have to do on their own.

Finally, I walk into the primary bedroom. Looking around, I stop my quick perusal when I see the old skateboard I gave him for his 15th birthday hanging on the wall above his dresser. I gasp at the sight.

It's only then that I realize I've never been in his room. I suppose it makes sense. What reason would I have to go into Ethan's bedroom?

Pulling the skateboard down from its hooks, I walk back to the bed and sit down, tracing my fingers along the green, blue, and black swirls and abstract images.

I made Mom take me to all the skateboard shops in Charleston until I found one that was completely blank on the underside. I spent weeks painting the board with intricate designs.

Of all the things I expected him to keep, this wasn't one of them. I didn't even think he liked it because I never saw him use it.

"You know he loved that board," Sam's soft voice startles me. I didn't hear him come in.

"I never saw him use it. I thought he didn't like it." I keep my attention on the board. "But here it was, hanging on his wall."

It looks just like it did when I gave it to him all those years ago. Gliding my fingers along the length of the skateboard, I finally meet Sam's gaze. I turn the board over so he can see the side I spent hours painting. "It looks like it did the day I gave it to him." My voice goes quiet when I mumble out, "I thought he threw it in his closet after his party and forgot about it." I furrow my brow as I watch him.

"Kat." Sam steps towards me, but stops and shoves his hands into his pockets. "He loved that board." His voice is tentative as if he's trying to calm a rabid animal. "He talked about how cool it was for so long after you gave it to him. He didn't use it because he always knew he didn't want to ruin it." When I look up at him skeptically, he adds, "When he moved into this place, the first thing he bought were hooks to hang it up."

My heart cracks and I can't hold back the sobs as I clutch the skateboard to my chest like it's a life vest. Sam immediately crosses the room and pulls me up into his arms. It's a bit awkward with the skateboard still in my grasp. He takes it from me, still holding me with his free arm, and sets the board down. He wraps me in both arms again and holds me until my tears stop, running soothing patterns along my spine.

I hear my parents in the living room and straighten up, pulling away from Sam. Looking at his shirt, I see I've left it wet from my tears. "I'm making a bad habit out of getting you wet." I sniffle.

"It's ok." He gently wipes a stray tear from my cheek, giving me a subtle smile. "I have lots of shirts. You can get all of them wet if you need." Sam winks at me, takes my hand, and leads me into the living room where everyone is gathered.

Why does it feel so comfortable, natural, for him to hold my hand?

When we walk into Ethan's living room, Dad's attention flickers from my hand interlaced with Sam's and up to my eyes. He quirks an eyebrow in question, which I ignore.

Sam drops my hand as Mom reaches for him and pulls him into an embrace. "It's good to see you, hun. It means a lot to me to have you here." Sam takes a deep breath, relaxing into Mom's arms.

She has always treated Sam like her own son. After his mom died, with how much time he spent at our house, my parents even bought a trundle bed to fit under Ethan's bed, so Sam had a nice place to sleep.

I love that she embraces Sam the way she does. I couldn't imagine how hard it was to grow up without his mom.

After we all say our hellos, we spend the next several hours going through each room. Mom looks through various documents we find, categorizing them based on bills and miscellaneous items.

Other than the paperwork, my parents don't want to get rid of anything. So instead, we box up the food in the kitchen, and Sam and Dan take it to a local shelter.

By the time we're done for the day, I've made a small pile of things I intend to take back to Columbia with me—the skateboard at the top of the pile.

Chapter 13

Fifteen Years Old

"God, I needed this," Liv groans as she stretches out on her beach towel. We're wearing matching hot pink bikinis with black polka dots. It's the middle of the summer. Liv has a perfect tan, and her blond hair looks lighter than it does in the winter.

We're both lying on our stomachs watching Ethan and Sam surf. Or try to surf. They haven't figured out how to stay up on their boards yet.

My focus stays on Sam. He's started developing muscles, and well, they are very nice to look at. His hair is short and looks spiky from the water. He is so cute, and I can't seem to look away from him.

"Kat, who are you staring at?" Liv follows my gaze, "Oh, Sam. Wait, Sam? Are you crushing on Sam?" Her voice is high-pitched with shock.

I smack her arm lightly and look around us to ensure no one is listening. The last thing I want is for any of the group we're here with to go telling Sam that I have a crush on him.

Seeing that no one is close enough to overhear our conversation, I finally look at her. She's looking at me with impatience. "Yes," I whisper to her. "I don't know when it started, but look at him... he's hot!"

"I guess it's kind of inevitable since he's always at your house."

"Please don't say anything. I would be so embarrassed. Oh my God, and if Ethan finds out? He would never stop teasing me about it."

"Your secret is safe with me. Do you think you'll try to get with him?"

"I don't know." I groan into my towel. "He's Ethan's best friend. Wouldn't that be weird?"

"No. I don't think so."

"Anyway, who are you crushing on this summer?"

Liv looks at me, chewing the inside of her lip. "Actually, that's something I wanted to talk to you about." Her voice is small and shaky. Liv is never nervous.

"What is it?" I try to have a reassuring tone.

"Well... I... I think that Emily is really pretty." She quickly looks down at her hands. I follow her gaze and see that she's wringing the towel. Liv likes Emily? Well, now that she says it, it makes perfect sense. I've always wondered if Liv was attracted to girls.

"Emily is so pretty, and she's nice," my voice relays the excitement I feel for Liv.

"Yeah?"

"Definitely."

"I think I have a small crush on her. I think she likes boys so it wouldn't work out." She sighs and then rolls onto her back, blocking the sun with her arm. She peeks under her arm at me. "Want to get in the water?"

I jump up from my towel. "Let's go."

***

P resent Day

I wake the next morning and groan at the realization it's Monday. All I want to do is stay in bed and not face anything this world requires of me. I also know that I've been away from work for a week and I have to return to Columbia tonight.

I don't know how I am going to leave my parents... and Sam, but I'm grateful that Liv and Talia will be there for me.

Since my trip home in August, I've been thinking a lot about moving back to Charleston. I spent two weeks just lounging around, hiking with Ethan, and going out on our parents' boat.

I knew I was going to break up with Philip soon, and the time away from him allowed me to think through what I wanted. But when I got back to Columbia, it took me a while to break up with him. Philip is just one less reason to stay.

I haven't talked to anyone about this because I don't want the outside pressure. I've always paved my own path and did what I felt was best. I haven't always made the best decisions, but I've always owned them. And this is one of those decisions I have to make on my own.

I stretch and see Liv curled up next to Talia, all three of us sharing my queen-size bed. The thought of the three of us crammed into this bed is comical, and I can't resist the quiet laugh that shakes my body.

Not wanting to wake them, I slowly and quietly get out of bed, grab my phone, and slip out of my room.

I make it to the kitchen and see Mom at the round table, head down on her arms.

Sitting next to her, I put my arm around her shoulders. "Hey, Ma. Can I get you some coffee and breakfast?"

She sits up and looks at me, tear stains streaking her cheeks. My gut clenches at the sight. "That would be nice. Thank you."

"I love you, Ma," I say before quickly kissing her cheek and getting up to start making the coffee.

"Love you, too."

I pull out pancake mix and breakfast sausage and get to work. While I'm cooking, Dad pads into the room and sits next to Mom.

"Hey, beautiful," I hear him say. "How long have you been awake?" I don't turn around, opting to give them a little privacy while I busy myself with breakfast.

"I'm not sure. I got out of bed around 5:00 a.m. I didn't want to disturb you."

"You could never disturb me, darling." I see Dad kiss Mom's cheek and rub her arm from the corner of my vision.

My parents have always been kind to each other. I'm sure they fought, but they never did it in front of us. I've always loved it when Dad calls Mom darling or when she calls him babe. They've been married for thirty-three years; I love that after all this time, they still clearly love each other.

Their relationship is probably the biggest reason I've never really gotten serious with any of the guys I've dated.

I want someone to love me with every fiber of their being, like I know my parents love each other. I want to know without a doubt that the person I am with will always be by my side and will always be a partner.

I'm not delusional; I know there will be tough times. I know we'll have arguments and disagreements. I just want to know that even in those challenging moments, he isn't going to just give up and walk away. Sometimes I wonder if I'm asking too much.

With the coffee ready, I pour three mugs, add creamer to mine and Mom's before setting the mugs on the table. Mom doesn't take as much cream as I do, but she also doesn't drink it black. Dad, on the other hand, does—it's disgusting.

Turning back to the stove to continue cooking breakfast, Dad interrupts the silence, "Kat, what time are you heading to Columbia today?"

"I think I'll leave around 3. I don't want to get home too late." I chuckle a little. "I wish I could stay longer, but I have a hearing on Thursday that I need to spend some time preparing for. And I don't know what else might have come in throughout the week that needs my attention. I know my office is picking up the slack while I'm gone, but I still feel like I need to be there."

"We wish you could stay longer, too, Kat. But your mom and I understand you have responsibilities and a life to get back to. I'm just glad you've been here this week."

"Me too, Dad."

"I've also been glad to see you spending more time with Sam. You used to be so close." I can tell Mom is trying to ask about Sam without actually asking.

"It's been nice having him here." I realize what I've said after it comes out, but I know it's the truth. It *has* been nice having Sam around. "We're going to get lunch before I leave."

"I'm so glad to hear that. You both need each other." I look at Mom, letting her words sink in.

Dad just gives me a knowing look. *Yeah, yeah. You saw us holding hands.*

Liv and Talia join us as I put the food onto the table, and we chat about the upcoming week as we eat. Dad asks a lot of questions about my hearing, and I'm grateful to have him listen to my ideas and offer me guidance. It's one thing I know I'm going to miss about Ethan.

Chapter 14

I spent the next part of the morning packing my belongings and loading them into my car, so I wouldn't have to worry about it later.

Liv and Talia gather their things and head over to Liv's parents' house to spend a few hours before they head back to Columbia as well.

Once my suitcase is packed, I slowly walk into Ethan's room. I go straight to his bookshelf and grab his copies of *The Outsiders* and *To Kill a Mockingbird*.

I used to tease Ethan whenever I saw him mark his books. *"Sacrilegious! You are torturing those poor babies!"* My books all show signs of being well-loved, but I don't crease the corners of the pages to hold my spot and don't write in them. Receipts and napkins happen to make great bookmarks.

But right now, I'm so grateful for his obsession with highlighting his favorite passages and writing notes in the margin. I can't wait to read the things he found insightful or that stood out to him.

I grab his Letterman's jacket before exiting his room and softly close the door.

I'm sitting in the kitchen, just breathing and staring out the window, when I hear the doorbell ring just before 12:30. As I reach the entryway, I see Sam walking in, Mom holding the door open.

Sam's wearing a fitted black T-shirt and dark jeans. *Always with the fitted shirts, this man.* I don't stop myself from looking at his muscled arms and tattoos. I hate to admit it, but his tattoos make me weak in the knees. He's devastatingly handsome.

Finally shifting my gaze to his face, I see him watching me. He quirks up an eyebrow in a *I saw you checking me out* way.

I groan, grab my bag, kiss Mom on the cheek, and walk out the front door. "I'll be back soon, Ma."

"Have fun, you two." She says it like she's in on a secret I don't know about. I roll my eyes as I walk outside.

Sam hurries along, getting to his dad's SUV first. He opens my door for me.

"Ever the gentleman." I tease.

"Always, my lady." He dips into an exaggerated bow, his eyes sparkling. I roll my eyes at his back but watch as he walks around the front of the SUV and climbs into the driver's seat.

"Soooo," I drag out as Sam pulls away from the curb. I have to know about this motorcycle accident he mentioned Saturday. "Motorcycle accident, huh?"

Sam snaps his attention to me and runs a palm across his face. "You caught that, huh?" As if I wasn't sitting there hanging on every word.

"Why didn't Ethan tell me?" This is the one question that keeps lingering in my mind. I understand why Sam didn't say anything to me. We hadn't exactly been speaking regularly enough for him to share that kind of information with me. But Ethan? Why didn't he tell me?

"Because I asked him not to," Sam says each word slowly, and I watch as the corners of his lips turn down slightly.

His words hit me like a punch to my gut. My palms start to sweat, and I feel the temperature in my cheeks rise. "You told him not to tell me? Wh... Why would you do that? Why didn't you want me to know, Sam?"

"It isn't that I didn't want you to know." Sam's words are rushed, and his voice rises slightly. He takes a deep breath. "Kat, we didn't exactly end things on great terms." His hands grip the steering wheel as he navigates the streets. "Despite seeing each other over the years since then, I know you've been avoiding me."

I was avoiding him. But that doesn't exactly explain why he didn't want me to know.

He takes another deep breath before continuing. "I was in a dark place. I was struggling daily with my accident and recovery."

He glances at me briefly before turning his attention back to the road. My eyes haven't left his face. I watch every expression flit across his handsome features. I get the sense he doesn't want to have this conversation, so I remain quiet.

"I'd never been in so much pain in my life before that. There were days it was hard to just get out of bed. My recovery was slow, with physical therapy kicking my ass every day. Truthfully, my mental health kind of tanked."

He sighs and I can't stop staring at him. I feel stupid realizing I had no idea any of this was happening.

"I didn't want you to know because... I didn't want that to be the reason that you finally let me back into your life. We have a lot to talk about." He shrugs. "I couldn't stomach my accident and recovery being the reason you—I think I would have always wondered if you felt like you had to talk to me rather than wanting to talk to me."

I let his words sink in, and I know he's right. I would have done anything for him if I had known what he was going through. I would have dropped everything and gone to him.

"I'm sorry, Sam. There's a lot about how things ended that I wish I could take back. You were a good friend to me, and I acted like a child. You deserved better than that. I'm sorry I wasn't there for you." I look at the road in front of us through the windshield, no longer able to look at him.

"That regret goes both ways, you know?" Sam gently bumps my arm with his elbow. I lean back into the seat, allowing my head to drop against the headrest. I interlace my hands in my lap to keep from fidgeting. "I wish I had handled things differently. I suspected how you felt. I shouldn't have sprung that news on you the way I did. It was insensitive. I'm sorry I hurt you, Kat."

We pull up to the restaurant, and I'm grateful for the opportunity to change the subject, even if briefly.

I get out of the SUV before he can open my door for me, and Sam shoots me a teasing scowl. When I give him one back, he laughs. "Come on, menace." He grabs my hand, and we walk into the restaurant.

Once we've ordered our food—brisket and cole slaw tacos for me, and a pulled pork sandwich for Sam—I look around the place. This BBQ joint has always been a favorite of mine, thanks to its casual vibes, great BBQ served on metal trays with paper liners, and fantastic drinks.

"About our conversation in the car." Sam looks at me like he's staring into my soul. I want to recoil afraid that he'll see my every thought of him, but I hold his stare instead. "That is one of the reasons I wanted to have lunch before you left today."

My attention is fixed on him, silently urging him to continue; my knee bounces slightly under the table.

"I don't want us to go back to how things have been the last few years. I've missed you. I want my friend back." Sam leans closer and places his elbows onto the table.

There's that word again...*friend*. "I'd like that, too." It comes out more guarded than I intended, and I know it's because I've never wanted to just be his friend. I try to mask my tone with a smile. If a *friend* is the only way to have him back in my life, I'll take it.

"Good." His smile is evident in his tone as he sits back again. "So, I'm going to text you and call you, and you are going to text me and call me, ok?"

I nod at him, knowing he's referencing my lack of responses to his texts and calls back in Seattle. "Yes. I'll text and call you."

I sip on the sweet tea the server brought me and use the moment to collect myself a little more. Even if we could be something more, right now, I need Sam as a friend. Maybe he needs me, too.

"Sooo," I drag out the word, "are you ok? I mean, after the accident?"

"I still have a pretty bad scar across my chest," he touches a spot along his ribs on the left side, "but otherwise, I'm good. Yeah."

"Will you show me? The scar?"

His expression is tight as he searches my face. "Some other time." Sensing he doesn't want to be pushed, I drop it.

We eat our food and chat the entire time. We talk about how Charleston has changed since we were kids. We talk about hanging out over Thanksgiving weekend if he can make the trip work with his schedule. We make plans to see each other over Christmas.

Once we're finished eating, he takes me back to my parents' house. I get out of the SUV, and Sam walks me to the door.

We stop in front of the door, and I turn to look at him, taking in his soft eyes. His body is rigid for a moment before he pulls me into a hug. He steps away sooner than I want him to. His absence makes me feel empty.

"Don't be a stranger, Kitty Kat." He kisses my cheek softly and then walks back to the SUV. I reach up and touch the place on my cheek where he kissed me and watch as he drives away.

Chapter 15

I drive back, stopping on my way out of Charleston to get gas and then to pick up takeout once I make it back to Columbia.

I grab the takeout and my suitcase from the car, leaving the things I brought from Ethan's bedroom and condo for another time.

Walking into the condo I share with Liv; she isn't home yet.

As part of my graduation gift from college and law school, my parents gave me a nice down payment on this place. Liv and I split the mortgage and share a small two-bedroom, one-bathroom condo. Our styles clash a bit, so our decor is eclectic. I like calming, neutral colors, and Liv loves bright colors that stand out.

We have a bright orange couch that looks like it belongs in the 1970s and a sleek, modern, black coffee table in front of it. Liv has bright green and orange coffee mugs she uses every day, while I prefer simple white dishes. Somehow, it all works.

I quickly message my parents to let them know I made it safely, and then send a text to Sam.

> Hey. I just wanted to let you know I made it back to Columbia.

> Thanks for letting me know.

I'm really glad I got to see you.

Me too.

Hopefully you can take a break over Thanks-giving.

Eager to see me again?

Is he flirting with me? God, I desperately want that to be the case. Not knowing, I decide to play it neutral.

Not eager, just want to make sure you see your dad more.

I'll do my best, Kitty Kat.

Why does his use of my nickname send shivers down my spine? A grin spreads across my face thinking about Sam.

I shoot Liv a message letting her know I'm home.

After eating dinner, I decide to unload the rest of the things from my car. It takes me two trips, and by the time I'm finished unpacking my suitcase, I hear Liv enter the condo.

"Hey girl," Liv shouts from the living room. "Did you already eat?"

"Yeah, I got Indian takeout. There's some left in the fridge."

I make my way into the kitchen and pull one of my favorite bottles of wine out of the fridge, which is covered in takeout menus—neither Liv or I cook very often—grab two glasses, and the corker before sitting down.

"So, tell me about lunch with Sam."

I tell her everything, including that we promised to stay in touch more often.

"And how do you feel about all of this?" She asks, and I know she's just trying to open me up and help me process everything.

This is a little game we play when we know the other is struggling with things. We ask questions about feelings and how we want to handle things rather than giving opinions. It's extremely helpful and extremely annoying.

I take a deep breath. "Honestly? He said we could be friends." I wrinkle my nose. "That word feels wrong. I don't want to be his friend—I've never wanted to be just friends with Sam."

"So, what are you going to do about that?"

"What is there to do about it? He lives in Chicago. I live in Columbia. I'm not interested in a long-distance relationship. But more than that, how would we even truly get to know each other again when we would only see each other a couple of times a year?"

"Do you think you could rebuild your relationship with him by texting and calling regularly?"

"Maybe. I think it depends. All I know is that I don't want to lose him again. Even if it means we're just friends. A lot has happened between us. There's a lot that we still have to talk about and work through. It's gonna take some time."

"It will take some time, but trust me, babe, it'll be worth it." Liv sighs and takes a sip of her wine, "I don't want to work tomorrow. I have this monster of a client that wants white everything in her *entire house*." She sticks out her tongue in mock disgust. "Fucking boring."

"Oh, what a terrible world you have to live in right now," I laugh out. It feels good to laugh when everything feels so heavy.

"Whatever, you know what I mean. My talent is being squandered on white pillows with white flowers embroidered on them." She sips on her wine.

"Not everyone wants an orange couch like you, babe."

"It's tragic, isn't it?"

"The couch? Yes."

Liv sticks her tongue out at me before standing up and putting her dirty dishes into the dishwasher. We both have early mornings so we say goodnight and make our way to our separate rooms.

As I lie in bed that night, my only thoughts are of Sam. His gentleness with me over the last few days. The way he took hold of my hand with ease, like we've been holding hands forever. The way his hand felt in mine. The gnawing absence I feel without him. I finally drift to sleep thinking about his small kisses on my forehead or my cheek.

***

I spend the next couple of days preparing for my hearing on Thursday and catching up on things my office couldn't get to while I was out. I wish I could have called Ethan a few times. Mostly just to have him talk me up about this hearing, or to just listen to me practice and give me feedback. My heart breaks a little more each time I reach for the phone to call him.

I try to shove Sam out of my thoughts. I know I promised we would talk, and we will. I just can't wrap my head around everything yet.

Thursday morning, I wake to a text from Sam.

> Good luck with your hearing this morning!
> Call me later and tell me about it.

I can't believe he remembered.

> Thanks, Sam. It's a pretty routine hearing and I'm expecting it to go well.

> I can call around 6 if you aren't busy then?

> I'll be impatiently waiting until then.

His response gives me butterflies, but I quickly push those feelings aside because I have to focus on my hearing today. I wasn't lying. It is pretty routine. But I'm still a relatively new attorney, and speaking in front of a judge still makes me sweaty.

I practice what I'm going to say in front of a mirror in my bedroom several times, and a few more times in the car as I drive to work. I don't know if this helps, but it helps calm my nerves, even if I still feel like I'm going to drench my suit in sweat when it's my turn to speak.

***

I got through my hearing and wrap up a few things when my mind starts drifting back to Sam. Glancing at the clock, I see it's 5:30 p.m. My stomach is in knots—*I've got 30 minutes left. Will it be weird or awkward?*

By the time I get home and change my clothes, it's already 6:00 p.m. I'm talking myself into picking up the phone and calling Sam, but my nerves have my stomach in knots.

In a moment of strength, or maybe weakness, I pick up my phone, put in my earbuds, and click on his number. He answers on the second ring.

"Hey, how was your day?" He sounds happy to hear from me.

"It was good. Long. But good."

"Did you eat dinner yet?"

"No, Mother Hen. I haven't eaten yet." I laugh as I walk into the kitchen and grab a bottle of wine and a glass. "I lost track of time and just got home."

"Tell me about your hearing while you get some dinner."

Heating my leftovers and eating, I tell Sam about my hearing and my job overall. He asks thoughtful questions, which tells me he's listening and engaged in the conversation. I don't feel like I'm boring him.

"Tell me about your day, Sam. Did you go hiking with your dad?"

"As a matter of fact, we did go hiking. We went along part of the Palmetto trail at Francis Marion and then stopped to grab some cheese biscuits for dinner."

"Oh my God. What I wouldn't give for some cheese biscuits. I can practically taste them!"

"Well, I happen to know where you can get some. Might require you to see a certain handsome older man..."

"Oh, I would definitely visit your dad while I grab some biscuits," I tease Sam.

"I didn't realize you were into *much* older men, Kat. When did that happen?"

I can't contain my laugh. "Just to be clear, I am *not* into your dad."

"What a relief." He chuckles. "So, tell me, do you have any plans for Halloween? A party you go to?"

"No parties. Usually, we have a few friends over, order pizza, and watch scary movies. We have a few trick-or-treaters, so we hand out candy too. What about you? Do you have any plans?"

"A friend of mine throws a party every year. So, I'll probably go to that."

"Like a costume party? Are you dressing up, Sammy?"

"Yes, a costume party," it comes out more like a growl, "and yes, I'll dress up."

"Wait. Samuel Harris in a costume? I *have* to see this!"

"Not a chance, Kitty Kat."

"Pleeeeaase, Sammy!"

"Begging won't help here."

"Ugh, you're no fun," I grumble. "Fine. At least tell me what you're going to wear."

"I'm not sure I want to tell you that."

"What? Why not?"

"Because I know you will use it against me at a later, very inconvenient time for me."

"I would never. I'm not that horrid! Please tell me."

"I'm gonna regret this," he mutters under his breath. "We're all going as versions of Britney Spears."

"Oh my God," I laugh out.

"I fucking knew I shouldn't tell you." I can practically see him run his hand through his hair.

"So. Um. What do I have to do to know which Britney you're going as?" I say it sweetly, knowing I am very unlikely to be told.

"Yeah. That part I'm keeping to myself."

"There isn't *anything* I could do for this tiny little tidbit of information."

"When you ask it like that..." His response causes heat to pool in my core.

Using my most seductive voice, "What can I do?"

"Fuck," he groans, and I think I might have him now.

Continuing the seduction, "Please?"

He clears his throat before responding, "The things I have thought about that wicked mouth of yours doing." His tone abruptly changes. "But I'm still not telling you. Good effort though."

"Damn it."

He laughs at my response. "You're such a menace."

"Don't think I'm not going to try to wear you down."

"Oh, I look forward to your efforts, Kitty Kat."

The problem with this little game I started is that it's left me feeling hot, bothered, and wondering why Sam has been thinking about my mouth.

We keep chatting and before I know it, it's 10:00 p.m. "Shit, I don't know how it got so late."

"I guess you need to get to bed?"

"A girl needs her beauty sleep."

"You will always be beautiful, sleep or not." His words cause butterflies in my stomach, and I feel the flush rise on my cheeks.

He thinks I'm beautiful? "Thanks."

"I'm glad you called tonight. It was nice talking with you."

"You too. Let's do it again soon?"

"Definitely. Goodnight, beautiful." My heart stutters at his compliment.

"Goodnight, Sammy." It feels right to use the nickname I gave him when we were kids.

***

The next morning, I wake to a message from Sam again. A smile forces across my face.

Good morning, beautiful!

I'm on my way back to Chicago. I hope you have a great day!

Checking the clock, he's probably already on the plane. I type out a quick message.

> Have a safe flight. Please let me know when you get home.

Sam finally messaged me a little after noon.

> Now who's the mother hen?

> I just made it home. Can I call you tonight?

> 6?

> Can't wait!

***

The next few weeks pass quickly. Sam and I continue to text and call each other daily. We talk about everything: how work was going, anything that happened that was out of the ordinary, and plans we have for the weekend.

Everything except the topics I most need to know: what happened in Seattle and why he didn't marry Claire. I have so many questions, but I don't think a phone call or text message is the right way to get answers.

Chapter 16

Twenty Years Old

    I'm glad the summer is here and I'm back in Charleston. I can't stop thinking about Sam and how I left things with him.

    I should have texted him or called him back. But what would I say? "I'm still in love with you, and it's ok that you're going to marry Claire?"

There's no way.

    I hear his voice, and I cringe internally. I'm not ready to face him. I know Claire is here, too. In my house.

    Claire came back with him to visit his dad for the week. She's helping Sam pack up some of his things to take with him to Chicago. Claire's family lives there; Sam got a job there so she could be close to her family.

    My heart aches at the thought of him leaving. With her.

    Sam showed up a couple of days ago, and when I saw Claire with him, my heart sank. It was all I could do to keep my composure until I could get away from them. I've been avoiding them as much as I can ever since.

    "Come on, Ethan, our dads say they have a surprise for us. Hurry up." Sam sounds excited; I wince at his tone.

    He's moving on. Without me.

    I know what the surprise is. Motorcycles.

    Our parents bought Ethan and Sam these nice BMW R nineT motorcycles as graduation gifts. Someone had two and was selling both, and our parents bought them, knowing how much Ethan and Sam would love them.

I was home when Dad rode up on the one meant for Ethan. It was pretty. Black with a tan leather seat.

"It'll be good for that cross-country trip they want to take," Dad beamed as he explained the purchase to Mom. She wasn't as enthusiastic about motorcycles as he was. I wondered if he wished he had kept his old bike.

Ethan and Sam have been talking about buying motorcycles for years and taking a cross-country trip at some point.

I can only imagine the look on Sam's face when he sees what the surprise is.

The hole in my heart widens, and I know I can't go out there and join in.

Seeing how happy he is.

Seeing him hug and kiss Claire in excitement...

No, it would be too much. I groan into my pillow. I'll be excited with Ethan later.

***

P resent Day

Sam and I have been talking on the phone for about an hour. He called right as I was walking into my place.

"I'm not sure how to explain it." I pause, trying to think of the right words. Sam doesn't interrupt, allowing me the space to think. "I guess I just feel like the world is slowly crushing me. Sam, I've never gone this long without talking to Ethan. I miss him every day."

Sam doesn't say anything for long enough that I have to confirm the call is still going. "I know what you mean." His voice is gentle. "I remind myself that he wouldn't want me to wallow in his death. I know it's easier said than done, but he would want you to be happy. To continue living your life and remember the good times instead of the fact that he isn't here."

"I know. I just—I don't know how. And I can't stop thinking about that last conversation. The things I would have said if I knew it would be our last." I'm pacing my room.

"Don't do that, Kat. You can't change anything about what happened. Obsessing over it isn't going to make it easier."

"It's just that," I stop pacing and sit down in the chair next to my window, looking down at Ethan's skateboard on the ground next to my char, "we never went a day without texting, and we would talk on the phone every couple of days. I can't tell you the number of times that I've been working on something at work and reach for my phone only to realize he won't answer my call." It crushes me every time, and I have to remind myself to breathe. I don't share that last part.

"I'm going to be in Charleston for Thanksgiving next week. Let's go for a hike—just you and me."

"I thought you weren't going to make it." It isn't a question. We talked about this a couple of days ago.

"My plans changed. I'm booking my flight tonight. I'll be there on Monday."

"I don't know, Sam. I was thinking about not going this year." I feel the dread seep into my words.

I know I should be there for my family, but I'm struggling to put on a brave face with everyone, as it is. My parents will see right through me, and I know they'll figure out that I'm not dealing with this very well. I don't want to burden them more than I know they already are.

"Kat." Sam pauses, causing me to worry that he's beginning to realize how deep my depression has gotten. "Kat, please go. I want to see you; your parents want you there. You don't have to be anything to anyone. You can stay in your PJs with your hair in a messy bun. Just go."

"I'll try." That's all I can manage right now. I quickly change the subject and then hang up with Sam as quickly as I can. I know he cares, but I can't talk about this any longer. Not right now.

It's Friday night, so I have a couple of days to think this over before he's in Charleston.

Chapter 17

The doorbell rings, startling me awake. The clock on my nightstand reads 9:00 p.m. I laid down around 6:00 p.m. but didn't mean to fall asleep. I'm still in my jeans.

Sam called a couple of times since I spoke to him on Friday, and I couldn't bring myself to answer his calls. I texted him short responses so that he didn't think I was totally ignoring him again. I know he's going to be upset that I didn't go to Charleston.

Liv and I had planned to drive over together, but when it was time to leave yesterday, I just couldn't bring myself to go.

I walk over to the front door and peek out the peephole to see who's there. Sighing, I open the door. "Sam. What are you doing here?" My tone is flat, laced with the exhaustion I'm feeling.

"You said you would be in Charleston for Thanksgiving. I got there this afternoon only to find out you didn't get in the car with Liv." I flinch at his harsh tone.

Without inviting him in, I turn and walk towards the kitchen to get a glass of water. I hear the door click closed followed by his footsteps trailing behind me.

"I don't want to be around everyone right now."

"Kat." His voice is suddenly gentle, which causes me to stop and look at him. God, why does he always look so good? "I know it's been hard, but—"

"You don't get it, Sam," I cut him off. "It's been a month. AN ENTIRE MONTH!" I realize I'm shouting when his face bleaches.

I blow out a breath before continuing.

"It's like no one cares. Everyone is just moving on, and… and I feel so lost. Ethan and I talked all the time. Do you know how hard it's been to want to tell him something and dial his number only to realize he's gone? Or to text him some stupid meme and realize it won't get to him? Every time I think about that last phone call, it feels like I can't breathe."

Did I say I love you?

"Yes. Yes, I do know what that's like." He looks like I've slapped him. His shoulders are high and his expression is tight. "Ethan and I talked all the time, too. Fuck, Kat. He was my best friend. I lost him, too."

I just stare at him—too angry to talk to him.

"Your parents lost him. And right now, they need you. We aren't all just moving on. We're doing the best we can to live while also dealing with the fact that Ethan is gone." He looks around the small kitchen, running his hand through his hair.

Sam fixes his attention on me again. He winces slightly at whatever he sees in my expression and sighs, exasperated.

What the fuck does he have to be exasperated about? I'm about to ask him—gearing up for a fight when he continues.

"We have a lot to talk about, Kat." I ball my hands into fists by my side, feeling the tension in my body. "Right now, you look like you need to sleep. I'll be here tomorrow morning, and we can talk while I drive us to Charleston."

My stomach drops, and I start to panic at the thought of him leaving. "Sam." I rush to stop him. "Where are you going?"

"One of the hotels in town that has a room available. Have any suggestions?" It sounds more like a challenge than a question.

I can't let him leave. "Stay with me. I mean here. Stay here. At my place."

Why do I feel like I just reverted to that 14-year-old girl with a crush on her brother's best friend?

I sigh, trying to clear my head. "I don't know how Liv would feel about me offering up her room. But you can sleep on the couch?"

He considers it, and for a moment, I think he's going to decline. "Thanks. If you tell me where I can find a pillow and a blanket, I'll take the couch." His expression loosens, and I see his body physically relax. "I'll get us breakfast in the morning and then drive us to your parents' house."

For some reason, his words cause the anger to flare up. "You don't need to coddle me, you know?" It comes out as little more than a grumble.

"Coddle you? You're kidding, right?" He snorts with disgust.

"No. I mean, I know I've relied on you a lot to get me through school and now everything going on with... Ethan." His name comes out choked and I clear my throat to try to stop the tears from starting. "The funeral and everything else." I wave my hand in the air as if gesturing to everything and nothing. "But I'll be ok."

He shakes his head. "I haven't been coddling you. Did you ever think that maybe I needed you sitting next to me, holding my hand, just as much as you needed me? Did you think that maybe I needed it more than you did? Because I've taken comfort from you, too.

"Every time I've reached for your hand. Every time I've hugged you. Every touch, every look, every phone call, every text has helped *me*. Has made *me* feel some semblance of normalcy in this fucked up situation." He looks at the ground and shoves his hands into the pockets of his jeans.

When he speaks again, his voice is so quiet I almost struggle to hear him. "I wasn't coddling you. I needed, need you."

Shit. I'm an asshole.

He turns to walk away. If I let him walk away, I'm afraid this will be it. I'll lose him for good this time. I can't let that happen, so I grab his wrist before he fully turns from me. "Don't go." He allows me to gently pull him towards me. "I'm sorry. I... what I said was selfish. I'm sorry. Please don't go, Sam."

Sam's shoulders are slumped forward, and he won't look at me—he just stares at the ground. But he doesn't say anything.

Finally, his eyes meet mine, but his expression is blank, his eyes are like two black holes.

I try again, softer. "Please don't go, Sam." Still holding his wrist, I reach my other hand up to cup his cheek and run my thumb gently across his cheekbone. I relax a little when he closes his eyes and leans into my palm.

Shifting my gaze to his chest, I'm not sure how long I watch it rise and fall with each breath he takes, the action somehow calming my ragged nerves.

I've been incredibly selfish with him. I know Ethan meant a lot to Sam. I just can't seem to get out of my own head and out of my own grief to see that Sam is struggling, too.

He hasn't cried, or at least, I haven't seen him cry, and he doesn't really talk about Ethan. I guess it's made me feel like maybe this isn't as hard for Sam. But that isn't fair. He shouldn't have to grieve the way I do for me to know he's hurting too.

Finally, he reaches up and brushes some loose hair behind my ear. I drop my hand from his cheek and raise my gaze to his. I remain completely still as Sam runs his thumb along the side of my face and across my jaw.

My breath hitches when his thumb glides along my lips. I want him to kiss me. I crave it. But he drops his hand and takes a small step back.

Once he finally meets my gaze, I see pain in his eyes, but his tone is soft when he finally speaks, "Ok. I'll stay. Go to sleep, Kat. I'll be here when you wake up."

I grab him a blanket and pillow from the cupboard and make sure he's settled in. Even though it's still early, I'm exhausted. So,

I say goodnight, point out which room is mine in case he needs anything, and head back to bed.

***

I'm not sure what time it is, but when I wake up, it's still dark outside. The clock glows 11:00 p.m.

Rolling over on my side, I stare at my bedroom door. Thinking about Sam sleeping on my couch. I can't believe how much I hurt him tonight.

I tell myself I just want to make sure he's still here when I get out of bed and quietly open my bedroom door.

This is stupid. Of course, he's still here.

Hesitating only for a moment, I convince myself I just need to see him so that I can go back to sleep.

But as I walk into the living room, Sam is sitting on the bright orange couch, very much awake, with his head in his hands, elbows on his knees. He's changed into running shorts, that show off his muscular thighs, and a loose T-shirt. He looks so sad, and the sight breaks my heart.

Hearing my approach, his eyes slowly meet mine. "Can't sleep?" Sam's voice is quiet as his eyes drop down the length of my body and back up. My hair is up in a messy bun, and I'm wearing tiny shorts and a tank top—my typical sleepwear. When his eyes land on mine again, they flicker, turning dark, but the look is quickly replaced with uncertainty as his lips turn down slightly.

"I was asleep, but I woke up. I'm not sure why I came out here." I quickly look down the hallway towards my room before looking back at him. Despite my unconfident words, I straighten my shoulders and step towards him. "I'm so sorry for what I said earlier. I'm so sorry for hurting you."

Sam stands up and walks towards me. "I'm sorry I was so harsh with you. I know you miss him, and I should have been more understanding with you. I'm struggling with this, too." He stops a couple of steps away from me, his arms crossed in front of him.

He looks down at the ground. "I think about him every day. About how it would be easier for everyone if it had been me instead of him." I'm struck silent by Sam's words. "You would be better off if he were here instead of me. I can't fill the void he left. Not with myself, not with your parents, and not with you." Tears stream down his face.

Easier if it had been him?

I slowly step towards Sam as he raises his hands and covers his face. I reach up and gently tug his hands down. His eyes are red-rimmed, and his hands shake slightly in mine. He still won't look at me.

Life would *not* be easier for anyone if Sam wasn't here. Do I miss Ethan? Yes. Do I wish he was here? Yes. But do I think anything would be different if Sam had died instead? No. I would be in a similar state of hell.

Except that Sam doesn't know what he means to me. Ethan—fuck, Ethan did.

Of course, he knew I loved him.

I hold his hands as I speak quietly, "Things would not be easier if it had been you, Sam. *Life* would not be easier for any of us." I kiss both of his hands before I let them go and softly place my hands on each side of his face. "Please look at me."

His eyes finally meet mine, and I continue speaking, "Don't ever say something like that again. Don't even think it." I plant a gentle kiss on his cheek. "Please don't ever think that things would be easier for me without you. *I* would not be better if you weren't here. I need you, Sam."

He breaks at my words. Sam grips my waist, pulling me to him. I hold him tight against me as his body wracks with sobs. Rubbing soothing patterns up and down his muscular back, I nuzzle my cheek into his chest, breathing in the faint scent of his cologne—pines and the salty sea air.

When his body stops shaking, I speak again, "I think I've been feeling pretty lost without him. I'm angry that he isn't here. I was upset about what you were saying, but I know you're right. I can't lose myself and lock myself up. I shouldn't have lashed out at you. That wasn't fair." The words are slightly muffled as I say them into his chest.

He grips me tighter. Sam's voice is little more than a whisper when he speaks again, "he would know what to say, what to do, to make things better. I'm so lost without him."

He leans back just enough to look down at me while keeping me locked in his arms. He kisses the top of my head before whispering. "You should go back to bed; I'll grab us some breakfast before we head out in the morning, so don't worry if I'm not here when you wake."

I shake my head no at him. He looks at me like he's about to argue. I speak up before he gets the wrong idea, "I don't want you to sleep on the couch." He flinches, so I hurry on. "I'm not kicking you out, Sam. You're much too big for the couch." I gesture toward it. "I'm asking you to sleep in my bed."

The surprise that flashes across his face makes me want to laugh, but this isn't the time for that.

"We can put pillows down the middle if that makes you feel more comfortable. But my bed will be way more comfortable than that thing." I gesture toward the couch again.

"Afraid I might get handsy with you?" He offers me a sad smile.

I look down at the floor to avoid his gaze when I speak because I wish he *would* touch me. "No. I..."

I'm unable to resist the blush rising to my cheeks in embarrassment when I realize he must be teasing me. I smack his arm. "Come on." I grab his hand and pull him towards my room.

Chapter 18

I don't know how I fell asleep with Samuel. Fucking. Harris. In my bed. But here I am, all but lying on top of him—my head on his chest, arm around his middle, and one leg between his. One of his arms is wrapped around me, the other is above his head.

Shit! I can't let him know I've practically attacked him while he slept!

Slowly, I work to extract myself from him and sigh in relief when he doesn't wake.

I make it halfway to my bedroom door when his voice startles me, and I let out an embarrassing squeak.

"Where are you sneaking off to?" His voice is gravelly with sleep.

The first thing I see when I turn around is his big grin with that heartbreaking dimple peeking out. His hair is slightly messy from sleep. I smile back at him. "I wasn't sneaking. Just didn't want to wake you." He looks like he doesn't believe me. "I was going to be nice and get you some breakfast."

Sam props himself up on one arm. "That's only fair since I didn't even get dinner before we slept together." He says it without any humor.

I choke on... nothing.

I'm. Choking. On. Nothing.

Sam laughs as I cough and try to remember how to breathe.

Once my coughing fit is over, I glare at him. "I don't think you deserve any breakfast after that."

"Hmmm." Sam looks around my room, and sits up fully, as if he's just realized where he is for the first time.

My bedroom is simple, with large paintings of bright blue flowers that add texture and brightness to the white walls.

Large windows on one side overlook the community garden. Dappled light shines through the sheer curtains hanging across the length of the window, in front of which a leather sling-back chair sits. Ethan's skateboard still sits on the floor next to the chair. I have a couple of books neatly stacked on a small round coffee table next to the chair. It's the perfect place to relax with a good book and a glass of wine. My favorite part is that the chair is large enough that I can easily curl up in it.

My bed is situated in the center of the wall. Nightstands that match the coffee table sit on either side of the bed. The only things I keep on my nightstand are my alarm clock, phone charger, and a reusable water bottle.

His gaze returns to me. "Thanks for letting me sleep in your bed. I was a little worried about that orange thing you call a couch. It was so lumpy, I don't think I would have been able to walk this morning." He's still smiling so big.

"Hey! That couch is well-loved. Don't insult it!" I accuse as I place my hands on my hips. Truthfully, it had seen better days, but Liv and I got it for a steal and have no plans to replace it.

He raises his hands in surrender, and I can tell he's barely holding back his laugh.

"Anyway... I'm going to start the coffee and make breakfast. I don't want to disappoint his majesty." I curtsey to emphasize my statement.

"I can think of a few things to ease my disappointment." His voice is so cool and collected. I'm not sure if he's joking.

Deciding to play along for a minute I raise an eyebrow in challenge. "Can you now?"

"Oh yes. Ones that I assure you, you would enjoy, too." I don't miss his wink. I'm melting into a puddle.

Is this real? He can't be flirting with me. Can he?

Trying to keep up my calm facade, I respond, "I don't know. It sounds like you're trying to convince yourself." I shrug, hoping I'm exuding nonchalance. I'm feeling anything but. I love this playful version of him.

Sam's out of bed in an instant, taking a few short steps towards me to close the gap, shocking me into silence. He leans in close and whispers in my ear. "Just say the word, Kitty Kat, and I'll prove my confidence is deserved."

I can't help but think of that dream. Sam holding me against the door, his lips and hands on me. His cock—my core heats, and I feel the wetness pool.

"I... um—" I shut my mouth because my brain clearly isn't forming coherent sentences. I look down at my hands to avoid his heated gaze.

"Just a moment ago, your body was wrapped around mine. Now you're shy?"

My gaze snaps back up to his. *Oh my God, I thought he was asleep.*

I internally slap my forehead in embarrassment. I feel my cheeks and neck flush. "I didn't mean to do that, and when I realized, I tried to move before you..." The words come out in a rush. "I thought you were asleep," I sigh.

He straightens to his full height, forcing me to look up at him. "I was definitely awake and more than comfortable with you lying on top of me." He searches my face. "But maybe another time." He shrugs and looks... disappointed as his eyes turn down and he frowns slightly. He takes a large step back from me. "I'll make coffee and breakfast while you pack." He stalks out of the room, exuding every bit of confidence, I don't feel myself.

My legs are jelly, and I have to sit on the floor until my heart is no longer beating out of my chest.

I take my time packing my bag and then take a long shower, trying to talk myself out of accepting Sam's offer. It would be effortless; too easy to allow myself to fully acknowledge the feelings I have for Sam. The feelings that have never left.

I'm not sure where this playful side of Sam came from. The only thing I'm confident about is that he's going to leave me with a broken heart again. I need to stop this.

I shove my feelings back down and only go into the kitchen when I know my resolve is in check.

***

After breakfast, we walk outside, Sam carrying my bag with my clothes. I start turning toward my car when he grabs my arm, his grip firm but gentle. He shakes his head. "Not so fast. You're riding with me."

"How will I get back without my car?" My feet are planted on the sidewalk halfway between my car and the SUV.

"Liv is already in Charleston and promised to get you back here safely."

Of course, he talked to Liv first.

Sam cuts me off when I start to protest. "It's decided. You're riding with me."

Knowing I won't win this battle, and not hating the idea of letting him drive, I follow him to his dad's SUV.

Sam stops at a coffee drive-through and orders us drinks before getting onto the interstate.

We're both quiet for a while when Sam breaks the silence. "Penny for your thoughts?"

I look at him, contemplating whether I want to tell him everything I've been thinking. "Just thinking about things." I shrug.

"Things." His gaze shifts to mine. "Care to share what those *things* are?"

"I have a lot of questions, and I'm just not sure when to ask them."

"Well, we have two hours in the car, so what better time than now?" He has both hands on the steering wheel as he navigates onto the interstate.

"The two-hours-in-the-car part is what has me nervous."

"That bad, huh?" He mocks a worried look. "What subject do your questions involve?"

"Seattle. Claire. Us." I look out the window, avoiding his gaze. I'm clutching my coffee with both hands as if it will somehow give me the strength to have this conversation. "Things don't add up for me. Sam, I want to trust you fully, but I don't know how to move forward without answers." I look back at him, gauging his reaction.

He grimaces. I can see the internal struggle flicker across his face as he chooses his next words carefully. "I haven't regretted words more than when I told you I only saw you as a friend. When I saw the hurt flash across your face, I wanted to take those words back immediately. That look still haunts me. Fuck, I almost told you the truth right then and there. But I knew I couldn't."

"What truth? I'm gonna need you to use more words." He flinches at my harsh tone. "I've spent the last several years trying to understand how you could go from spending almost every waking minute with me to telling me you didn't care for me. That I was only your brother's kid sister."

"Kat, I was dating Claire." He runs a hand through his hair and then takes a sip of his tea. "Fuck, I was talking about getting engaged to her, and you, you *are* Ethan's little sister."

I suck air in through my teeth and look down at my coffee. I refuse to go down memory lane with him if he isn't going to give me anything to work with here.

Sam shakes his head. "I told Ethan I was falling for you when we were in high school."

Ok. This is something; I sit straighter.

"I asked him if I could ask you out, and he lost his shit. He made me promise not to pursue you. When he found out you were going to school in Seattle, he told me he would cut off my balls if I ever touched you." His words are fast, like they've been bursting to get out, and the dam has finally broken.

I'm surprised by his answer. Not because of what he said. I'd suspected his feelings were mutual. That's honestly why this has been so hard. Why I've kept my distance. I've felt crazy thinking I misread the signs.

I'm also not surprised by Ethan's role in this. He was always protective of me.

No, I'm surprised Sam's being this transparent. Finally.

Deciding to push him since he's being open, I ask, "Why didn't you marry Claire?"

"Because she wasn't what I wanted." His gaze shifts to me briefly, and I catch the vulnerability in his eyes. "Claire was great. I thought she was everything I wanted."

Please tell me how great Claire is... "But?"

"But," he drags out the word, "after we got engaged, I couldn't get what you said to me at the jewelry store out of my head. I kept replaying your words in my mind over and over."

He takes another sip of his tea, and I think he's doing it to compose his thoughts.

"I didn't realize how often I talked about you to Claire—how often I kept bringing you up in conversations." Sam looks at me briefly before returning his eyes to the road. "She called me out for it. I hadn't really thought things through when I proposed. I hadn't really thought through why I did it or what the rush was.

"She went on a girls' trip for a week, and it allowed me the time and space to really think about what she said. To think about my feelings and to think about you." He looks at me again and smiles softly.

"I realized then that I couldn't marry her while I still thought about you, still wanted you." He looks over his shoulder and moves into the left lane, passing a slower car.

I don't dare say anything.

"I loved Claire," Sam continues once he's maneuvered the SUV back into the right lane. "I just realized I was more in love with the idea of her than I was with *her*." He places his left hand at the top middle of the steering wheel and leans into his elbow on the center console.

"I felt like an asshole for dragging her through all of that. When she got back from her trip, we sat down and had an open conversation about everything. I know she was hurt. She moved out that week, and we haven't talked since." He looks over at me, his eyes are bright and his posture is relaxed. He said the words so smoothly, almost as if he had practiced them.

I remain silent as I think about what he said. "You moved to Chicago for her."

"Initially, yes. But I stayed because of my career." He keeps his eyes on the road.

"That makes sense, I guess." I take a long sip of my coffee. "Ethan told you not to date me?"

"Yeah. The night we went to the homecoming dance." He places his right hand on the steering wheel again, glances over his shoulder, and signals as he changes lanes one more time. He sneaks a peak at me under his impossibly long eyelashes.

"God, I was so angry that Kevin stood you up. But at the same time, I was glad about it. It gave me the chance to step in and show you how I felt. After the dance, we got back to your house, and I was talking to Ethan about it. It was one of the worst fights we've had—but ultimately, I agreed I would back off."

"But you didn't back off, Sam!" I hurl the words at him, my voice rising.

He grimaces. "I started suspecting how you felt about me, and so many times, I wanted to tell you I felt the same. I should have stayed away from you, but I couldn't. I also couldn't break my promise to Ethan. Watching you date Kevin was, well, it was hard for me. I hated him. Especially after he broke up with you, I hated that he had you and let you go." He glances at me quickly before returning his eyes to the road.

I look over at his hands gripping the steering wheel. It's one of the first times we've been in a car together since we started talking again that he hasn't been holding my hand. The thought makes me want to reach out to him, but this isn't a conversation I want to have while touching him. I need that small amount of distance so I can get all of this out.

"I thought you had feelings for me," I say quietly. "I could never figure out why you seemed to be holding back. Then you started dating Claire, and I never thought it was serious enough with her to make you want to get engaged."

"It was a rash decision on my part. I think I was trying to force something with her that just wasn't there. After you rushed off, I decided my promise to Ethan wasn't worth losing you. I had planned to tell you how I felt, but I couldn't do it over text, and you wouldn't talk to me. I knew I'd messed things up with you. I had to keep trying, I couldn't lose you. Even though I ultimately did lose you."

I watch Sam drag his hand through his hair and watch the strands fall back into place, only slightly messy.

"If I'm being honest, I'm not sure that I would have broken things off with Claire, even if you knew how I felt."

"Because of Ethan," I sigh and look out the window.

"Because of Ethan," he repeats. We're both silent for what seems like an eternity.

I drink more of my coffee and watch him raise his to-go cup to his lips. I can't count the number of times I've thought about those perfect lips, plump in all the right places, so kissable. I bite my lip as I see a small amount of moisture that he licks off as he sets his cup back into the holder.

I look out the window again before I do something I'll regret later. I guess I understand why Ethan told Sam to back off—Sam was a bit of a ladies' man in high school. Not in the player sort of way. He was always dating someone, and I know he had girls lined up just waiting for their chance.

"Anything else that's holding you back from *trusting* me?" His words are tight.

"Trust probably wasn't the right word to use. I trust you..."

"Just not with your heart." It isn't a question.

"Sam." I look at him, searching his face. There isn't an ounce of teasing in his expression. I know my words hurt him; I've been trying, and failing, to process what happened with only my side of the story. He broke my heart, and it's never fully mended.

"Why are you telling me all this now? Other than I asked you."

"Because I lost Ethan. I can't—" His voice cracks, and I think he's trying to hold back tears. "In a lot of ways, you and Ethan were the only family I had. My dad was always so busy. After my mom died, your family took me in. You all made me yours.

"I want you in my life, Kat." He looks at me, showing me how serious his words are. "In any way I can have you. If that means we only text and call each other and see each other when we're both in Charleston, I'll take it. I'm done with this distance we've built. If I have to spill all my secrets to you, I'll do it. I just want you back." His tone is matter of fact, as if he'll fight me on this if I try to say no.

I have no intention of denying him. Because I want him in my life, too. I reach for his hand, giving it a little squeeze. "I don't intend to lose you again, Sam."

His lips lift in a small smile. "Can I ask you something?"

"Yes." I drag the word out. I'm nervous. Dropping his hand, I pick up my coffee cup and take a sip, trying to hide my nerves.

"I know I hurt you. I know that's why you initially kept your distance. But Kat, it's been seven years. Why have you kept away from me for so long? Why have you continued to avoid me?" I can feel the hurt in his words; it guts me to think of how much I've hurt him.

I look out the window, not able to meet his eyes for this. "At first, it was because I was embarrassed. Then..." I pause, trying to search for the right words.

I don't want to share this with him. But, with how much he shared with me and how vulnerable he was, he deserves to know the truth.

Finding my resolve, I straighten my shoulders, look at him, and continue, "I stayed away because I've never stopped wanting you. I couldn't seem to put my feelings aside. Knowing how you felt about me, at least based on what you said that day, I stayed away because I couldn't be that silly girl pining after a guy who didn't feel the same way. I stayed away so that I could move on."

"And did you? Move on?" I wish he would look at me so I could see his expression.

"No." The words are barely louder than a whisper.

"Good." He picks up my hand and brings it to his lips. He places a gentle kiss on the back of it before putting it on the center console, his fingers intertwined with mine.

When Sam and I were in Seattle, he hardly ever took my hand in his and certainly never kissed me. The only time I can remember him kissing me on top of my head was when we went to the Space Needle and even then, I'm not sure he meant to do it.

Looking down at our interlocked hands, I revel in how my hand fits perfectly in his. I smile at how comfortable this is.

We spend the rest of the drive talking and singing along to our favorite songs on his playlist. Mostly it's me singing along, but he seems happy to contribute occasionally.

I feel lighter knowing his side of what happened. Knowing that he did have feelings for me. Knowing his reasons doesn't make the pain go away, but it makes it easier for me to process the past.

Chapter 19

S am drops me off at my parents' house and then drives over to his dad's for the rest of the day.

Mom and I go grocery shopping to pick up last-minute ingredients, and then we spend the rest of the day preparing for Thanksgiving dinner, which she's hosted at our house for as long as I can remember. She invites extended family and close friends, and everyone brings their favorite dishes.

She's always cooked the turkey, ham, and baked pies. Once we were old enough, she recruited Ethan and me to help with the prep work. At this point in my life, I could bake a cherry pie with my eyes closed.

We prepare well into the evening. Mom and I sigh in relief when Dad comes in with pizza he picked up from one of our favorite shops.

We all sit at the small dining table, Mom keeping an eye on the oven. I'm reaching for a slice of pepperoni when she breaks the silence, "So," she drawls, "Sam dropped you off?"

"Yes," I respond just as slowly.

"He left to pick you up yesterday. He stayed the night?"

"Yes." It comes out measured. I know she's building up to something, and I'm waiting to relax or run.

"Anything going on there we should know about?"

I sigh and sink into my chair. "I don't know. Maybe?"

"Before Ethan," she clears her throat and the corners of her eyes glisten, "you and Sam weren't talking. Now he *spends the night* with you?"

"Ma, what are you really asking?"

"Are you dating? I've seen you holding hands and hugging a lot recently."

"No, we aren't dating. We're friends." I look over at Dad, who's just sitting there watching us, a smile on his face. I roll my eyes and focus back on my pizza.

"Hmmm." She looks at me and raises a brow in challenge

"Ma," I let the exhaustion from this conversation bleed into my tone, "he lives in Chicago, and I live in Columbia. That isn't exactly a great way to have a relationship. Speaking of which, I've been thinking." I want to change the subject. "How would you guys feel if I moved back home for a bit—just until I got a new job and an apartment?"

My parents both look at me in surprise. I've been thinking about this move for a while. I like Columbia, but even before Ethan died, I've felt like something was missing. Now that he's gone, I want to be closer to my parents.

"You can always move home, baby girl. But why would you need to find a job when you know you can come to work at my firm?" Dad's voice is strained, and his eyes are pulled together, like I should have known I could work for him.

"Dad, it's not that I don't want to work for your firm."

"But?"

"But I don't want handouts. I never have. That's why I went to school in Seattle and why I got a job in Columbia. I wanted to make it on my own. I don't want to be successful because my dad got me a job."

"Baby girl, you know it wouldn't be because of me. I know how hard you work. And the truth is, we need someone now that—" He clears his throat. "I've been meaning to list an open position because we could use the help. Really, you would be doing me a favor."

Need someone. Because Ethan isn't there. I try to quickly school my features as my stomach drops.

I can't replace him. I don't think he meant it that way, but it's how this all feels. "Well, nothing is set yet. I've just been thinking about it. I miss you guys, and it would be nice to be back in Charleston."

Not understanding the direction of my thoughts, Mom jumps in, "Hypothetically speaking, of course." I can feel the excitement radiating from her.

"Of course," I repeat, winking at her and giving Dad a knowing look.

Mom ignores my teasing. "If you were to move home, when do you think that would happen?"

"I don't know. I haven't talked to Liv. I can't leave her hanging. I could keep the condo, and she could continue living there, but we are currently splitting the payments, and I would need that money to pay for something else."

"That's completely fair. You would give notice mid-December?" she asks as if it's been decided. A done deal.

"Yeah. That would be ideal. I want to talk with Liv before I make any solid decisions or plans," I remind Mom because this isn't set in stone yet. Otherwise, she might start making plans of her own.

"Kat, you take your time thinking this through but know that no matter what and no matter when, you can always come home. And you always have a job."

"Thanks, Dad. That means a lot."

It seems like now would be a good time to transition. I broke things off with Philip, so I don't have a boyfriend keeping me there. I like my boss, and most of my clients are great, but I'll never let a job tie me down.

The only thing that's keeping me in Columbia is Liv. I know she'll understand and support my decision. She always has. It's one of the things I love about her.

The only thing that's holding me back is me.

***

Thursday morning, I slowly make my way downstairs when I hear guests arrive. My uncle on Dad's side, Richard, his wife, Candy, and their adult son, Billy, his wife, Susan, and their five-year-old daughter, Eliza, are here. I say hi and hug each of them in turn.

"Gram, can I help make the dinner?" Eliza's high-pitched voice rings out. Eliza is adorable with blonde ringlets and bright blue eyes. She's carrying this well-worn stuffed puppy that she talks to as she walks around the house.

Candy looks to Mom for a response. "Of course, my dear. How about you wash the potatoes, and I cut them?"

"Yay!" she sings as she runs off to the kitchen.

Hearing the doorbell, I rush over and am greeted by Dan and Sam. Both have their arms full of bags and ingredients. Dan always makes this delicious sweet potato casserole. I would never tell Mom this, but it's my favorite Thanksgiving dish.

"Can I help bring anything in?"

"No thanks, Kat. This is everything." Dan makes his way into the kitchen while Sam hesitates for a minute.

"I'm so glad you're here, Kitty Kat. You aren't even wearing pjs." Sam smiles softly. I'm wearing black leggings and an oversized blue sweater that hangs off one shoulder. "You look great, by the way. Charleston suits you." His smile is contagious, and I feel like I can breathe a little easier now that he's here.

"Thanks for dragging me here kicking and screaming."

"Between you and me," he leans in and whispers, "I brought rope and duct tape in case I had to tie you up to get you here." He winks at me and kisses my cheek. I force myself not to reach up and touch the spot that his lips just touched.

I shake my head and follow him into the kitchen. I am *not* thinking about Sam in my bed Monday night. Or how he felt under me when I woke up. I am *not* staring at his ass through his jeans and definitely *not* thinking about what Sam would look like out of those jeans.

Shit, I need to get a grip. This is a family holiday, for fuck's sake!

The kitchen looks like a tornado hit it, or a starved toddler. It's absolute chaos with people filling each empty corner and food covering the counters.

I stand in the doorway as Sam sets everything he was carrying down on the counter and steps back to my side. We share a knowing look, one that says we don't want to be in the chaos.

"Hey, pretty girl, will you and Sam set the table?" Mom doesn't even turn around, yet she knows I don't want to be in this circus we call a kitchen.

Sending her a silent thanks, I reply, "Sure, Ma." Turning around, Sam and I head back out to the formal dining room, where we work to pull the ends of the table out to fit another couple of leaves in. Once that is done, we head towards the hutch and start pulling out the dishes we use for holiday dinners.

"Sam, will you grab the wine glasses? I can't reach them."

"You got it, short stuff."

"Not everyone can be a sexy giant like you, Sam." I freeze, realizing too late what I just said. I look at him in horror.

"So, you think I'm sexy, huh?" That thirsty smile of his only adds fuel to the fire burning in my core.

"Definitely not. I think you need to have your hearing checked." I know my attempt at recovery fails when his smile widens and he winks at me.

He steps towards me until he's close enough that I have to look up at him. It would be all too easy to go onto my tippy toes and brush my lips against his.

With that thought, I look at his lips. They look soft, and I wonder what they would feel like on mine. His lips tilt up at the corners in a wicked grin. Caught off guard, I look up at his eyes and see they are burning with desire.

God, he's gorgeous.

Before I can process what's happening, he leans in and whispers in my ear. "Kitty Kat, you need to stop biting that lip of yours unless you *really* want me to be sexy."

I didn't even realize I was biting my lip. My face flushes.

"Sam, I..." He steps back, and I feel the cool sting of rejection. I look at the ground to hide my embarrassment.

Gently, he lifts my chin with his fingers. "Kat," his voice is soft, "the first time I kiss you isn't going to be in a place where either of our parents can walk in on us. I want to take my time with you. Uninterrupted." He runs his thumb along my bottom lip; the action causes shivers to run along my spine. "But make no mistake. I want to kiss you. Thoroughly."

Before I can respond, he turns around and starts pulling the wine glasses down from the top shelf. I'm frozen in place, my body forgetting how to move, as my heart pounds out of my chest.

Chapter 20

*E*ighteen Years Old

"Kat, for the hundredth time, I'm not trying to ditch you somewhere. It's not that much further. Hang in there; it'll be worth it. I promise!" Sam looks down at me, and I know he's getting frustrated.

I groan audibly; he rolls his eyes in response. He won't tell me where we're going, but I swear it feels like we've been trying to get there all day.

That isn't true. It hasn't been that long. But this is the second bus we're getting on, and I'm starting to think he's just taking me somewhere to ditch me, so he doesn't have to deal with me anymore.

Maybe try to get me confused and lost, so it takes me longer to get back to my dorm.

Truthfully, I wouldn't blame him. If I didn't have to be around myself, I would probably ditch me, too.

I've been miserable since Kevin broke up with me a couple of weeks ago. I've only left my dorm room to go to class. That is, until Sam showed up at my room a couple of days ago and forced me to study with him.

Today, he practically dragged me out of bed. He waited in the hall as I showered and got ready because he didn't trust me not to go back to sleep. I probably would have. Whatever.

"I didn't even get coffee before you made me go through all of this," I whine and wave my hand, gesturing at nothing in particular.

"I'll get you coffee when we get there," he laughs.

I shove his arm a little more forcefully than I intend to. He just grabs my hand and leads us onto the bus. He doesn't let go as we take our seats. His hand in mine feels nice. Comforting.

Suddenly, a jolt of pain spikes in my chest. Kevin will never hold my hand again.

Sam must sense the direction of my thoughts because he lets go of my hand and softly says, "Everything's going to get better. I know it's hard right now. But it'll get better." His smile just makes me think he pities me.

I wish I were back in my dorm with only Ben and Jerry *to keep me company. I look out the window instead of responding; he sighs next to me.*

We sit in silence for the rest of the ten-minute bus ride.

We're in downtown Seattle when we finally get off the bus. I stop to look around briefly, taking it all in. The buildings are so tall; the air is slightly salty from the ocean nearby.

It's a rare sunny day in Seattle, and I guess I can appreciate being outside. Coffee would still make this better.

Even I can't stop internally rolling my eyes at my poor attitude.

"Come on. This way." Sam gestures for me to walk next to him. We walk close enough to each other that I can feel the warmth seeping off him. Even though I'm not in the mood to be dragged all over the city, I feel comforted by his proximity.

I always have.

I brush off the thought. Of course, he feels comfortable. I did grow up with him, after all.

We continue our journey on foot, and Sam stops at a small coffee stand, where he orders a vanilla latte for me and a chai tea for himself. He remembered my favorite drink. *I look at him in surprise, but quickly look away when he turn towards me; I pretend to look at a building in front of us.*

When our drinks are ready, we continue walking.

I take my first sip and groan. It's so good. I realize Sam is looking at me, a smirk on his face. "You sure you aren't trying to ditch me?"

He rolls his eyes dramatically. "You're exhausting sometimes," he growls out.

It isn't until Sam stops walking and looks up that I realize we're standing in front of the Space Needle.

"Wait, are we going to the top?" I beam up at him.

He just smiles down at me.

I'm giddy as we make our way to the observation deck. I'm in absolute awe as I look out at the 360-degree floor-to-ceiling windows. Briefly looking around the area, I can't decide where I want to look first when Sam takes my elbow and guides me to the side overlooking the water.

"Wow. It's gorgeous!" I gasp as I gaze out at this incredible view. I look up at Sam, and he smile down at me, that stupid dimple in his left cheek making an entrance.

"I knew you would love it. I also got tickets to the Chihuly Garden and Glass. But we can stay here for as long as you want, Kitty Kat." He dips his head and looks at the ground.

I step close to him and hug him around his waist. He wraps his arms around me, and pulls me in closer to him.

"Thank you, Sammy. I've wanted to come here since I moved to Seattle. Thanks for planning this and putting up with my grumpiness. This means more than I can tell you."

"You're very welcome." He kisses the top of my head, and before I can process his sweet kiss, he quickly steps back. I think I see a blush forming on his cheeks, but he turns from me before I can fully take him in.

Sam has never kissed me before.

We spend a few hours just admiring the view and chatting about how different Seattle is from Charleston. It isn't until we're leaving to go to Chihuly Garden and Glass that I realize I haven't thought of Kevin once. I couldn't be more grateful for Sam.

***

Present Day

Once our Thanksgiving feast is ready, we all sit together at the table. I'm sitting between Mom and Sam.

We have a tradition of going around the table and saying one thing we are thankful for that year before we start eating.

Dad always starts. "Well, I just want to thank you for being here. It's difficult this year because we have an empty chair." He clears his throat before continuing, "I'm thankful this year for all of you. For your support. Your grace and, most importantly, the love you show us every day." I smile at him. Every year, he always shares thoughtful things for which he is grateful.

Ethan and I always put little effort into what we said—usually something about bikes, video games, or ice cream.

"This year, I'm thankful for good memories that I'll carry with me always." Mom's voice is sure, but I see her eyes glisten with unshed tears.

It's my turn, and I'm not sure what to say. I should have been thinking about it. Especially since I knew this was coming. My leg bounces under the table until I feel Sam's warm hand on my knee; he gives it a reassuring squeeze. I don't dare look at him.

I internally chastise myself for not thinking this through and speak without knowing what to say, "I guess…" Looking around the room, I try to come up with something I am thankful for at this moment. "I'm thankful for open doors and new opportunities." I look down at my empty plate and shrink into my chair, trying to make myself smaller so the attention moves on from me.

I worry my words sound disingenuous. But I guess it's true. I *am* thankful for this new friendship, or whatever it is, with Sam. I'm also excited about the possibility of moving back to Charleston.

"I'm thankful for renewed friendships and the possibility for a new future." I see Sam looking at me out of the corner of my eye. I can only assume his words are meant for me. I tune out everyone else while I try to unravel Sam's meaning.

Thinking back to our conversation on our drive here, I believe he told me the truth—that he's had feelings for me just like I've had for him. But somehow my mind still wants to fight that.

I've dated a lot since that terrible night in Seattle. But I've never really gotten close to anyone. There's always been a part of me that felt like something was missing with these other guys.

Philip is a good example. He's the opposite of Sam in nearly every way. I think that's why Philip felt comfortable. Felt... safe. I don't think I ever truly opened myself up to Philip. At least not where it mattered.

Despite his asking several times, I refused to let him meet my parents, even though we had dated for a little over a year. My family is everything to me, and I refused to share that piece of myself with him.

Because deep down, I knew we wouldn't last—he wasn't Sam. I knew Philip couldn't fill the void left by Sam's absence. I wonder if Sam has felt the same.

We eat dinner—the conversation never lulls. By the time we're done, I've eaten more than I should have. I'm feeling exhausted, so after I help clean up the leftovers and the dishes, I make my way towards the couch in the living room. Snuggling into the couch corner, I lay my head on the arm.

Dad follows me in, sitting on the opposite side.

I look at him out of the corner of my eye and mumble out, "Where's everyone else?"

"Playing board games." He rubs his hand across his face, and I peek at the group that I can see at the formal dining table. Sam catches my attention and winks at me. I duck my head to hide my blush.

"I wanted to talk to you about moving back to Charleston." I sit up and give Dad my full attention. "You know you can always move home. This is your home, and you are always welcome here. But if there is any chance you're hesitating because you don't want to live here specifically, you can always move into the condo."

"Ethan's condo?" I sit taller on the couch, "But I thought you guys sold it."

"We still have it. Every time your mom and I talk about listing it, she says it isn't the right time. We paid it off with Ethan's life insurance. It's just sitting empty, and you wouldn't have to pay for it." He runs his palm across his face again. "Well, not empty; a lot of his stuff is still there." He looks a little guilty. "We've been over there several times, and we've been going through Ethan's things, trying to sort through them. But it's been hard to say goodbye." I scoot over to him and give him a tight hug.

"Oh, Dad, I wish I were closer so I could have helped with all of this. I don't know how I feel about moving into his place, but it would make things easier." I give Dad a sheepish smile. "As much as I love you and Ma, and as much as I love this house, I don't want to live with my parents, you know?"

I pull my legs onto the couch and sit cross-legged. I look over at the dining table and see Mom smiling at something someone said. I look at Sam again and see he's watching me. He smiles at me before returning to the game in front of him.

God, he's like a beacon, and I can't seem to keep my eyes off him.

"I know, baby girl. The condo is yours if you want it. No pressure. Just an option."

Moving into the condo would be a great way to keep paying half of the condo in Columbia while also being able to afford a place here. I wouldn't feel like I'm letting Liv down or leaving her hanging. "Thanks, Dad. I would love that." I lean my head against the back of the couch and stare at the ceiling. It might be weird, but it would make things a lot easier.

Chapter 21

"Kat?" Mom's voice is gentle and quiet.

"Ma? Is everything ok? What time is it?" It's still dark in my room, and I feel my body stiffen with the panic forming in my gut.

"Everything's fine, pretty girl. It's 4:00 a.m. Sorry to wake you. Are you still ok with helping me at the bakery today? It's going to be very busy with all the shoppers. I could use the extra hands."

In my haze, I remember Mom asking me to help her last night and realize I forgot to set my alarm. Sitting up slowly, I see she's already showered and dressed. "Sure, Ma. Do I have time to shower?"

"Of course. I'd like to leave in about thirty minutes, if that works for you."

"Yeah, ok. I'll be ready." I watch Mom leave my room before I stretch and climb out of bed.

By the time I make it downstairs, Mom has a to-go mug full of coffee ready for me. Taking my first sip, I groan into my cup. She made it just the way I like it.

"Do you mind if we eat something at the bakery? We had some leftover croissants from Wednesday. I offered everything to Cassandra, but she only took a few things home with her. I probably should have brought everything else to the house and added it to the Thanksgiving feast we had." I get the feeling she's talking more to herself than to me by the end.

Mom gives the leftover baked goods to her employees. But on Wednesday, she worked with only one other person, and they closed early. Mostly selling rolls and desserts for Thanksgiving.

"I don't mind at all. I love your croissants." She makes amazing croissants. They're so flaky and buttery, even when they're a couple of days old. I'm secretly crossing my fingers that there are a couple of cream cheese ones left so I can devour them.

Mom's bakery looks small from the outside. It's on one of the main shopping streets in Charleston, nestled in between a bookstore and a coffee shop, the perfect combination, in my opinion. When the bakery opens, its windows are filled with glass displays showcasing the available items for the day. Right now, they're empty.

I look up at the sign above the shop door, "The Little Loaf" is in pink letters with black whisks on each side. I've always loved the sign. I smile at it as we walk inside.

We're the first ones here, so Mom unlocks the door, and we step inside. I'm immediately hit by the smell of sugar and flour. The scent is intoxicating and cathartic.

I spent a lot of my childhood in this shop. When I was young, Mom would measure out ingredients, and I would get to dump them into the large commercial mixers. As I got older, she let me knead the dough and shape cookies. Now, I've helped Mom here so many times that I can make almost anything with her, as long as I have a recipe, that is.

I start wiping down the counters, cleaning the cases, and sweeping the floors. The shop is thoroughly cleaned at night before locking up, but Mom always likes to go over everything each morning to ensure it's spotless.

She prepared croissants and muffin batter before locking up on Wednesday, so she pulls those out of the coolers, puts the muffin batter into muffin cups and into the pre-heated oven and lets the croissants proof before baking them. She moves on to mixing ingredients for various items she plans on selling today.

Soon, Cassandra and Susie walk in the door and start helping to get things ready.

Now that everything is clean, I shift my attention to making frosting for the red velvet and chocolate cupcakes that will be ready soon. Mom insists on using buttercream frosting on most of her cakes and cupcakes. It's one of my favorite things, and I may or may not have sampled the delicious frosting.

Before I know it, the bakery is packed with early shoppers. I spend the next few hours working the cash register and boxing up cakes and other baked goods. It isn't until I sit down for a break that I realize it's 2:00 p.m.. Checking my phone, I have a message from Sam.

I heard you are helping your mom this morning, but I'm hoping to sneak you away for a hike. What do you think?

I don't want to leave Mom too soon, but things are slowing down now that the lunch rush is over. "Hey, Ma, Sam wants to pick me up to go hiking. Do you think you need me here much longer?"

She looks around before she answers, "I think we're in a pretty good spot now. Thanks so much for your help today." I kiss her on the cheek and type out a response to Sam.

Good timing. I can leave whenever you're ready. But can you pick me up here and take me back to my parents' house so I can change before we head out?

Be there in 10.

While I'm waiting for him, I walk over to the coffee shop and order a latte for myself and a tea for Sam. As I'm waiting in line,

I hear a familiar voice behind me. "Kat? Is that you?" Turning around, I see Chris, an old friend from high school; I haven't seen him in years. Chris dated my friend Sophie for about a month during our senior year. I always thought he was nice, just not a great match for Sophie.

She was all drama and very serious; Chris was a big goofball, always trying to make everyone laugh. His dark brown hair is cropped short and reminds me of the military haircuts I've seen. He has an athletic build but isn't particularly muscled. He has dark brown eyes and dark skin.

"Chris! I haven't seen you in ages. How have you been?" We hug each other briefly.

"I've been good. You look amazing. Your mom still owns the bakery next door, I take it?" He reaches up and brushes flour from my cheek. I blush at the contact and shrug, trying to act like it's no big deal.

"Yeah. I was helping her this morning. It's always busy the day after Thanksgiving."

"That's amazing. I was just finishing up some shopping with my sisters." He waves in their direction. "We're grabbing coffee and then going over to your mom's shop for some snacks before heading back to the house to take naps." I catch his sisters looking at us, so I smile and wave to them. "Maybe I'll see you over there?"

"I'm actually on my way out. I'm just grabbing coffee first." Hearing my name called, he walks with me over to the counter where the finished drinks are placed.

"How long are you in town for? I'd love to catch up." He offers me a shy smile.

"I'm going back to Columbia tomorrow." He frowns so I quickly add, "But I'll be here for a week over Christmas. Maybe we can do something then?"

"I'd love that." We say our goodbyes, and by the time I walk out, Sam is waiting at the curb.

Chapter 22

"Who was the guy you were talking to in the coffee shop?" Sam asks in greeting.

"It's good to see you, too, Sam." I roll my eyes at him, handing over his drink. "I got you a chai tea latte."

"Sorry. It's good to see you. Thanks for the drink." He takes the cup, sets it into his drink holder, and leans over to plant a quick kiss on my cheek. "So, who's the guy?"

Rolling my eyes again, I let out an audible sigh before answering, "Chris Polk. I'm not sure if you would remember him. He was in my grade and dated Sophie a bit during our senior year. I don't think I've seen him since graduation."

"Oh. Cool." Sam says it like he thinks it's anything but cool. "Does he still live in Charleston?"

"Yeah. I think he's a CPA and works for his dad's accounting firm downtown. He said something about hanging out." I don't know why I added that last part.

"Do you want to hang out with him?"

"Maybe. I mean, it might be nice to catch up. We were friends at some point."

"Hmmm," is his only response.

We drive the rest of the way to my parents' house in silence, and I can tell Sam is stewing over Chris. I try to ignore the tension radiating off him and look out the window instead.

Once at my parents' house, I quickly change and meet Sam back downstairs. I find him standing in the living room, looking at the bookcase.

"Do you think your parents have read all of these?" He gestures vaguely at the books.

"I don't know." I look where he's pointing. "My mom almost always had a book in her hands when I was growing up, so I assume so."

He continues looking at the titles.

"Do you still read?" I ask him.

He turns his attention to me before responding, "Yeah. I don't watch a lot of TV and read books instead. But I don't own a lot of books. I like to support my local library. I tend to go on the weekends and pick up a few that I'll read over the next week."

"A few?"

"I can usually finish two or three books a week." My mouth drops a little in surprise. "I like to wind down after work by reading. It's a great way to stay creative but in a way that doesn't feel like I'm still working."

I tilt my head to the side to contemplate Sam's reading habits. I haven't read for pleasure nearly as much as I used to. Now my days are full of reading legal documents, but I still read a handful of books each year. "I don't really read for pleasure as much anymore."

"That's surprising! You used to always have a book with you."

I shrug in response and look back at the books.

"Are you ready to go?" He holds his hand out, gesturing towards the door.

"Yes." He grabs my hand, and we walk out of the house. His hand is warm and comforting.

Sam suddenly stops, and I barrel into him. "Why is my dad here?"

Peeking around him, I notice my parents are chatting with Dan on the sidewalk in front of the gate that leads to the driveway and backyard.

How did Mom get here so fast?

Before I can respond, Dan shouts out, "Hey, kids, come to the back with us." Sam looks at me over his shoulder, giving me a "I don't know what's going on" look before he leads us to the backyard with our parents.

An intricate wrought iron gate sits at the sidewalk and leads to a long driveway spanning the length of the house and ending at the two-car garage on one side and the backyard on the other.

As we walk down the long drive, I spot Ethan's motorcycle parked halfway down the driveway, a helmet hanging off one of the handles.

Sam and I stop walking when we are standing right in front of the motorcycle—the twin to the one Sam was driving when he was in his accident.

Mom looks down at mine and Sam's interlocked hands and smiles as she looks up at me.

"What's going on?" Sam's quiet voice breaks my thoughts.

"We want you to have Ethan's bike." Dad gestures between himself and my mom.

Sam drops my hand and starts shaking his head. "N... No. I can't take this." He gestures at the bike before rubbing the back of his neck with one hand while he shoves the other into his pocket.

"Sam, honey. Ethan would want you to have it." Mom's voice is strangled. She clears her throat and then continues, "We," she gestures at herself, Dad, and Dan, "want you to have it."

Sam steps forward, tentative, as he glides his palm along the seat. "Are you sure?" His voice is timid as he looks at my parents, tears in his beautiful brown eyes. I want to go to him. I want to comfort him. But my feet won't move.

"Yes. Absolutely." Dad uses the voice he uses when something is decided. Leaving no room for argument.

"I don't know what to say." Sam's voice is rough and wobbly, and it's all it takes to bring me to action. "Thank you." I move toward him and wrap my arm around his, my hand stroking his bicep. He looks down at me, giving me a weak smile. Tears form in Sam's eyes.

He hugs my parents, and Mom tells him she loves him. Dan hands Sam the keys, gives him a quick hug, and then follows my parents into the house.

I stand in silence, watching as Sam walks around the motorcycle. His expression flits between awe, devastation, and concern.

I watch as he gently sets the helmet onto the ground, straddles the seat, and places his hands on the handlebars. He looks up at me, devastation etching his features. "I haven't been on a bike since my accident." His voice is so small. Stepping forward, I run my hand along his back.

"You don't have to take it if you don't want it. But they are right." He looks at me like I'm his lifeline. "Ethan would want you to have it."

"It doesn't feel right that the last time I was on a bike was when I almost died. And now..." His voice wavers. "Now, your parents are giving me Ethan's bike, and—" he chokes on the words. "And he *did* die in an accident. I... I don't know how to..." He cuts off abruptly and looks back down at the motorcycle, one hand drifting down to rest on the tank.

I'm not sure what to say, so I keep rubbing his back in soothing circles.

"Fuck." It's a little more than a whisper. He covers his face with his hands as his body shakes.

I stand frozen again for just a moment before I awkwardly wrap my arms around him. I hate seeing him this way. Embracing him is the only way I know how to comfort him. There are no words I can say that will take his pain away.

He slowly drops his hands from his face and shifts his body, moving himself off the bike. Once he dismounts, he pulls me into a hug, both of us allowing our tears to run freely.

I'm not sure how long we stand there like this, wrapped up in each other's arms. But it isn't until our tears have stopped that I hesitantly disentangle myself from him.

"I don't feel like hiking anymore. Do you maybe want to watch a movie instead?" My voice is thick, and my throat feels raw, like I've been yelling for hours.

"I'll do whatever you want to do, Kat, as long as I get to be with you." His eyes are red-rimmed, the color so light I can see the green that forms a circle on the inside of his irises. I grab his hand, and we make our way back into the house.

Pulling him behind me, we slowly go up to the third floor.

Chapter 23

Once we get up to the loft, Sam looks around like he isn't sure what to do. He watches me as I sit down on the couch, right in the middle. I pat the seat right next to me, and he slowly sits down.

I glare at the space he's left between us. I'm not sure if this is because he doesn't want to be that close to me or if it's because he's trying to be respectful.

"How am I supposed to cuddle with you when you're sitting so far away?" I meant to say it in a flirty way, but it comes out wrong.

"You want to cuddle?"

Fuck, the look on his face breaks my heart. It's the same look he got when he watched Ethan and Mom during small, intimate moments. Like when Mom would brush a stray hair out of Ethan's face. Or when she would walk by and randomly squeeze Ethan's shoulders.

Sam looks lost.

Starving for attention, he doesn't know how to ask for.

Without hesitating, I scoot right next to him, lift his right arm, and put it around my shoulders. I shimmy next to him, getting as close as I can, and then lean my head against his chest.

I feel his body relax and his breathing even out. I love that his body reacts this way to me. It reminds me of the times we would snuggle up on one of our dorm room beds and watch movies together.

The memory makes me want to move away and protect myself, but I know he needs this. He needs human contact. A soft touch.

We both do. So, I shove those feelings back down and try to think only of this moment.

Using the remote, I pull up our movie app and start scrolling through the digital movie list. "Action? Horror? Comedy? Roooo-mance?" I waggle my eyebrows at him. "What sounds good to you, Sammy?"

"I don't care." He shrugs and sounds defeated. "Something happy?" His voice is slightly brighter.

"Comedy it is." I randomly choose an Adam Sandler movie from the list and press play. Before we get through the opening credits, Mom comes up the stairs and tells us they are going to dinner with Dan.

"Pizza?" I give Sam my best, "I've been a good girl and deserve pizza," look. Sam grants me a slight chuckle. It doesn't reach his eyes, but it's progress.

"Only if we can get extra pepperoni." He winks at me.

"You got it." I pull out my phone and order from the website, choosing the delivery option. "I got a couple of Diet Cokes, too. It'll be here in about 20 minutes." I hear Sam's stomach grumble. "Which sounds like it couldn't come soon enough." I elbow him lightly in the stomach and laugh.

We decide to wait until the pizza comes to start the movie so that we aren't interrupted. I adjust my position so that I have one leg folded under me, slightly propped on his thigh, while the other dangles off the couch.

I turn towards him, searching his face. "Sam, I'm so incredibly grateful that you survived. I'm so sorry I wasn't there for you. I'm sorry I was so stuck in my own feelings that I couldn't stop and be your friend, not only when you needed me, but for all of the times in between and after." I look down at my hands in my lap. "I wish I could take it all back. I wish I could go back to that night and stop the words from exiting my mouth."

He takes my chin in his long fingers and gently raises it, forcing me to look at him. "Don't ever apologize for speaking your feelings. Don't ever apologize for telling me you love, *loved* me." *Oh Sam, I do love you.* "I've cherished those words. They've given me hope that someday you'll forgive me and let me be back in your life. Those words kept me going on some of my toughest days." He tightens his arm around my shoulder.

"Ok," is all I say in response.

He leans into me until his mouth is only inches away from mine. His eyes search mine, and my breath catches at his proximity. I could lean in just a little, and our lips would be touching.

"I want to kiss you, Kat." His eyes alight with playfulness. "Can I kiss you?"

A breathy "yes" is all that comes out before he closes the short distance, and his lips are on mine.

Oh my god!

Sam is kissing me.

The kiss starts out gentle, a caress. His lips are soft, just like I thought they would be. He swipes his tongue over my lips, and I open for him, allowing him to deepen our kiss.

I'm not sure which one of us turns the kiss frantic. But we can't seem to get close enough to each other.

Like we're both drowning, and the other is the air our lungs desperately crave.

I want to mold my body to his.

Sam's hands are on my back, pulling me into him while my hands explore his neck before running through the soft strands of his hair.

I don't realize I've climbed into his lap until I'm straddling him, his hands moving from my back to my hips. He shifts us onto the couch so that I'm lying down as his body presses gently against mine; his hands are on the couch above my head.

I feel his body press into mine, not enough that it becomes hard to breathe, but enough that I feel his rigid length through my leggings. I can't stop my hips from moving, trying to create friction for my most sensitive parts.

He breaks our kiss and hisses, "Fuck." Sam looks at me, eyes searching mine. "Kat," he groans my name, "I want whatever you're willing to give me. But I don't want to do anything you'll regret later. You set the pace here. You choose which pieces you let me have."

His cautious gaze ignites something within me, and I grab his shirt in a fist and pull him back into me, crushing my lips to his. He moves his hips in time with mine; our movements create delicious friction, causing my core to tighten.

My hands run up and down his back in slow strokes. *God, this feels so good.*

I reach up and grab his left hand, placing it on my breast. He immediately starts massaging my breast before circling my nipple through my thin tank top and bra. He removes his mouth from mine and trails kisses along my neck and throat.

He grabs the top of my loose tank top, pulling down slightly, and looks at me, asking permission. With a quick nod of my head, he pulls my shirt and bra down, exposing my breasts.

He gives me a satisfied look before taking one nipple into his mouth. He sucks and nips in the most tantalizing way.

God, I think I'm going to come like this.

His hips continue moving with mine when I reach my hands down, gripping his toned ass, and pull his hips into me harder.

"Sam," I moan. "Sam, I... I think I'm going to... fuck... I don't want you to stop." I can't form the words as my brain short-circuits at the feeling of his body against mine.

He adjusts his position, creating space between us, and I groan at the loss. "Do you want to keep going like this, or do you want my fingers?" he says, breathily.

Not even a heartbeat later, I enthusiastically respond, "Fingers."

He gives me a wicked grin and moves his hand into my leggings.

"No panties?" He looks at me in surprise.

I shake my head. "I don't like them." I let my knees fall open more, giving him better access.

"Fuck," he groans as he crashes his mouth to mine, his thumb finding and circling my clit.

He slips one finger inside of me, and I moan at the contact.

He moves his finger in and out a couple of times before adding another, curling them to hit that perfect spot.

The tension continues to build in my core, and my body clenches. "That's it, I want to see you come on my fingers," he breathes into my neck.

He takes my nipple into his mouth again. The sensation of his fingers stroking in and out of me, his palm rubbing against my clit, and his very skilled tongue on my nipple has me writhing under him.

"Come for me, Kitty Kat."

That stupid nickname is my undoing. My release barrels through me, and I call out his name; his mouth is on mine again, capturing my scream. He continues sliding his fingers inside of me, dragging out my orgasm.

Once I come down from my high, he drops his head to my shoulder. "That was...." I'm a little breathless. I chuckle slightly and move my hand to cup his length through his jeans.

He slowly lifts his head from my shoulder and smirks. He gives me a quick and chaste kiss. "I don't expect anything, Kat. Watching you come undone at my touch, that was enough for me."

I smile at him, grip his T-shirt, and start tugging at it so I can remove it. But he grips my hand and shakes his head.

He looks at me in horror, but it's gone in a flash.

I don't understand what just happened.

What did I do wrong?

I don't get the chance to ask him because the doorbell rings, announcing the arrival of the pizza.

"I'll get that," he says too quickly as he kneels above me, creating distance between our bodies that I don't want. He adjusts my bra and shirt, covering me, and leans over to place a soft kiss on my lips.

Without another word, Sam heads downstairs to greet the delivery person.

I don't even know where to start with what just happened. I never meant to… I never meant for *any* of that to happen. But Sam, shit.

I can still taste his lips on mine. Feel his mouth on my nipples. God, I feel the ghost of his hands on me, *in* me.

But why did he stop me, and why did he look terrified?

I'm still in stunned silence when Sam comes back upstairs—pizza, plates, and our sodas in hand.

"You ok, Kat?" His voice is laced with concern.

"Sam, I… I don't know what to say." I feel embarrassment flush across my cheeks. Looking down at my hands, I start picking at one of my nails.

"Do you regret what just happened?" His question surprises me, and I look into his eyes. They are wide, and he seems nervous about my answer.

"No." It comes out small. "Not at all. I—it's just, you seemed upset when I was taking off your shirt. I don't want you to feel like I took advantage of you." I shrug.

He barks out a laugh. "*You* take advantage of *me*?" He sets the food on the coffee table in front of the couch. He sobers as he sits next to me. "I meant it when I said I want whatever you are willing to give me." He takes my face in both of his hands and places a gentle kiss on my lips. "Kat, I wasn't upset with you."

He runs his hand through his hair and looks towards the TV hanging on the wall. When he finally looks at me again, I see the vulnerability in his expression.

"I haven't exactly shown anyone my scars. Ethan and my dad have seen them, and the doctors and nurses, and my tattoo artist." He adds the last part almost as an afterthought. "But, that's it." He reaches for my hand, interlacing his fingers with mine.

No one else? No friends or girlfriends? The thought surprises me. That trip was years ago. But now that he mentions it, I don't think I've seen him in a tank top recently, and certainly haven't seen him without a shirt.

I look down at our interlocked fingers and I'm in awe at how strong this man is in front of me. And yet, he's shown me so many pieces of himself over the last few days. Vulnerable and emotional pieces. It makes me love him even more.

The thought terrifies me.

Sam's voice breaks through my thoughts. "So, I wasn't upset. I guess I'm just nervous about it. I—" he takes in a long breath and blows it out, "I don't want you to see my scars and pity me or turn away from me."

I cup his cheek with my free hand; my heart warms as he leans into it. "Sam, I will not pity you or turn away. But I also won't push you to do something you aren't comfortable with. I'm here when you're ready."

He sighs and turns his head, placing a kiss on my palm.

I drop my hand to my lap and look down at our interlocked fingers again. "Do you, um... do you want to continue what we started? I promise to leave your shirt alone."

I keep my gaze averted from his face. Not because I'm ashamed, but because I don't want to see his expression if he rejects me. I couldn't take it after what we just did.

He gently lifts my chin with his index finger and searches my eyes before speaking, "Don't think for a second that I don't want you. I do. I want *all* of you. I want to take my time with you. I want to taste every inch of you." He runs his thumb along my lips before placing his hand on the back of the couch. "I don't want to fuck this up again. So, I want to go slow, if that's ok with you."

I give him a slight nod in agreement.

"Next time, Kitty Kat, I'm going to take my time memorizing every curve of your body." He kisses me softly. "For now, let's eat and watch that movie. You owe me some cuddling time."

Chapter 24

N*ine Years Old*

"Ethan, what are you doing here?" I'm sitting on the concrete wall in front of my class. I've been sitting here since the boy in my class pushed me down, and I couldn't stop crying.

"Mom found out what happened and asked the counselor to let me sit with you for a bit. You ok?" He sits next to me and drapes his arm over my shoulders.

I can't stop the new stream of tears that roll down my cheeks. "I don't know why Michael is so mean to me," I choke out.

"I'm sorry, Kat. Do you want me to talk to him?"

"NO!" I shout.

"Ok, ok. I won't talk to him. What can I do?" He runs his hand along my hair, and I lean into him.

"I don't know."

"Are you hurt? Do you want me to walk you to the nurse's office?"

"Will that be ok? I don't want you to get into trouble. I scraped my knee, and it really hurts." I point down to the scrape that's still bleeding a little.

"Yeah, my teacher said I could come out here until you were ok to go back to class. I'll walk with you there. But then, I probably need to get back."

"Thanks for being here for me."

"Always, sis."

Ethan helps me walk to the nurse's office and tells her where I'm hurt. Once the nurse calls me into her small exam room, I watch as Ethan walks out of the waiting area to go back to his class. I'm so glad he takes care of me when I need him.

I don't know what I'll do when he isn't at the same school next year. Thankfully, I don't cry at school very often.

***

P resent Day

The next morning, Liv picks me up, and we head back to Columbia. As we drive home, she tells me about her week at her parents' house, and I tell her about mine.

I tell her about my time with Sam, omitting the part about me coming on his fingers. I know she would be excited, but I'm not ready to delve into what this means yet.

I want him. That fact is clear.

But he lives in Chicago, and I live in Columbia. We see each other less than a handful of times a year; I'm not sure how that would work out for either of us. Even when I move back to Charleston, it'll still be hard.

So, instead of delving into my evening escapade with Sam, I broach another subject I'm scared to talk to her about. "Liv?"

"Yeah, babe?"

"I need to talk to you about something."

She glances at me before responding, "Why do you sound... I don't know... off? What's wrong?"

"I'm just, I don't want you to be disappointed." I frown at her.

"You're my best friend and a badass lawyer. Just say it!" She gives me a wide smile before quickly turning her focus back on the road.

The laugh that escapes my lips is automatic. "I've been thinking for a while about moving back to Charleston. Truthfully, I had planned on talking to you about all of this before Ethan died. But then everything happened, and I just didn't know how to bring it up."

"Kat." She takes my hand and looks at me meaningfully. "You know I always want you to follow your heart. I'll miss you desperately, but if Charleston is where your heart is? You should definitely go."

I smile and look out the window. "I talked to my parents, and it turns out that they never sold Ethan's place, and it's paid off. They said I could live there, which means I can afford to keep paying half of our place."

"Oh my God, woman! Is this why you were nervous to tell me?"

"A little," I say sheepishly.

She gives me this look that tells me something is up her sleeve. "It's actually good timing because Talia and I have been talking about moving in together. Her lease is up in January, so I was going to talk to you about her moving in with us."

"That's great, Liv! Yes, she can definitely move in!" I'm genuinely excited about this next step in Liv and Talia's relationship. Especially with some of the turmoil they've been navigating with Talia's family.

"So," her tone loses its prior excitement, "when are you thinking about moving back to Charleston?" Her mouth is drawn downwards in a slight frown, and she slumps into her seat. I know she'll miss seeing me every day just as much as I'll miss her.

"I think I'll give notice at work in December and then have my last day be around mid-January. I know it's more notice than anyone needs to give." I shrug and fiddle with my fingers in my lap. "I want to give them as much time as I can so they can work out the transition and possibly find my replacement. That should also give me enough time to wrap some things up."

"You're gonna move into Ethan's place?"

"I guess so. It'll be better than living with my parents." I grimace at the thought of navigating whatever is going on between Sam and me with my parents always around. "I think it might be a little weird." I sigh audibly. "You know, they kept all his furniture and clothes. I don't know if I can move into his place with all his stuff still there. And you want to know what's even weirder?"

She looks at me, raising an eyebrow, and nods her head for me to continue.

"Well, I decided to work at my dad's firm." I scrunch up my face in mock disgust.

Liv just laughs.

Fucking. Laughs.

Playfully, I push her arm. "Shut up. I hate you."

"Bitch, you fucking *love* me." She flips her hair over her shoulder in jest. I smile at her dramatic nature.

"I do love you. I don't know what I'm going to do without you being at my beck and call. What am I going to do without your sass? Who's gonna make me blueberry waffles when I'm sad? Or watch *Gilmore Girls* reruns with me?"

"You really are going to be helpless without me. Good luck with that." Her laugh is contagious.

Chapter 25

Seventeen Years Old

I'm nervous as I walk out on stage. I've practiced this song more times than I can count, but not in front of this many people.

I peek out into the stands, trying to find my parents. Ethan is in Columbia, attending his first year at the University of South Carolina. This is the first performance he won't be at, and the thought makes me sad. There are too many people, and I can't see where my parents are sitting.

I'm singing a solo in a regional competition with other high school students. I chose Castle on a Cloud *from* Les Misérables. *It's one of my favorite songs, and I know I'm ready.*

When it's my turn, I stand in the middle of the stage, waiting for them to open the curtains. When they finally do, I take a deep breath and hit every note.

When the song is over, I know I did my best. I don't know if it's good enough to win one of the soloist awards, but I won't let that get me down.

Once the curtain closes, I walk off the stage and hurry to find my parents as the event sponsors set up for the next performance.

It takes a couple of minutes to check in with my high school choir director; my parents stand off to the side, waiting for me. They're beaming at me as they wait for me to finish up with the choir director.

I feel the sting of unshed tears as I see the figure towering over Mom's shoulder: Ethan.

I rush over to them with a huge grin plastered on my face. "Ethan! You made it!" I hug him, and he squeezes me tight with one arm.

"Of course I did. I couldn't miss my baby sister's performance." He steps back and hands me a bouquet of pink tulips, my favorite.

"For me?"

He shakes his head. "You were amazing, kid. I knew you could sing, but damn. You really did great." His smile warms my heart.

"Thanks. I'm so glad you were here for it."

"Me too."

***

P resent Day

Sam and I spent no more than a few hours together on Christmas. He almost didn't show up at all.

His boss demanded that he stay and work through the holiday on a last-minute project for one of the firm's top clients.

He took a redeye and landed in Charleston in the early hours on Christmas Day, only to hop on another redeye back to Chicago that night.

I knew he was angry about the situation, but we did our best to make the most of it.

After exchanging gifts, he fell asleep while we watched a movie in the loft. I wanted to talk to him but didn't have the heart to wake him. Instead, I helped him get comfortable with his head in my lap and ran my hands through his hair as we watched Christmas movies.

"I refuse to work for an organization that thinks so little of my personal time," he complained to me the next day, his voice gruff with exhaustion from traveling and spending the day working. "It's one thing to significantly lower my ability to take a vacation. But over fucking Christmas?! Kat, I have to get out of here. I just don't know if I should find a different firm to work for or just bite the bullet and open my own."

"I know you're upset. Just don't make any rash decisions while your emotions are running high."

His voice lowers. "It's not exactly a rash decision, Kat. I've been thinking about this for a while. Everything was fine until they replaced my boss. Now, I just think my timeline has shifted up."

"I'm sorry. I didn't mean that the way it came out." I pace in my room, feeling anxious for him.

"I know. I'm just frustrated and feel a little stuck right now. I miss being in Charleston. I miss my dad. I wanted to spend time with you, and I'm mad that I slept the entire time."

"I wanted to spend time with you, too, but I'm not upset that you slept. It was enough for me that you were there."

He sighs, and I picture him dragging his hand through his hair. "I'm nervous about transitioning out of this job. What if I fail?"

"What if you don't? Sam, you've shared some of your designs with me, and they're incredible. *You* are incredible. And whether you choose to join another firm or start your own, I'm confident that you'll succeed. Don't stay in a toxic job."

He's quiet for a moment before speaking again, "Thanks. I—thanks, Kat."

Over the past month, Sam and I have fallen into a comfortable routine of texting in the morning and talking on the phone in the evenings. He hasn't made any solid plans for his future. Of course, I want him close to me. But I won't pressure him.

I can't believe I went so long without him in my life. I can't take that time back, but I'm glad to have the chance to move forward with this friendship.

Chapter 26

Fourteen Years Old

I never realized how popular Sam and Ethan were until this year. I knew Ethan always had a date whenever he wanted to go out. But this?

They practically have an entourage with the number of girls that follow them around campus like puppy dogs begging for treats.

Even some of the girls in my grade are in awe when they learn Ethan is my brother and that Sam hangs out at our house all the time.

The number of times I've heard "Oh my God, how do you handle being around Sam all the time? He's so hot!" I just roll my eyes.

I get it, they think my brother and his best friend are hot. I've also seen them both pick their noses, fart, burp, and cry. Whatever.

It's my freshman year, and I'm just glad all my classes have at least one of my friends in them, so I don't have to deal with the swoony girls on my own.

Liv, Sophie, and Kristen are great at coming to my rescue and changing the topic away from my brother and his best friend.

Sam and Ethan are juniors this year, both on the track team. And both got muscular between their freshman and sophomore years. It isn't a surprise that the girls all fawn over them.

I would be lying if I didn't say I think Sam is hot, too. But the constant ogling and fawning over my brother is just too much.

***

P resent Day

Time flies by, and next thing I know, my parents are at my apartment in Columbia, and we're loading up Dad's truck with my things.

Since Ethan's condo is furnished, I won't be taking any furniture with me. But I still have a lot of personal items I've collected over the last few years.

Liv and I spent as much time together as we could over the last few weeks. Even though I know we'll see each other, and we promise to talk all the time, I'm going to miss seeing her every day.

I'm nervous about going back to Charleston. I'm anxious about living in Ethan's condo. And I'm stressed about working at Dad's firm. Despite my nerves, I'm glad I'll be closer to my parents.

Once we've loaded everything into Dad's truck and my small car, Liv and I say our goodbyes. I wish I could say it was a tear-free experience, but it wasn't. Not even close.

We both ugly cried as we clung to each other. Dad, uncomfortable with the entire situation, had to intervene and remind us that we would still see each other and could still talk on the phone. "You know, video chat is a great invention you may not have heard of yet," he teased us.

Now here I am, driving back to Charleston, blasting my 2000s pop playlist. I wonder if I would have actually made the jump and moved back to Charleston if Ethan were still alive.

His death scared me. I'd spent a significant portion of my adult life thinking I wanted to make it on my own. And I did in many ways. But the result was also distance from my family.

I'd like to think that Sam and I would have started talking again eventually. But I also know it wouldn't have happened as soon as it did if Ethan's death hadn't brought us back together.

In many ways, Ethan has been my anchor.

Even in death, he's guiding me along.

There isn't a day that goes by that I don't think about him. I guess the pain is easing up a bit with each passing day. I wonder if there will be a time when I don't think about him. The thought makes my heart ache.

A call interrupts my playlist, and I hit the answer button when I see Sam's name pop up on my radio screen.

"Hey, how's it going?"

"Good. How are you, Kitty Kat?" His voice is playful.

"Good." I pause and take in a couple of steadying breaths. "I'm sad to leave Liv and Columbia."

"I know. It's a big change for you, and I can only imagine that you're both excited and sad about it. I know you'll miss Liv. I'm proud of you for making this change even though it'll be hard at times."

My throat feels like it's closing up, and I choke out a response, "Other than Seattle, I haven't ever lived away from Liv. And I've definitely never lived on my own before. I don't want it to feel lonely."

"Living on your own for the first time can be hard. When Claire and I broke things off, and she moved out, some days were very lonely." My gut clenches at the thought that Sam was ever lonely. "Those were the days when I would call Ethan and make him play video games online with me. Or I would make plans with my friends just to get out of the house. I'm here anytime you want to talk."

"Thanks, Sammy." My voice is small as I continue to languish over Sam's loneliness, knowing that I played a part in that.

"As for Liv, it's going to be hard being away from her—just remember she isn't fully gone. She's a phone call away, and you can visit her on the weekends. Actually, have you thought about making plans with her so you have something to look forward to?"

"I haven't." My words are slow and tilt up at the end. "That's a great idea."

"You know," he drags it out like he has something up his sleeve. "The flights from Chicago to Charleston aren't too expensive most of the time. I could fly over more often, I mean, if you want." He sounds hopeful that I'll say yes.

"You would do that?"

"For you, Kitty Kat, anything." His comment about inexpensive flights gives me an idea.

"Maybe I could visit you, too. And you could show me around Chicago?"

"Yes. 100 percent, yes. Let's do that! This weekend?" He chuckles. His excitement over the prospect makes me excited, too.

"Maybe not this weekend, but I am serious. Would you want me to visit you? I've never been to Chicago."

"I would be thrilled if you came for a visit. But fair warning, I live in a one-bedroom, so we'll have to share a bed again, cause I'm not letting you sleep on the couch. And this time, I expect you won't sneak out of bed when you wake up with your body wrapped around mine."

I choke on air and instantly think back to that morning. About how good it felt to wake up with Sam's arm around me, my head on his chest. About that night over Thanksgiving and how much more I want him.

"Only if you buy me dinner first." It comes out sounding braver than I feel.

"I'll buy you every damn dinner in existence if you visit me."

I don't hold back the laugh that bubbles out at his enthusiastic response. "Deal."

Chapter 27

I spent my first night back in Charleston at my parents' house. We were all too tired to unload things, and I wasn't exactly ready to sleep at Ethan's—*my* place yet.

I wake early the next morning, drive over to Mom's bakery to pick up an assortment of muffins—blueberry, chocolate, and an almond-poppyseed for Dad. Once I have the muffins, I head next door to grab coffee for the three of us.

I'm lost in my thoughts, waiting in line to order coffee, when a familiar voice cuts in, "Kat?"

Shaking my head to clear the fog, I say, "Chris. Hey!"

"You ok?" His brow is furrowed.

"Were you talking to me for a while?"

"Not a while," he chuckles. "But long enough, I could tell you were in your own bubble."

"Sorry about that. A lot is going on, and my head is a bit messy right now."

"Want to talk about it?"

I laugh uncomfortably. "I'm moving back to Charleston. Well, *moved* back. Last night, actually. I'm picking up breakfast for my parents and me before we head over to my new place to unload some stuff from my dad's truck."

"Kat, that's amazing!" Chris's face beams in excitement. "Do you want any help? I'm free all day."

"Um," I rub my neck, "there isn't much to move." His face drops as I'm speaking, so I hurry and add, "we were supposed to meet up for lunch or something over Christmas, and I know things got busy. I won't have things settled enough to cook dinner tonight. Do you want to get pizza?"

"Definitely," he perks back up. "Do you want to come to my place? Or I can pick you up, and we can go out."

"How about we go out. You choose where?"

"Perfect. Text me the address, and I'll pick you up around 6?"

"Sounds great. See you then!"

We part ways, and I head back to my parents' house. I'm excited to hang out with Chris. He was always fun to be around, and he treated Sophie very well.

Sophie and Chris were never a great match, and when they broke up, they stayed friends for a long time. I make a mental note to text Sophie and talk to her about going out with Chris.

Shit, this isn't a date, is it?

That's something I should have cleared up with him before he walked out. *I'm sure he knows.* I hope.

The thought that Chris might think this is a date causes a gut-wrenching feeling of guilt.

Sam and I have been getting closer, especially after what happened over Thanksgiving, and then our call yesterday. We live so far apart, and it's not like we've made any commitments to each other.

I would be lying if I said I didn't have feelings for Sam.

I've *always* had feelings for Sam.

I can't dwell on what might be or could be. So, I shove my conflicted feelings down and vow to try to make the most out of whatever tonight is with Chris.

***

My parents and I eat the muffins and drink our coffee before heading over to Ethan's—*my* place.

We spent a couple of hours unloading boxes from Dad's truck and clothes from my car.

While dad picks up sandwiches for lunch, Mom and I relax on the couch.

Looking around, I see pieces of Ethan, from the large abstract painting over the couch to the fake potted plants on the built-in shelves.

I don't know how I'll ever remove all these remnants of Ethan without feeling like I'm throwing him away.

"You ok, pretty girl?" Mom's voice breaks my contemplation.

"Yeah." The word is little more than an automatic response. But then I look at her, and the confession sits on the tip of my tongue. "All of this is a little... strange. I keep looking around this place, and it's nice, but—" I pause, searching for the right words.

"But?" Mom encourages. She's lounging on the couch facing me, with her knee propped onto the couch, and her arm dangling along the back. I adjust my position so I'm facing her.

"This is Ethan's place. The place *he* chose. It has all his furniture in it." My voice cracks a little, and I swallow the lump in my throat. "I'm so grateful to be able to live here. It's just going to take some time, I think, to settle in and feel like I'm not intruding on his space."

"You know you don't have to stay here, right?" Her expression is soft as she looks at me. "If it doesn't feel right, you can live at home." I fiddle with my fingers as she speaks. "We can sell this place, and you can use the money to buy something else." Her voice is shallow, like selling this place is the last thing she wants to do, but I know she doesn't want to make it feel like she's forcing this on me. It's not. I don't feel like it's being forced on me.

"I know, Ma." I place my hand on her arm in a reassuring way. "I think having some of my stuff mixed in will help it feel more like my home. I'm also a little nervous about living by myself. I went from living with you all to living with a roommate in school to living with Liv."

"It's a lot of transition at once, I suppose." She looks around before speaking again, "You should get a cat to keep you company."

"That's a great idea! I should get a couple of cats. Kittens. That way, they'll like each other," I laugh. I'm not going to get a cat.

After lunch, my parents head back to their house, leaving me alone. It's still a few hours until Chris picks me up, so I decide to start unpacking.

I connect my phone to the Bluetooth speaker system that Ethan had installed—there are speakers in every room—put on my favorite playlist, and grab a box labeled "Clothes." I set the box on the bed in the primary room and walk over to the closet, opening it only to realize Ethan's clothes are still hanging up.

I don't have the mental capacity to go through his things right now, so I shut the closet doors, pick up my box, and head to the guest room. I open the closet; I'm relieved to find it empty.

This will have to do until I'm ready.

I make easy work unloading my clothes, one box at a time.

Britney Spears' Work Bitch, playing through the speakers, is interrupted by an incoming call.

Thankfully, my phone is in my back pocket, so I don't have to search for it. I answer it as soon as I see Sam's name on my screen.

"Hey, hang on. I need to connect this to my headphones." I hurry into the living room where I left my purse and rummage through it until I find my headphones. Once they're situated and connected, I turn my focus back to Sam. "Sorry about that. I know this is a first-world problem, but I can't handle holding my phone to my ear."

Sam's lighthearted chuckle makes me smile. "You're such a princess at heart." He laughs again. "So, are you all settled in?"

"Settled? Not exactly. But I unpacked my clothes."

"Whoa, slow down there, tiger. You don't want to overwork yourself." I can hear the smile in his voice. I wish I could see him.

"You're in a good mood."

"I'm always in a good mood when I talk to you, Kitty Kat."

"Whatever. What did you do today?" I sit down on the couch and prop my legs on the coffee table.

"I slept in, got some tea, and went grocery shopping. I just finished at the gym, and now, I'm relaxing. I have a few minutes before I need to leave to meet up with some friends for a movie and dinner, and I wanted to hear your voice."

I smile at his words. "Slept in? You heathen! I ran into Chris this morning while I was grabbing muffins, and he's picking me up later to go to dinner."

I regret the words as soon as they leave my mouth; I try to recover by quickly asking, "What movie are you going to see?"

"Kat I—" His voice is tight, strangled, and he sighs audibly. "I hope you have a great time with Chris. You deserve to have a great night out. Sorry, I just remembered I told Clive I would pick him up, so I need to leave early. Have a great night."

The shift in his tone is so significant that I feel it in my bones. I want to do anything to change it back to what it was at the beginning of this conversation.

"Sam. What's—"

"I'll text you tomorrow. Good night, Kat." And the line goes dead.

"What the fuck?" I'm left stunned.

Chapter 28

I can't believe Sam just hung up on me. He said goodbye but didn't even give me a chance to say anything.

He must be upset that I'm going out with Chris tonight. But it's not like it's a date. Right? *Is it a date?* I kick myself for not clarifying this point.

I'm not interested in dating Chris.

No, I'm only interested in dating a certain six feet, three inches, brown-haired, brown-eyed, tattooed man who just hung up on me.

With Chris, it would just be nice to have a friend in Charleston. Sophie and Kristen both moved away a couple of years ago. With Liv in Columbia, and Ethan—I don't have anyone left.

Before I can continue much further down this rabbit hole, I get a message from Sam.

Sorry I cut our call short.

I really do hope you have a great night.

Have fun with your friends, Sam.

He doesn't send another text, and I'm left reeling. Instead of spiraling with my thoughts, I dial Liv's phone number.

"Fucking finally! Do you know I've been waiting all day for you to call me? Did you forget about me already? I know the whole *out of sight, out of mind thing.* But my God, woman. It's only been one day!" I hear Talia laugh in the background, and the sound helps me relax.

"Sorry, Liv. I promise I haven't forgotten you... yet. But give it another week, and I make no guarantees."

"I swear to whatever god exists, if you even think about forgetting me, I'll... I don't know what I'll do, drive to Charleston and cry at your door until you let me in."

"You know that just makes me want to pretend I've forgotten you, right?" I laugh at the vision this conversation creates. "Then you'll have no choice but to move to Charleston and be my roommate again."

"You know I would, but I can't leave Talia. Did you know she has no idea how to operate the espresso machine? I have to teach her immediately, cause you know I can't be held responsible for making *my own coffee.*" She says the last words slowly, enunciating each one.

"Oh, you poor thing! Whatever will you do?" The sarcasm drips from my words.

"What are you up to? Are you unpacked yet? I know you hate boxes and clutter."

"No, not yet. I unpacked my clothes. But I wanted to talk to you about something." I take my feet off the coffee table and lean forward, my elbows on my knees.

"What's up, girl?" She's serious now.

"I just had a weird conversation with Sam, and I'm not sure what it means, or how to, I don't know, fix it?"

"Tell me everything."

I relay the conversation to her, including my interpretation of his tone. She listens quietly until I finish.

"So, what did I do wrong?"

"Ok, first, Chris, as in the guy Sophie dated senior year?"

"Yes?" It comes out like a question.

"Well, I mean, he was always a cool guy, but that seems weird, and we need to talk about that decision later. As for Sam. When are you going to realize that he's in love with you?" Now she's scolding me. I bet if she were with me in person, she would be shaking my shoulders, trying to force the words to sink in. "He has been in love with you for a long time."

Sitting up, I lean back into the cushions. "Liv, come on. He's not in love with me." I'm exasperated with this conversation already, and I can't stop it from seeping into my voice. I know that Sam said he had feelings but didn't act on them because of Ethan, and he seems to be... different, but I don't want to rehash this with Liv now. I'm not delusional to think our budding friendship changes anything—even after Thanksgiving.

"You know, for how fucking smart you are, sometimes you're incredibly dense." I flinch at her harsh tone.

"Olivia, don't be rude," Talia says in the background. I can almost picture Liv rolling her eyes in response. I want to be mad at her, but, somehow, I'm not.

"I know you haven't talked to him for several years until recently." She's softer now. "But you have to remember that I have. He asks me about you all the time. He's always wanted to know how you were doing. If you were happy. But the thing he asked the most?" She doesn't wait for me to provide an answer, "When I thought you would talk to him again." She sighs and I sit straighter. "Whenever I told him I wasn't sure, and to give you time, I knew it broke his heart."

I can practically see her pacing in the living room. Conflict makes her antsy.

"I know your reasons for keeping your distance, but it's been hard watching the two of you want each other, and for you to shut him out so thoroughly."

"I knew you talked. I didn't realize it was that often."

"Every couple of weeks, or so. Anyway, I don't have to talk to Sam now to understand what's going on in that gorgeous head of his. He's upset because he doesn't want you to go out with Chris. That man wants you all to himself. But you know he's a good guy, and instead of telling you what *he* wants, he's giving you the space to find someone *you* want. Even if that someone isn't him."

I let her words sink in for a minute. "Liv, I freaked out when I thought that maybe Chris thinks this is a date. I don't want to date Chris." I get more confident as I speak. "I'm not sure what exactly I want from Sam. I know it isn't just friendship. But he lives in Chicago."

"And that's why he's trying to give you space."

"I don't want the space." I breathe out and walk into the kitchen to grab a glass of water. "I want Sam. I want him here." The words come out before I can thoroughly think through them. But it's true. I do want Sam. I'm also scared of my heart breaking again when he inevitably decides he doesn't want me.

"I have some thoughts, but I'm gonna keep those to myself for now." I take a glass from the cupboard and fill it with the tap.

I ignore her jab. "Ugh. Why does everything have to be so complicated." It isn't a question.

"It doesn't have to be. Just think about that. Now explain to me why you're having dinner with Chris."

"Because I don't want to be by myself. I don't want to be lonely."

"Girl, that does not mean you jump at the first guy that walks by."

"Oh my God, that isn't what happened. I don't want to date him. I just thought it would be nice to have a friend." I pause to guzzle the water in my glass.

"Then you need to tell Chris that, and you definitely need to tell Sam."

We chat for several more minutes until it's time for me to shower and start getting ready for my not-date with Chris.

I can't get Sam out of my mind as I get ready, and I have to stop myself several times from picking up the phone to call him.

I'm about to lose the battle when I hear a knock on the door.

Opening the door, Chris is standing on the other side, wearing navy pants and a black polo shirt. He looks nice.

"Hey, Kat." His smile is warm. "You look nice." I'm wearing dark skinny jeans and a grey sweater. My hair is pinned on one side and draped over the opposite shoulder.

"Thanks, Chris. So do you." He blushes at my compliment, and I know I'm in trouble. That kind of reaction can only mean he thinks this is a date. *Shit*.

"Well, are you ready?" He holds out his arm for me to take.

"Yes. Let me just grab my purse." Walking into the living room, I pick up my purse where I left it on the couch and sling it over my shoulder, intentionally placing it between us to discourage any touching. I don't want to put him off, but holding his arm as we walk out to his car feels too intimate.

On our way to the pizza place Chris chose, we make small talk—discussing the weather, my decision to move back to Charleston, and my new job with Dad's firm.

The conversation feels a little forced, but not overly uncomfortable.

Still, I'm relieved when we pull up to the restaurant.

***

The restaurant has an old-fashioned feel to it, with high tables, and TVs hanging throughout with various sports games playing.

Beers on tap line the entire length of one wall. It's the kind of place where you order at the counter, and then they bring the food to you.

"This is my favorite place to get pizza," he says, giving me a shy smile. "They have these amazing calzones that you have to try sometime."

We order our food and find a table to sit at. As we wait for the pizza and our beers, the silence turns awkward. I'm not sure if it's because of the atmosphere or the company. But I can't stop myself from averting my gaze from Chris. I'm looking at anything but him.

"So," he says awkwardly, "do you still talk to Sophie?" Finally, my gaze meets him, and he looks as uncomfortable as I feel.

"Yeah. We aren't as close as we used to be, but I see her every once in a while, when we're both in town, and we talk maybe once a month or so. It's been hard to keep up our friendship since her parents moved away after she graduated."

"Hmmm," is his only reply.

"Do you?"

"Do I what?"

"Do you still talk to Sophie?" God, I just want our food to come so we can eat and not have to fill the silence with weird chatter.

"No."

And we're back to awkward silence.

Our beers show up first, and I'm all too grateful for the momentary reprieve.

Suddenly, Chris starts laughing; I just gawk at him. *What is even happening right now?*

"I'm sorry, Kat. I don't know why this is so uncomfortable. But I see the look on your face, and I know you're feeling the same way. I don't even know why I asked you out. I guess I was just feeling a bit nostalgic or something."

I sigh in relief at his confession.

"Let's just eat the pizza when it comes, and then I'll take you home, ok? No pressure. Just a couple of old friends catching up."

"I'm sorry, Chris."

"No, you have nothing to be sorry about."

We spend the rest of dinner chatting about our respective jobs, our hobbies, and what we've been up to since graduating from high school. The conversation doesn't come easily, exactly, but it's better than where it started.

When we finish eating, Chris drives me home. He doesn't walk me to the door but stays by the curb until I'm safely in the building.

I'm relieved it's over and hurry up to my condo where I change into some comfy clothes, slip on Ethan's Letterman's jacket, make popcorn, and turn on *Mulan*. I always watch Disney movies when I need some comfort.

I watch the first fifteen minutes and realize I can't stop thinking about Sam and how uncomfortable our call ended. I can't handle the weirdness any longer, so I send him a quick message.

I hope you're having a great time with your friends tonight.

His message is almost instantaneous.

Back from your date already?

Or are you messaging me while he's droning on about how much hair gel he uses?

Hair gel? I breathe out a laugh before sending my response.

It wasn't a date. But yes. I'm home now in my pjs, watching Mulan.

Mulan, huh?

Don't start with me, Harris.

Wouldn't dream of it, Kitty Kat.

Can I call you in about an hour? I should be home then.

Only if you promise not to tease me about my movie choices.

Deal.

***

By the time Sam calls me, I've almost finished Mulan. I pause the movie and put in my headphones before answering.

"How was your guys' night?"

"It was fine." He doesn't sound like it was fine. "Listen. About earlier? I'm sorry I ended the call so abruptly. It was rude of me," he sighs before continuing, "I have no right to be jealous. But I was, and I know I wasn't a good friend to you. I'm sorry."

He was jealous? I can't imagine that Liv was right—that Sam is in love with me. The feeling is too foreign. "You were jealous?"

"Of course, Kat. After Thanksgiving, and our call the other night about you coming to Chicago, I just thought—" He blows out another breath. "I don't know what I thought. But yes. I was jealous that Chris got to be on a date with you."

I take a deep breath, trying to wrap my head around what he's saying, and lean forward on the couch.

For some reason, my mind drifts to that phrase I've heard so many times: people show you who they are. I think it's meant more in the negative context, but it still seems relevant right now.

Sam wouldn't have kissed me if he didn't want me. He wouldn't have made me feel, well, Sam isn't that cruel.

I need to believe what he has been telling me for a few months now. I need to think that Sam wants more, too.

"Sammy, I wish it were you instead of him," I say too quietly, but his quick intake of air tells me he heard my words.

"Kat," he says my name like a prayer, "it isn't fair of me to hold you to anything. I know I can't expect you to wait for me. I won't ask you to be mine when we live so far from each other."

Be *his*?

"I want you to be happy, and I promise I'll try my best to support you when you go on another date." He sounds gutted as he speaks, and my heart cracks.

What I wouldn't give to be there with him. To take his face in my hands. To kiss him. To wrap my arms around him.

I'm not sure how to respond. My brain is stuck on the merry-go-round of Sam's words. *He was jealous. He won't ask me to be his. Sam wants me to be his? He wants me to be happy.* He *would make me happy.*

"Did you finish Mulan?" I know he's trying to change the subject as if he knows my mind is spinning. Or maybe his is, too.

"Almost," I answer automatically and without emotion.

"Kat, I'm so sorry. Please forgive me for how I acted." His pleading stops the spinning.

"Sam, it's ok. You don't need to keep apologizing." I roll my neck, trying to stop the tension that's creeping into my head. "I guess I'm trying to reconcile what you're saying with everything else." I stretch out on the couch and pull the blanket up to cover my chest. "I wish you were here," I say finally.

"Do you? Wish I was there?" He sounds shy. Uncertain.

"Yes. Everything has been easier when we're in person."

"'Cause you can't keep your hands off me?" he teases.

"Pretty sure it's the other way around, buddy." We both laugh. "Maybe because I can see your face and your expressions? Maybe because I can feel your words instead of just hearing them?"

"If I were there, what would you do?"

"Honestly? I would make you sit on the couch next to me, I would snuggle into your side and listen to your heartbeat." My words surprise me—because they're true.

He groans out, "God, that sounds amazing. Especially after the night I've had."

"Wait, you didn't have a good night?"

"No. I was an asshole to you. I spent the entire night regretting how I acted *and* wishing I could be there to punch Chris in the face just for being with you." He lets out a dark laugh. His possessive words cause my core to tighten and my heart to beat so fast it's a surprise it isn't beating out of my chest.

"Sam," it comes out too breathy. "I feel like I'm stuck in this impossible situation."

"Yeah. So, what are we going to do about it?" His defeated tone matches my feelings about the subject.

"You're older than me. Aren't you supposed to have all the answers?"

His laugh breaks some of the tension I'm feeling. "I have some solutions, but none that are easy, I'm afraid."

"Care to share with the class?"

He sighs audibly, "Well, either I have to let you go, and you move on with someone else, which I can't do, or I move back to Charleston." He says it in such a matter-of-fact way.

His first option feels like a knife to my gut. If only he knew how much I've tried to move on with someone else, only to be pulled back into his orbit, even if we weren't speaking.

"Is moving back to Charleston an actual option for you?"

I hear the smile in his voice when he responds, "I think so. But it's complicated."

"It always is," I say in defeat. The thought gives me hope. If he were in Charleston, things between us would be a lot less complicated.

Chapter 29

The next morning, I'm nervous as I walk into Wilde, Oaks, and Harris, PLLC. I'm so anxious that I couldn't eat breakfast.

I love Dad, and Steve Wilde and Dan are great. It's just that I never thought I'd be here. I never thought I'd wake up one morning to find myself working for Dad at his firm. I've always hated the whole nepotism thing. But here I am.

I know I deserve to be here in the way I deserved to be at my last firm. I'm a hard worker, and I've always put in the time and work to get to where I am.

As I step off the elevator and look at the glass doors leading to my new place of employment, I cringe inwardly as I stare at "Wilde, Oaks, and Harris, PLLC" splashed across the glass doors in black, bold lettering. I suppress a groan and try to muster a genuine smile.

My biggest concern this morning is navigating the people who worked with and loved Ethan. He was so charismatic and got along with everyone he met. He was respectful of everyone and stood up for people when others wouldn't.

Even though I don't want to admit it, I'm worried my new colleagues are going to get to know me and be disappointed that I'm not more like he was.

I'm just a poor man's Ethan.

I'm not outgoing like he was, I would rather sit at home reading a book than go out any day. I just want to go in, do my job, and then go home. I know things are going to have to be different here.

Ethan was a spitting image of our dad, down to their extroverted personalities.

I take a deep breath, pull open the doors, and walk through.

A woman, who must be in her early 20s, immediately greets me. She has short blonde hair and bright blue eyes. She smiles at me and stands from her chair behind the large mahogany reception desk.

"You must be Kat! Or do you prefer to go by Katherine? You look just like your dad and Ethan." She gets a horrified look on her face as my brother's name leaves her lips. "I'm so sorry." She looks down and starts fiddling with her fingers. "I'm so sorry about your brother."

Trying to lessen the guilt pouring off her, I make sure to use a calm and friendly voice. "Thanks, and please call me Kat. What's your name?

She looks back up at me and smiles. "Kat. My name is Clarisse. Welcome to your first day. I'll show you to your office so you can get settled in. Each Monday morning, the firm gathers in one of the conference rooms. I'll point it out on our way to your office, and we have a meeting to review any significant cases for the week. That's at 9:00 a.m. After that, I'll give you a full tour of the office."

I've never actually been to this building before, so I don't know what to expect.

Dad's firm was in a completely different building from the last time I showed up at his work. That was back when I was in high school. Since then, I've never really had a reason to go to Dad's office.

"Thanks, Clarisse. That sounds great." She steps around her desk, and I fully take her in. She's petite, probably a little over five feet, if I had to guess. She's wearing this A-line black dress that is incredibly similar to my own. I grin as I take in her hot pink ballet flats.

This is something that Liv would do—wear a conservative outfit only to pair it with something flashy.

"Right this way." She gestures to a hallway hidden by a large wall behind her desk. She makes small talk as we walk down a long hallway, passing several offices along the way.

The first thing I notice is the glass walls connecting the offices to the hallway. *No privacy here. My impromptu dance sessions are out.* I'm curious about the soundproofing. *Will I hear the commotion outside my office? Or whoever is in the neighboring office?* I really hope not.

She points out the conference room for the meeting in just under an hour and continues leading me to my office.

"And this one is you," she says brightly, gesturing toward the large space.

"Thanks so much, Clarisse. See you in the conference room?"

"Yep, see you then!" She leaves me standing there and walks back towards the front of the building. I take in my name already on the glass by the door and smile a little. At my last place, it took several weeks to get the names changed out on the office doors. Even though I'm dreading this, I know Dad is excited for me to work with him.

Walking into the open door, I set my bag on one of the black leather chairs sitting in front of one side of the large L-shaped white desk and slowly take the space in.

It's minimal with no decor. On the opposite side of the interior glass wall are large, floor-to-ceiling windows that overlook downtown Charleston. I *love* the view.

I turn back to my desk and am startled to see Dad leaning into the open doorway, watching me. He has a massive grin on his face that I'm compelled to return.

"Hey, Kat. What do you think?" He's wearing his standard black suit, which he paired with a blue button-down shirt, and a black tie.

"Hey, Dad. It's nice. Larger than my last office." I look around again and take in the white bookcase that matches my new desk. Someone *really* likes white. "Do you have any issues with me bringing in some pictures and maybe a plant or two?"

He chuckles before responding, "It's a little too bland for my taste, too. Of course. You can bring in whatever you want." I make a mental note to bring in my Seattle pictures as soon as possible to bring color to the washed-out space.

"Thanks, Dad. Um…" I gesture at the door, and he steps inside my new office, closing the door behind him. He sits on the black loveseat by one of the walls opposite the desk.

Feeling awkward about sitting in the desk chair, I opt for one of the chairs in front of my desk. I awkwardly shuffle it so it faces the loveseat and sit down.

"What's on your mind, baby girl?" He shifts uncomfortably.

"Well, you know I love you, and I'm proud to be your daughter." I take a breath. He just stares at me with a blank expression. "I feel weird about you being my boss and calling you Dad." I examine his face and watch as it transforms into a huge grin that crinkles the skin around his eyes.

Suddenly, he starts laughing. I just stare at him, trying to understand what is so funny about what I just said.

"I'm sorry, baby girl," he says in between bouts of laughter. "It's just that I thought there was something seriously wrong when you gave me that serious face of yours."

"I *am* serious, Dad." I pout.

"I know. I'm sorry." He stops laughing and looks at me with a serious expression. "Ethan called me Dad all the time. And everyone here knows you're my daughter. A lot of the folks working here have kids. It isn't something you need to feel uncomfortable with." He looks at me with a bit of heartbreak in his eyes. "But I'll understand if you want to call me by my first name instead. Please don't call me Mr. Oaks."

"I just don't want everyone to hate me because they know I got this job because of you. I want them to value my work and my accomplishments."

He sits straighter. "Kat, you think I would have gotten the other partners on my side to hire you if they didn't know you were more than capable? They know. Shit, I brag about your work accomplishments all the time. They've been asking me since you passed the bar when you would be coming here. Everyone is excited to have you." His pride is written on his face. Hearing Dad's words makes me feel a lot better. "I know it's still early but just wait. Give them a chance to love you, just as I know they will. I think you'll find how well you fit in."

"Ok, Dad. Thanks for the pep talk. So, where's my computer?" I gesture at the space on my desk where only a monitor sits.

He laughs again. "We do a little orientation here. So, we'll have an IT guy come and set up your laptop with you. He'll show you how to navigate some of the systems and make sure everything is working. If you want to set up your phone, he can help you out with that, too. Or if you want a tablet to travel with, just let him know. His name is Conner. He should stop by your office after your tour with Clarisse."

"Oh. That sounds nice." My last firm didn't have an IT person, so this will be a new adventure for me.

Chapter 30

My morning goes by quickly, and Dad was right, everyone's been nice. It isn't until Conner leaves that I realize it's around noon, and my stomach growls from hunger. The thought of going out for food makes me miss Liv.

Who am I going to get lunch with now that we live in different cities?

Resigned to having lunch without my bestie, I push my chair away from my desk and make my way down to a sandwich shop I saw on the first floor.

I'm walking to the cashier to place my order when I hear a familiar voice. "Hey, Kat, fancy seeing you here."

I give him a polite smile. "Hey, Conner. I saw this place as I was coming in this morning. Have any recommendations?"

Conner is tall, a little shorter than Sam, and a little older. He's handsome with dark brown hair and dark green eyes that seem to sparkle with mischief. I laugh internally that here I am comparing another man to Sam again. I fiddle with the strap of my bag as I wait for his response.

"Yes, I highly recommend the turkey avocado club. I swear it's the best one in Charleston." He smiles back at me.

"That sounds great. Thanks!"

"Do you want to sit with me? For lunch?" He looks at my feet briefly and then back up to my face. Not in a raking up my body way, more in a way that suggests he's nervous.

"That would be nice. I hate eating by myself."

"Me too. I figured you would be having lunch with your dad today. First day at the firm and all."

"He had to take a client out to lunch." I shrug.

"Well, lucky me!" Conner smiles at me. His smile is nice. Charming. It does nothing for me.

I order, and once my sandwich is ready, I head to the table Conner chose. I sit down in the seat opposite him, open the paper wrapped around my sandwich, and take my first bite. "Oh my God. This is delicious!"

"Right? Best one in Charleston." He smiles at me. His smile is disarming and makes me feel instantly comfortable.

"So, how long have you worked at the firm?" I take another bite and hold back a moan; it's so good.

Conner rubs the back of his neck. "I guess about eight years now. I graduated from college and was hired by the firm to set up the network, and they liked me enough that they kept me on part time." I feel a little awkward knowing he worked with Ethan, too.

I frown into my sandwich at the thought, trying to school my features so he doesn't notice.

"I'm sorry about Ethan. He was a great guy and even better to work with." I guess I didn't school my features soon enough.

"It's kind of weird for me to work with so many people who knew him and worked with him." I take another bite to avoid saying more and look out the window. I haven't asked anyone, but I assume the office I'm in was Ethan's old office. I want to ask Conner, but it feels weird.

"I can only imagine how hard all of this is for you. You know your dad talks about you all the time. He's been wanting you to work here since you graduated." I'm grateful for the change in topic.

"I always got that sense from him, but he never asked me to work for him. I think he knew I wanted to go off on my own."

"What made you change your mind?" His question sounds genuine and not like the accusation my mind wants to interpret it to be.

"I was homesick," I sigh. "I haven't lived in Charleston since I moved away to go to undergrad. I missed it. Then with Ethan… I just didn't want to miss out on more experiences with my family." I'm not even sure why I'm telling him all of this. I hardly know him. "I didn't plan to work here. I was going to move back into my parents' house while I found a different firm to work for. My dad suggested I work for him, and it just kind of felt right, I guess."

"Well, I'm glad you did." I look up at him to see his bright smile.

We finish our food and make our way back upstairs to continue our workday.

When I get back to my office, Pam, my new paralegal, is waiting for me. "Hey, Kat, do you have a few moments? I'd like to chat with you."

I gesture for her to walk into my office as I say, "Yes, of course!"

Pam looks around briefly and sits down in one of the black leather chairs in front of my desk. I make my way around it and sit in my office chair.

"What's up?" Pam is about my height, with short brown hair and eyes so dark, they're almost black. She's older than me, but no more than five years.

She sits up straight in the chair, and the action makes me wonder if it's a nervous reaction or if she just has good posture. I fight the desire to correct mine to match hers.

"I wanted to chat with you about how I can best support you. I don't know if you knew this, but I worked with Ethan a lot. I was his paralegal." She looks down at her hands, and the action makes me think she's trying to compose herself.

I knew Pam worked with Ethan and had been mentally preparing for a conversation like this.

"Ethan talked about how great you were all the time. He enjoyed working with you." It's the only thing I can think to say. She looks back up at me, her features softening at my words.

"I enjoyed working with him, too. I'm sorry about your loss."

"Thanks." I shrug.

"Well, I wanted you to know—I've worked here the longest, out of all the paralegals. Whenever a new attorney joins, the partners offer me the opportunity to assist them. When I heard you were coming in, it was an easy choice." Her hands are linked together in her lap. She sits so still. "I want you to know that I asked to work with you because Ethan talked about you all the time. I feel like I know you already."

I'm not sure what to say. I never expected Pam to ask to work with me. And all because of Ethan. I swear he's helping me out when he isn't even here anymore.

I can't resist looking away from her as I feel the tears prickle at the corners of my eyes.

I stare through the windows overlooking the city beyond and take a moment to compose myself. The last thing I want to do is cry at work.

Finally, I look back at her and appreciate that she doesn't seem affected by my moment of despair; she just lets me work through the emotions. "Thank you," I finally say to her. "This means a lot to me."

We continue chatting about working together. We cover Pam's preferences and mine, and I'm glad to know that most of our work styles seem to overlap. I'm grateful to have her.

***

B y the time five rolls around, I can't believe how quickly the day went and how little I feel like I accomplished. With nothing keeping me in the office past five, I clean up my workspace and head home.

While I'm walking to my car, I receive a text from Sam.

> I can't wait to hear how your first day went.
> Call me when you get home?

> It was nice. I think I made a friend. I'll call you in about 30?

> That's great! Drive safe.

I call Liv on my way home and tell her about my new lunch friend.

"Fuck off right to hell for replacing me so quickly after leaving me!"

"Damn right I replaced you quickly! You know I can't have lunch *by myself.*"

"Whatever. I hate you. I'm just sad you have a new lunch friend, and here I am forced to eat lunch by myself."

"You could make a frieeeend." My voice comes out sing-songy.

"Pfff, making friends is overrated. Only you and Talia appreciate my spicy ass."

"You know I love you, but I don't want anything to do with your ass, babe."

"I know. You only want Sam's ass." *Yes. Yes, I do.* But I'm not giving her fuel for her sass right now. "On a serious note. Do you think you'll be happy there?"

"Yeah. I think so. I mean, it's a bit weird being there with my dad, but everyone is friendly."

"I'm so glad to hear that, Kat. As much as it pains me to say this, I'm glad you're back home. I know you were kind of miserable here."

I thought I hid my feelings well, but as always, I can't hide anything from her. She sees it all. "Thanks, Liv. My only regret is not making you move with me."

I finish telling her about my workday and my conversation with Pam. Liv tells me about the family dinner she had the night before with Talia's family. Things seem to be slowly getting better, but there's still tension.

I wait to call Sam until after I've changed out of my work clothes and made myself dinner—a cheese quesadilla.

"Hey, Kitty Kat. Did you get dinner yet?" Sam says by way of greeting when he answers my call.

"As a matter of fact, Mother Hen, I ate a quesadilla before I called."

"Good. Now tell me everything about your day."

So, I do. When I get to the part about Pam, he interrupts me, "Pam? Ethan's paralegal?"

"How do you—forget about it. Yes, Ethan's paralegal. Anyway, she told me that she asked to be my paralegal because of Ethan. He talked about me." The last part comes out wobbly.

"Of course, he talked about you. He loved you." His voice is so gentle, and I feel the words seep into my soul.

"Thanks, Sammy. I think I needed to hear that."

"I'll remind you any time you need it."

At some point in our conversation, I left the dining table, changed into my pjs, and sprawled out on my bed.

I look at the clock and see it's nearly 10:00 p.m. when Sam groans, "I don't want to hang up yet."

His confession has a smile cracking across my face, and my heart beams. "I don't either."

"Kat, our calls every night are the highlight of my day. When I'm having a bad day at work, I just know I need to push through a little longer because soon I'll be able to hear your voice, and everything will be better."

"Really? I feel the same way." I pause for a moment, a thought bubbling to the surface. "Sammy?" I move, so I'm sitting cross-legged on my bed.

"Yeah, Kitty Kat?" He is starting to sound tired, and I waver on broaching this next subject.

Deciding I need this, I push forward. "I was thinking. How would you feel about me visiting you in a couple of weeks? Just over the weekend? I could leave work early on Friday, fly over, and then fly back home Sunday evening?" I chew on my lip as I wait for his response.

"When should I pick you up from the airport?"

I laugh. "Well, I haven't booked anything yet, but—"

"I can help you book the best option. Let's do it before we hang up."

"Yeah, ok. Um, let me find my laptop." I get out of bed and go into the dining room, where my laptop sits on the kitchen counter.

Sam and I discuss the best flight options, and I book a flight from Charleston to Chicago.

"Fuck I'm excited to see you! I don't know what I'm going to do with myself for the next two weeks." I wonder if he's raising his fists in excitement. The thought makes me smile.

"I've missed you. It'll be nice to spend some time together."

"I've missed you, too. I know you have an early morning, so I won't keep you any longer. Goodnight, Kitty Kat. Sweet dreams."

"Goodnight, Sammy."

Chapter 31

*S*ix Years Old

Tonight is my parents' annual holiday party at the house. They invite some close friends and a few of the firm's bigger clients.

My parents won't let us join the party, so Ethan and I are hiding upstairs, listening in and trying to peek at the festivities. Sammy is home sick with his mom.

Holiday music is playing on the speakers throughout the house, and I can't stop myself from singing along when Rockin' Around the Christmas Tree *comes on.*

"Shhh. They're going to hear us if you keep singing." This isn't the first time Ethan has scolded me tonight for singing. But I can't help it.

We sneak a little further down the stairs to try to catch a glimpse of the party. Several people pass by the stairs without noticing us, so we sit quietly and watch.

I love seeing everyone in their holiday outfits, especially the ladies.

While the men mostly wear sports jackets, polo shirts, and slacks, the ladies wear pretty cocktail dresses. I love the ones with sequins on them because they shimmer.

We stay like this until our dad catches us. His voice is firm but gentle: "Back to bed, you two." He leans close to us and whispers, "You can stay up and play video games in the loft if you don't tell Mom." He winks and watches as we go back upstairs.

Ethan and I sit on the couch in the loft, playing video games and singing along to the holiday music drifting up from the party.

***

P resent Day

"I'm headed to the doors now. What are you driving?"

"It's a blue Toyota 4Runner. I'm right out front; you can't miss me. Fuck, hurry up, I can't wait any longer."

A smile creeps across my face at Sam's impatience. "Patience, my dear Watson. I'm nearly there." I'm dragging my carry-on behind me and trying to navigate the slow walkers in front of me. I want to shout at them to move, but I maintain my cool. "Oh, I see your SUV! Oh my God, Sam. You drive the same SUV as your dad!"

"Yeah, well, it's a good vehicle. Wait, why can't I see you yet?"

As soon as the words leave his mouth, I finally spot him walking around the front of the SUV. I nearly drop my bag as I rush the rest of the way to him and wrap my arms around his neck.

He picks me up and twirls me around while placing a rough kiss on my cheek.

"I've missed you. Now get in the car so I can give you a proper welcome without all these people watching." His words cause butterflies to form in my stomach.

Once my bag is in the car, Sam helps me into my seat, and takes off his jacket, he pulls away from the curb.

I keep fiddling with my hands when Sam takes one of them in his, brings it to his lips, and places a small kiss on my palm. "Why are you nervous?"

I avoid his gaze when I speak and look out the window. "Just, I don't know, you and me, spending the entire weekend together." *Alone.* I don't say the last part.

"Nothing to be nervous about, Kitty Kat," he says, kissing my palm again before lacing his fingers through mine and settling our interlocked hands on the center console. "I have some cool things planned, but we can also skip all those things and spend the entire weekend watching Disney movies, if you want. I'm just glad you're here."

He gives me a shy smile.

I shift my focus to him and watch as he navigates the traffic. My gaze catches on the tattoos on his right arm, peeking out from under his light grey T-shirt.

"I'm dying to know what your tattoo is," I blurt out. "The one on your right arm."

He smiles over at me and lifts his sleeve to give me a full view of his tattoo. The bottom is a chain of daisies, and above the daisies—"Is that the Space Needle? And the Seattle skyline?"

He chuckles softly, "Yeah. It's one of my favorite places. I got this a little after I broke things off with Claire. I guess I wanted a memory of happier times." He shrugs.

Happier times. Seattle, with him, were some of my favorite times, too. "And the daisies?" I trace the flowers lightly with my fingertip—his bicep flexes as his body shivers. I quickly pull my hand away from his arm. "Sorry, my hands are cold from the airplane."

He clears his throat. "The daisies were my mom's favorite flower. I wanted something to remember her."

I trace one of the flowers with my index finger again, holding myself back from dropping a kiss on each one. "I'm sorry, Sam. I can't imagine how it's been for you without her. I don't remember much about her, just that I loved to hear her laugh."

"It was a long time ago. But I miss her." He shrugs and pulls down his shirt sleeve. "Are you hungry? I was thinking about taking you to one of my favorite restaurants."

"That sounds great." He laces his fingers through mine again as he drives. "You gonna tell me what version of Britney Spears you dressed as for Halloween, yet? I *did* fly all this way."

He smirks at me before responding, "Not a chance."

Chapter 32

Twelve Years Old

Ethan and Sam are so engrossed in playing Mario Kart *that I know I have enough time to sneak into Ethan's room and read his new comic books.*

Ethan's always been hesitant to let me touch his comic book collection because he "doesn't want me to mess them up."

When he isn't looking, I read them anyway.

I know he got a new X-Men *one, and I can't wait to see if it has Rogue in it. She's my favorite* X-Men. *Something about her long auburn hair with the white in front. And her ability to absorb the powers, memories, and energy of those she touches? So cool!*

The third floor is split, with my room on the left of the stairs and Ethan's on the right. Between the bedrooms is a full bathroom and an open space loft where the TV and a couch are, so we could play video games or watch movies with our friends.

I walk past the loft where Ethan and Sam are and try to act like I'm going into the bathroom. Once I'm past them, I continue and sneak into his room. Thankfully, his door is open.

I hurry to Ethan's bookshelf, where he keeps his comic books stacked in neat piles, and grab the X-Men *one on top. Flipping through it, I see Rogue isn't in this one, so I put it back and hurry back out of his room before I'm caught.*

***

P resent Day

"When did you start swearing so much?" We're sitting at the restaurant Sam chose, a casual taco joint. We've finished eating and are now sitting in the cool air outside, chatting and enjoying our margaritas.

"Um, always?" I exaggerate the words. "I always swear, Sam, but maybe it's gotten worse since working with my dad. Everyone there swears like it's going out of style. I don't think I've heard my dad say fuck so many times in my entire life. Did I tell you about the first time I heard him say fuck at the office?"

"No, but tell me more." Sam leans forward and places his elbows on the table in front of him. I lean in, too.

"I was walking by his office, and his door was open. He was talking to another associate; I think something went wrong on a big case. He shouted the word, and I immediately turned to look at him." I'm laughing as I tell the story. "He wasn't yelling at the associate; he just yelled the word. Anyway, he saw me and went stark white. He looked like he had seen a ghost, then all of a sudden, his cheeks were blazing! He later begged me not to tell my mom."

"He did not." Sam's eyes crinkle with his laughter.

"He did." We're both laughing now. I love how easy our conversations are. Even the silence feels comfortable.

His voice turns serious, "Listen, I was thinking. When I get back to Charleston, can I take you on a proper date?"

"Is this not a *proper* date?"

"No, Kitty Kat. Picking you up from the airport and getting dinner after is *not* a proper date," he scoffs and leans back into his chair.

"So, what is a proper date then?" I pick up my margarita and take a small sip.

"One where we both dress nicely. I'll pick you up for dinner and something fun. Or maybe I pick you up on my bike, and we go for a long ride and have a quiet picnic somewhere. Then at the end, I walk you back to your door and kiss you goodnight."

My stomach is doing somersaults at the thought of being on the back of his motorcycle, my legs hugging his muscular thighs, my arms around his waist. The vision both terrifies and excites me. My voice is husky and thick when I finally respond, "I'd like that a lot."

"Good, cause I don't know what I would have done if you said no."

"Probably groveled." I smile at him.

He half laughs and half groans. "Is that what you want, Kitty Kat? For me to grovel on my knees at your feet?" His voice is almost a purr, and my lady bits are screaming at me for attention. *His* attention.

I'm feeling bold. "Sammy, there are many things that cross my mind that would be much better than groveling if you're on your knees at my feet." I'm trying to use my most seductive voice.

"I can think of several things I'd like to do when I'm on my knees in front of you, too."

When. Oh fuck.

Sam's gaze shifts to something behind me. I'm about to turn and look at what's caught his attention when I hear a female voice purr, "Sam, is that you?"

She stops at our table, her back to me, so I can't see her face. She's clearly dismissing my presence with this simple act. It infuriates me.

She's slim, taller than me, with black hair cut in a short bob.

"Hey, Tiffany, what—"

"Sam, you look amazing. It's so good to see you." Her voice is too breathy, like she's trying too hard to be seductive.

It grates on my nerves.

The way she keeps saying his name puts me on edge—*I'm so glad you know his name.*

I look from this woman to Sam, who gives me an apologetic smile.

"Tiffany, this is—" Sam stops talking as *Tiffany* places her hand on his shoulder and runs her fingers along his arm.

I see red.

My body goes rigid as I watch this woman touch Sam. My Sam.

Who is this woman? And why does she think it's ok to touch MY DATE?

I want to rip her hand off his body.

I want to stab my fork in her eye.

I clench my hands on top of the table, so I don't do something stupid.

Before I can say anything, Sam grabs hold of *Tiffany's* wrist and removes her hand from his arm. His jaw is tight, and his nostrils flare slightly.

"Don't do that, Tiffany."

"But Sam," *Tiffany* whines, "I've missed you."

Did she just whine? God, she's annoying.

"And you," his voice is stern as his eyes narrow, "are interrupting my date." I don't think I've ever heard this tone from Sam. It would terrify me if it were directed at me. But right now? My core heats.

Tiffany glances over her shoulder and eyes me.

I hate to admit that she's gorgeous, with dazzling blue eyes and high cheekbones. I feel slightly self-conscious about myself with this woman, who could definitely be a model. Before she shifts her attention back to Sam, Tiffany's lips curl in disgust at whatever she finds in me.

"I miss you, Sam. I want another chance." She's back to her purr. At least she isn't touching him again.

Another chance? They dated?

Sam ignores her and watches me. He reaches across the table and takes my hand in his.

Uncomfortable with this situation, I want to pull away from him when he gently pulls my hand to his lips and kisses my knuckles.

Sam's eyes are fixed on mine as he says, "You need to leave, Tiffany. I'm not interested in anything with you." He kisses my knuckles again and smiles that full-watt smile at me, and the fucking dimple makes my breath catch.

I relax a little as he continues to watch me until she finally gets the hint, huffs out her distaste at being rejected, and stalks off.

"You know I can't stop thinking about that night over Thanksgiving." Sam plants another kiss on my knuckles. "You writhing below me." His eyes are black, and his smile turns wicked.

He's trying to take my mind off *Tiffany*.

"Sam, who was that?"

"She doesn't matter."

I glare at him.

"Someone I briefly dated a long time ago," he sighs. Sam leans back in his chair, but keeps his hand wrapped around mine.

"You're not interes—"

"Absolutely, not. Why would I want anything to do with her when I can't stop thinking about your wet pussy soaking my fingers." He leans forward again. "The feel of your hard nipples in my mouth. The way you moaned my name as you shattered below me. I can't stop thinking about how you will taste as you cum on my face." His smooth voice has me desperate for his touch. "Have you thought about that night, Kitty Kat?"

"I..." My brain is short-circuiting at this incredibly sexy man and the way his words turn me on. I briefly look around the restaurant to ensure no one can overhear this conversation.

"Tell me." He demands.

"Yes," it comes out breathy.

He shifts in his seat, sitting up and looking around the restaurant, like he's just realized where we are. His voice is husky when he speaks again, "Do you want to order dessert, or should we go back to my place, where you can be my dessert?"

Fuck. "Check, please!"

Chapter 33

We barely make it into Sam's apartment before his mouth is on mine. He didn't hesitate when I demanded he take me home and give me the proper welcome he promised me at the airport.

His kiss is hungry as he devours my mouth, maneuvering us into his apartment.

I'm guessing it's taking too long because he picks me up, my legs instinctively wrapping around his waist as he carries me to his bedroom, his lips never leaving mine. He breaks the kiss as he sets me down on the bed.

"Are you sure about this? As much as I want you, I would be just as happy holding you while you sleep." His eyes are dark with need.

I know if I told him I didn't want to go forward with this, he would stop, without hesitation. He'd do anything I asked him to.

The thought makes me want him more. *Fuck, he's perfect.* "Sam, I want you." It comes out breathy. I clear my throat, trying to remove the lust from my voice. "But will you give me just a moment to use the restroom?"

He runs his hand through his hair and nods at me, stepping away so I can stand. "First door on the right." He waves behind him absentmindedly.

I make my way down the hallway and stop to look over my shoulder at him sitting on his bed. I close the bathroom door and lean against it.

I just need to calm my nerves for a moment.

I've wanted all of Sam for so long, and our teasing and flirting over the last few months have me coming undone.

I'm not sure how long I stand in the bathroom; every time I feel myself calm down, I think of Sam sitting on his bed waiting for me, and I feel coiled like a spring all over again.

I splash cold water on my face as a last-ditch effort before giving up entirely. Patting me face dry with a hand towel hanging on a hook by the door, I step out of the bathroom.

Sam hasn't moved an inch. His gaze watches my every move as I walk back into his bedroom.

Slowly, I make my way towards him and stop when I'm standing in front of him. I nudge his legs open so I can stand between them.

I run my hands through his hair. Closing his eyes, he groans at my touch. Leaning down, I press my lips to his in a soft and chaste kiss. When I start to pull away, his hands grip my hips.

He stands up, forcing me to take a step back. His eyes are soft and reverent as he takes me in.

In a flash, his gaze turns feral, and he pulls my body to his. I feel his hard length against my stomach, and I can't wait any longer.

I pull his mouth down to mine and try to devour him through that kiss. My hands rub along his arms, his back, to his chest.

"Sam," I moan into his mouth. He pulls back and looks at me with a grin that says he knows exactly what he does to me. "I want you."

In one motion, he spins us around so he's facing the bed. He gently pushes me until my legs hit the bed, but he doesn't push me down.

Sam grabs the hem of my shirt before pausing. His eyes meet mine, questioning, asking for permission.

I nod, and he lifts my shirt over my head. Sam moves towards my jeans, unbuttoning them and pulling them down with ease, leaving me in nothing but my pink lacy bra and matching panties.

Sam's gaze drop slowly. His eyes are nearly black when they meet mine again.

Reaching behind my back, I unclasp my bra and let it fall to the floor. When I get to my panties, his hands stop mine. He smiles seductively at me, showing that stupid dimple that melts my heart.

"Let me." He starts to lower my panties, gently guides me to sit down, and kneels before me. Placing his hands on my outer thighs, he trails kisses from my right knee to my thigh and higher.

"Sam, please." I'm breathless as he tortures me with his mouth.

He shushes me, "Patience, Kitty Kat. I want to memorize every curve of your body." I want to give him that time, but my body is on fire as his lips trail closer to my core.

Before he gives me what I want, he starts the process over with my left knee, trailing slow kisses up my thigh.

I'm writhing below him as he holds me in place. Once again, he stops right before my apex. I'm about to protest again when he looks up at me. I'm lost in him; my vision hazy with lust.

"You are so beautiful."

Before I can respond, he pushes my thighs apart, giving him more space. He circles my clit with his thumb; the sensation causes my back to arch. He slowly pushes a finger inside me and pumps in and out a few times, his eyes never leaving my face.

I drop my head back and look towards the ceiling when I feel Sam's warm mouth on my clit, sucking and swiping his tongue along my sensitive nerves.

"Oh, God. Sam, that—fuck, that feels—" I grab his hair and pull at him gently. I'm already so close, and he's barely touched me.

Adding another finger, he continues moving in and out of me, his mouth never leaving my clit.

The tension continues to build inside of me with each slide of his fingers, each suck and pass of his tongue. I want more. I want... him.

He curls his fingers inside of me, hitting that perfect spot, "Come for me, Kitty Kat." Sam's rough voice is my undoing. I clench around his fingers, screaming his name. He continues moving his fingers inside me, as his mouth and tongue continue working my clit, prolonging my release.

Slowly, he pulls his fingers out of me, raising them to his mouth, and sucks them clean. "You are delicious," Sam punctuates each word. "I would die a happy man if I could taste you every day."

Fuck, that's hot.

"Scoot back and lie down," he says gently. His eyes are still blazing.

It's only now that I realize he's still fully clothed. I shake my head at him. "Let me see you first." He starts unbuttoning his jeans, and I place a hand over his chest where I think his scars might be. "All of you, Sam. I want to see all of you."

His expression immediately turns agonized and pained. But slowly, he takes off his shirt, revealing the scar beneath. I make sure to keep my expression schooled before I look at it. I don't want to give Sam any reason to hide from me.

Sam's scar is jagged and runs from above his left collarbone, past his pec, before curving down his ribs. I figured it was bad when he said he was in physical therapy for a while, but I never imagined this.

I gently touch where his scar meets his collarbone and look at the jagged edges. He goes rigid at the contact, and tears prick my eyes.

This is Sam, *my Sam*, and he's terrified.

"Did I tell you the doctor said I could have lost my arm?" He clears his throat as I shift my gaze to his. I'm stunned by his words. His eyes search mine, finding whatever answer he needs before continuing, his voice little more than a whisper. "Even then, I'm lucky to have full function after the accident. I could have died if I had gotten to the hospital even a few minutes later." I return my gaze to his scar.

God, I almost lost him, too.

Getting to my knees, I trail kisses along the length of his scar, starting at his collarbone and stopping only when I reach the opposite end by his ribs.

I lean back and catch him staring at me, wonder, and something else. He leans down and kisses me. His lips are soft and gentle like a caress.

He removes his jeans and boxer briefs. My eyes trail over his body and stop when I meet his rigid length.

Fuck, I'm going to enjoy this.

I can't stop myself from touching him. Wrapping my hand around his cock I begin to stroke. He sucks air in between his teeth, but too quickly, he grabs my hand and stops my motion.

"I want to be inside you, Kat. Now be a good girl. Scoot back and lie down." His voice is husky.

I can't resist him when he sounds like that. I do as he asks and lie down in the middle of the bed. I watch as he rolls on a condom I didn't realize he had opened.

He crawls up the bed and hovers over me, bracing himself with his arms. He leans down and takes my mouth in his. Kissing me like it could be his last.

I watch as he takes his cock in his hand and lines it up with my entrance. "Are you sure?"

My answer comes immediately as I flash him a seductive grin. "Absolutely."

He smiles, and slowly, he enters me. He closes his eyes and doesn't move as I watch him breathe in and out.

"Sam?" Concern laces my tone, and he looks at me, his eyes blinking.

"You feel… amazing. I just, fuck, I need a moment."

I reach up and run my palm along his cheek, and he starts slowly thrusting inside of me; his pelvic bone hits my clit as he moves.

"You are so wet. Is all of this for me?" He kisses my collarbone.

I nod eagerly, "Yes," I pant. "All for you." I run my hands slowly up and down his back, and have to remind myself not to dig my nails in.

I expect Sam to set a hard and fast pace, but I'm not disappointed when he takes his time, slowly moving in and out as I meet him thrust for thrust.

A soft moan slips from him. "God, you feel—"

"I feel what? Tell me how I feel," I whisper the words as I kiss his collarbone.

"You're pussy is clenching me so tight. I don't know how I've gone this long without being inside of you." I feel the heat rising to my cheeks as I take in his words. "You take me so well, Kitty Kat."

My core continues to tighten, and I dig my nails into his back.

He chuckles lightly. "Eager little thing, aren't you?"

"Stop teasing me, Sam." My tone is scolding.

"Never," he whispers in my ear as his hand explores the curves of my hip, my stomach, until he reaches my breast. His other hand still holds his body up to give me enough room to breathe under him.

He trails kisses along my jawline, nipping at my earlobe before kissing my neck. He takes one nipple into his mouth and begins sucking and gently biting.

My fingers claw into his back again as I feel my body start to tense under the impending orgasm. He speeds his pace, which I match.

"Come for me," he whispers into my ear as my body tenses. He continues thrusting in and out of me as my climax crests, my pussy clenching around his cock. He kisses me, swallowing my moans.

Once my body starts to come down, Sam lifts my legs, wrapping them around his waist; he grips my hips with both hands as he deepens his thrusts. He continues moving in and out a few more times until he finds his own release, causing me to crest again. He groans as his cock twitches inside of me.

Slowly, he pulls out of me, and I groan at the loss of him. He lies next to me and pulls me into him, wrapping his arms around me. We lay like this, wrapped in each other's arms, catching our breath.

Too soon, Sam gets up and walks into the bathroom, returning with a warm, wet cloth. His gentleness as he cleans me up, placing soft kisses on the inside of my thighs, causes my core to heat again.

Chapter 34

"Wait, what do you mean you're moving to Charleston?" Sam is making blueberry waffles as I sit at the bar top in his kitchen, sipping on the perfect cup of coffee.

I stare at the muscles on his bare back as he cooks. They ripple as he moves, highlighting the scratches I left on him last night. I wince a little at the red marks; my mind drifts to the way his body molded to mine in such a perfect way. Heat pools in my core at the thought.

"I mean, I'm done. I can't do this anymore." His words pull me from my overheated trance. "These guys are making my life increasingly miserable by the day. So, I'm doing it. I'm moving back to Charleston and starting my own architecture firm."

Standing up, I walk over to Sam and start planting soft kisses on the scratches along his back. A shiver runs down his spine at my touch. "Sam, that's great! I'm so proud of you! So, when is the big move?"

He turns around and pulls me into him, his strong arms wrapping around me. "My lease is up at the end of March."

"Wow! That's so soon. Are you going to stay with your dad while you find a place out there?"

Sam kisses the top of my head, my cheek, and finally, my lips. I lean into him and groan into his mouth when his hands work their way down my back and to my hips. He squeezes gently before stepping back slightly. He glances over his shoulder at the waffle maker.

"My dad's insisting that I stay with him. He begged me to move home and never leave again," he chuckles. *I love that sound.*

Sam turns from me, and I watch as he takes a waffle out of the waffle maker and adds more of the mixture to cook.

I wrap my arms around his waist and lean my head onto his back as he shifts to flipping bacon—I marvel at this man, making me breakfast, taking a moment to listen to his heartbeat and feel his body move slightly as he breathes in and out.

"He's missed you. Every time I've seen your dad since I moved back, you are pretty much all he talks about. 'Kat, what are you doing to convince my boy to come home?'" My attempt to imitate Dan's voice has us both laughing.

"He doesn't sound like that."

I step away from him and lean against the counter behind us. "That was the best impersonation you've ever heard! Don't try to deny it, Harris."

"That was the *worst* impersonation I've ever heard. You need to practice more."

"Whatever, jerk. Anyway. I'm so fucking excited to have you back home!"

"Me too."

When the next waffle is cooked, Sam pulls two plates from the cupboard, placing a waffle and a couple of strips of bacon onto each one. He hands me the plates, and I walk back around to the barstools while he grabs the syrup—the pure maple kind. My mouth waters as I bring my plate up and smell my waffle.

He laughs as he makes his way around the counter to sit next to me. "Does it smell good?"

"It smells delicious," I sigh as I cut into my waffle and take my first bite, groaning as the flavor assaults my taste buds in the most delectable way.

"So," he says when he finishes his own bite, "I have a couple of things planned for today. There's a lot to do and see in Chicago. But with this short trip, I didn't want it to be overwhelming." He pauses to eat more.

"Care to share these plans with the class? Or you just gonna keep that to yourself?" I lightly jab his ribs with my elbow.

He exaggerates a groan and rubs where my elbow hit him. "After that, I might just make you suffer and keep it to myself."

I shrug nonchalantly and hurry to take another bite. Sam laughs and wraps his arm around my shoulders, pulling me in close to him. He places a kiss on my temple and releases me.

"I bought tickets for one of the river tours. After that, I thought we could grab lunch and then head up to the Observation Deck. We'll have some time between the river tour and the Observation Deck—we don't have to get lunch right away—but I know you'll be hungry, and we can walk around the city, if you want."

"That sounds great!" I smile at him and continue eating.

"It'll be a bit cold on the river tour, so we'll need to bundle up. But I think you'll like it."

I nod absentmindedly. I know he isn't going to be working at his architecture firm much longer, but I have this weird longing to see his office. I want this part of Sam that I've never experienced before. "Would it be possible for you to show me your office?"

"You want to see my office?" He sounds skeptical.

"Yeah. Is that weird?" I scrunch my face at him.

"Not weird. I can make that happen. But first, finish your breakfast; I have some other plans before we leave this apartment." He winks at me before turning his attention back to his food. I'm torn between scarfing this down and calling it quits now.

Making my decision, I push my plate away from me, stand up, give Sam a sultry look, and walk towards his bedroom.

I don't make it far when I hear the scraping of a chair and Sam's bare feet tapping quickly against the wood floors. Sam scoops me up into his arms, taking my breath away, and carries me into his bedroom.

Chapter 35

"Sam, this is gorgeous!" I gasp as I snuggle into his side. His arm tightens around me as we listen to the guide talk about the various buildings and architectural history of Chicago. "Have you done this before?" I peel my eyes from the view to look up at Sam, who's smiling down at me.

"Only once, and it wasn't as great as this time."

I frown at him. "What makes this time better?"

"Well, last time I went by myself." He shrugs and looks out at the river. "It was just after Claire and I broke up, and I needed to clear my head. I'd been hearing about this for a while and decided it would be a great way to break up the monotony. This time is better because you're here."

He squeezes his arm around me a little tighter. I kiss his jaw before snuggling into him more.

We spend the rest of the river tour with Sam pointing out some of his favorite buildings and what he loves about them. His enthusiasm reminds me of when we were kids; he would stop and stare up at houses and buildings, just admiring the designs. I love this side of him. I've missed it.

We finish the river tour and head further into the city. We slowly walk through downtown Chicago, hand-in-hand. He stops in front of one of the buildings, and I look up at the high-rise in front of us.

Sam's body tenses next to me, and I'm about to ask him what's wrong when he answers my unasked question. "This is where I work," he sighs.

"Shall we go up?"

"Yeah, ok."

Sam leads me up to the 95th floor; we walk through the double doors, Sam using a keycard to unlock them, and then walk through the floor until we reach his office.

Sam's been weirdly quiet and distant since we stopped in front of the building a few minutes before.

"I'm sorry, Sam. I don't want you to get in trouble for bringing me here. Do you want to go?"

Sam lets out a breath. "No, it's not that. We can be here. I think it's just this place. It makes me feel off." He brings my hand up to his mouth and places a soft kiss on the back of my hand. Sam opens the door to his office and walks in, pulling me behind him.

My eyes immediately fall on the pictures hanging on his wall, specifically, the one that matches a picture hanging in my office. The picture is from one of our hikes to Mt. Rainier. We had stopped by a small river with the mountain in the background. The pine trees inked down his left arm remind me of the ones from this area.

Sam must notice my attention because he stands behind me and wraps his arms around my waist. "That was the picture you took when we were hiking Mt. Rainier."

"I know." I look at him over my shoulder. "I have this same picture hanging in my office, too."

"You do?"

I turn back to the picture, taking it in. "Yeah. I'm surprised you have it hanging here."

"It was one of my favorite hikes with you." He kisses my cheek, and we stand there for a moment, looking at the picture. It seems so strange to think all this time we've both had this picture hanging in our respective offices. A little piece of our past life.

Did he have this before or after he broke things off with Claire? I'm about to ask when I hear voices coming from the outer office. Sam shifts away from me and steps into the hallway.

"Steven, hey. I'm surprised to see you here on a Saturday," Sam speaks to someone I can't see yet.

"Me? What the fuck are you doing here, bro?" a deep voice, Steven, I presume, responds as a figure steps into view.

Steven is a little shorter than Sam, with blond hair and brown eyes. He reminds me of a much taller, male version of Liv. "Well, well, well, who is this stunning creature?" He's looking at me like a predator, and I'm his prey.

"This is Kat. Kat, this is my colleague, Steven." Steven steps forward, pushing past Sam, and pulls me into a hug. I stand there frozen in place, my arms at my sides, unsure what to do. Sam clears his throat. "Dude, back off from my girl." Sam pulls on Steven's arm, who finally releases me and takes a step back.

I watch as Steven looks me up and down, drinking me in. I can't stop the blush from rising on my cheeks when I see Steven's assessment of me. I don't think I'll ever get used to men finding me attractive.

"What is a beautiful woman like you doing with a dope like him?" Steven points his thumb at Sam, who walks over to me and puts his arm around my shoulder. Claiming me. Marking his territory.

I look up at Sam, who's glaring at Steven, and can't contain my laugh, "Please don't start a pissing contest." Sam's gaze snaps to mine, surprised. I elbow him in the ribs lightly. "I thought you were going to get me lunch?"

"Mmmm." He kisses the top of my head. "Yes, Kitty Kat, let's go get lunch." Sam grabs my hand and pulls me toward the door. He tilts his head towards Steven and says his name as we pass, leaving Steven in Sam's office. After my jealousy last night over Tiffany, jealous Sam is adorable.

Chapter 36

Eleven Years Old

"Ma!" *I shout for her as I walk into the kitchen, where I know she's making her morning coffee.*

"Yes, pretty girl?"

"If I have to listen to Ethan screech out 'these wounds they will not heal' one more time while he's in the shower, so help me! He sounds like a dying cat."

Ethan's been on this Linkin Park kick since he bought one of their posters at a music store a few weeks ago. He came home with posters of Linkin Park, Twenty One Pilots, and Panic! At the Disco and showed them to Mom and me.

"What are you going to do with those posters?" I asked him.

"Hang them in my room. Obviously!" Ethan sounded exasperated when he responded.

Mom laughs a little. "He can't help it. It's just puberty, and he'll grow out of it. Maybe not the singing in the shower part, but he'll start to sound better again."

"Ma," my tone is incredulous, "he does this every morning. I don't know how much longer I can take it." I plop into one of the chairs at the small table in the kitchen and place my head in my hands. "I swear even the spiders are covering their ears," I grumble.

"I know you can handle it. Be gentle with him and try to remember he can't help it right now."

***

P resent Day

I wake the next morning half lying on Sam—my head on his chest, my arm around his waist, and one leg swung over his.

Sam has one arm around my shoulders, holding me to him. His breaths are deep and even, and I know he's still asleep.

Not wanting to wake him, I breathe him in, the faint pines-and-salty-sea-air scent that is all Sam is intoxicating. It's a mixture of his cologne and his deodorant, leftover from the day before.

He smells like home.

I listen to the faint sound of Sam's beating heart and allow it to soothe me. I don't know if I'll ever be tired of hearing his heart beat.

Slowly, I move my hand up his chest to meet the scar that runs from his collarbone down to his ribs. The scar that almost took him from me.

What would Ethan think if he knew Sam and I were not only talking to each other but also sleeping together? I know he told Sam to back off and not pursue a relationship with me.

Would he be mad at Sam? At me?

It might take him some time, but I want to believe that Ethan would accept this. Would accept Sam and me.

What are we?

Is he my boyfriend?

Or are we just having fun?

My fingers lightly trace the portion of Sam's scar that runs just under his pec as my thoughts spiral into what all of this means.

I feel Sam stretch slightly as he tightens his arm around me. "Good morning, beautiful."

I meet his eyes briefly before dropping my chin and snuggling into him more. I close my eyes, reveling in Sam nuzzling his face into my neck as he inhales deeply.

"You wouldn't happen to be overthinking things over there, would you?" His voice is husky, and the sound makes my lady bits want to grovel at his feet, begging for attention.

"No." *Busted.* "I was thinking a normal amount over here."

"Right." I hear the distrust in his voice.

I look into his eyes but quickly drop my chin again.

"Hey," he says hesitantly. "You ok?" he gently lifts my chin so I'm looking at him.

I quickly respond to reassure him, "Better than ok, Sammy." I tilt my head forward and kiss his bare chest.

"Wait," I pull back enough to look into his eyes again, "are you ok?" *Does he regret this weekend?*

He chuckles softly before kissing my forehead. "I don't think I've ever been happier."

I don't fight the smile that forms on my face at his words. This is a literal dream come true. If only I could tell younger Kat just to hold on, that she would end up with Sam. Younger Kat would never believe me.

"I was just thinking about Ethan."

"Tell me more."

"Just that he told you to stay away from me, and here we are. I don't know what this is," I gesture vaguely at us, "but I was wondering what Ethan would think." I look at my hand and lightly retrace Sam's scar again. He doesn't flinch or tense up like I would have expected. "I was just wondering if Ethan would be mad at me."

Sam's quiet for long enough that I think he won't respond. He finally says, "He wouldn't be mad at you, Kat. Me, on the other hand?" Sam rubs his hand up and down my arm in soothing circles. "He'd be furious with me. At least initially. I think he'd come around once he realized how much I love you. At least, I hope he would."

Did Sam just say he loves me? Isn't it too soon for that? I'm not sure he realized he said it. I don't dare look at him, so I keep my focus on my hand tracing his scar.

Not understanding the direction of my thoughts, Sam continues, "Ethan could never be mad at you. Especially not for this. As for what this is, I was hoping I could call you mine."

I meet his gaze again, searching his expression. "Yours?" It comes out in a croak.

Sam's body tenses under mine. "Yeah, I mean, unless you don't want that?"

I lightly brush my lips along his. "Yes, I'm yours." I look back down at my hand and continue lightly tracing his scar, running my fingers down to where it ends at his ribs.

Sam kisses the top of my head, and his body relaxes again. "Are you truly interested in exploring today before you leave?"

"What else do you have in mind, Sammy?"

"I was thinking," he says slowly, "I would much rather stay here where I can keep you all to myself. Preferably without clothes," his hand dips from my arm to my bare waist where my tank top has shifted up, "but I can be persuaded if you really want to leave this bed and go out."

"Mmmm. I'd love to stay here for as long as we can." I playfully nuzzle my face into his chest. My stomach makes its presence known at that moment, growling loudly. Sam chuckles at the sound. "But I suppose my body is going to need to be fed, sooner, rather than later, I'm afraid."

"I can either make you breakfast or I can have it delivered."

"I thought you didn't want to leave this bed? Or was that just posturing?"

"Delivery it is."

***

True to his word, Sam and I spend the majority of the day in his bed, only leaving for brief periods. We cuddle, talk, and watch *The Princess Bride*. We both laugh at the jokes and quote our favorite parts.

I avoid packing until the very last moment—I want to soak in as much of Sam as I can before I know we have to say goodbye. We won't see each other for a month—not until he moves back to Charleston. The thought of us living in the same city again sends a surge of electricity through my body.

When it's time for Sam to take me to the airport, the air feels thick as my mood turns somber. I don't think it's just me who feels this way.

Being with Sam this weekend makes me feel more connected to him. More trusting that his feelings for me are genuine.

Maybe we have a chance to move beyond the past. Maybe Sam really is choosing me this time.

Sam parks along the curb when we get to the airport. "Fuck, I don't want you to leave," he says as he kisses my forehead, my nose, my cheeks, and finally my lips. "I want to keep you here and never let you out of my sight."

"My dad would frown upon you kidnapping me."

"Ugh. Fine. Leave me if you must." Sam nuzzles his face into my hair.

"I don't want to leave either. I want to stay here and never leave your sight. A month is a long time. But I think it'll be here faster than we realize. Besides, you're going to be busy packing."

Sam runs his hands along the length of my back, stopping just before the curve of my ass. "I'm not packing anything. I'm hiring movers for all of that. Packing sounds like the worst time, so I'm not doing it," he laughs.

Sam grips my hips and pulls me towards him. Once my body is flush against his, he lightly tugs on a few strands of hair before tucking them behind my ear. He looks down at his watch and then back up to me. "Time to go, Kitty Kat," he sighs. "As much as I want you to stay, I know you can't miss your flight."

I tighten my arms around his waist and bury my face into his chest, trying to hold back the tears I feel prick the corners of my eyes. His arms tighten around me again. I'm not sure how long we've been standing here, breathing each other in, when I release him and take a step back.

"Text me when you land and call me when you're home?"

"Of course. Don't go falling in love with someone else before you move back to Charleston." The words are out before I realize what I've said. I try to laugh them off as if it were a joke. But truthfully, I'm worried he might do just that.

"Never, Kitty Kat," Sam tries to reassure me. He takes my face in his palms and places a soft and chaste kiss on my lips. "Never," he repeats.

I gather my suitcase and make my way through the airport doors. Looking back at Sam, I find him watching me. I give him a small smile and wave goodbye.

As I walk through the airport, I can't stop the few tears that slide down my cheeks.

Chapter 37

S am moved back to Charleston a week ago. He put his furniture into a storage unit and has been living at his dad's house.

We're supposed to have our first *proper* date today. Except it isn't a date because Liv told Sam I refuse to sleep in the primary bedroom.

So, Sam's bringing my favorite Chinese takeout and is helping me clear out Ethan's things. I've been dreading this since Sam told me we were changing plans on Wednesday.

I immediately called Liv to complain. *"Kat, you can't just avoid that room for the rest of your life. I know it's hard, but having Sam help you will make it easier."*

Fucking. Whatever.

But I know she's right.

Sam knocks and then lets himself in. He's looking sexy as hell in loose running shorts that show off his muscular legs, and a hunter green AC/DC t-shirt that shows off his muscular arms and tattoos. I want to trace my fingers along the trees painted down his arm.

I drag my eyes down the length of his arm and see he's carrying a few bags of food as he makes his way in. "Think you ordered enough food?" I laugh as Sam pulls out container after container, placing them on the kitchen counter.

"Well, I figured we should eat before we get started, and then I thought it might take a while, so I got extra in case we get hungry again."

"So thoughtful." My voice is dripping in sarcasm. *I don't want to do this.*

He steps away from the food and makes his way to me, determination in his steps. "I know this is going to be hard, but I'm here. Every step of the way, I'm here." He wraps his arms around my waist, pulling me into a warm and comforting hug.

I blow out a breath, "I know. Thanks for being here." I wrap my arms around him and snuggle into his chest. "Can we just stay like this for a bit?"

"We can stay like this for as long as you want." He kisses the top of my head the way he always does. I hear his stomach grumble with hunger and begrudgingly step out of his warm arms.

"Better feed you before you turn into a bear," I tease.

"I think you'd like me as a bear." He winks before stepping back to the food. He pulls plates out of the cupboard, and even though this is the first time he's been here since I've lived here, I realize this isn't his first time here. He knows exactly where the plates, cups, and silverware are. My chest tightens at the thought.

"What's wrong?" His voice is laced with concern as he looks over at me.

I sigh, trying to collect my thoughts. "I just realized that you must have been here a lot since you know where everything is. It took me a couple of weeks to figure out where everything was."

I don't tell Sam that his knowing where everything is just reminds me of all the time we've lost. *Was I being selfish for not talking to him for so long? Probably.*

But more than that, it reminds me of the time I've lost with Ethan. I should've been here more. I should've moved back to Charleston after I graduated from school. I should have been a better sister.

"Hey." Sam's voice is gentle, too gentle, and it causes my heart to crack again. I don't notice I'm crying until he wipes a tear from my cheek. "Don't do that. Don't beat yourself up for not being here as much. You and Ethan made things work on the terms that made sense for both of you. He never resented you for not being in Charleston, and he wouldn't want you to be upset about it now." Sam is only half right about all the turmoil I'm experiencing right now.

Sniffling, I say, "Thanks. Why are you so good to me?"

"Because you're worth it." Sam softly kisses my lips. "Now let's eat. I even brought plum wine for you." He winks at me and puts a little of everything on two plates.

Beaming at the mention of plum wine, I exclaim, "You, Samuel Harris, are a godsend."

Once we finish eating, I try to delay the inevitable by drinking more plum wine. Sam catches onto my tactics and takes the bottle from me. "You can have this back once we're finished."

I just sulk at him.

"I'll make you a deal." I perk up a little, but I'm still pouting. "I'll let you have half a glass once we tackle the closet and dresser, and then another half once we figure out what to do with the mattress."

"I can think of a few things to do with the mattress." I waggle my eyebrows at him. I'm a lightweight, so it doesn't take much to make me tipsy, and apparently, one and a half glasses of plum wine is all that I need to hit on Sam.

"I would love nothing more than to do some of those things with you. But, we need to get this over with." He stands up, decision made. He holds out his hand to me. I take it and let him pull me to my feet.

It doesn't take us long to go through the closet and dresser. We have trash bags ready for items that need to be thrown out and those in good enough condition to be donated.

I keep a stack of Ethan's T-shirts, thinking it might be cool to make a quilt or something out of them for my parents. As promised, once we're finished with Ethan's clothes, Sam has some plum wine ready for me. But I don't take it.

It's been several months since Ethan died, and it's not that I'm over it; you don't get over death. It's just that things feel easier, lighter, with Sam around.

I move over to the bed and pull off the bedding. Sam inspects the pillows and, finding them suitable enough, puts them into the donate pile.

"What do you think about the mattress? It looks like it's in good condition."

"I can't sleep on his mattress," I say matter-of-factly.

"It's the same size as the one in the guest room. Why don't we swap it?"

"Sammy?"

"Yes?"

"Could we swap out all the furniture? I've gotten used to the stuff in the guest room, and I think it would make sleeping in here a little easier."

"That's a great idea. How about we start with moving the guest room furniture into the living room, and then we can move this stuff out and set it up as we go?"

"Ok." I was worried he might think my request was silly.

We spend the next couple of hours rearranging furniture. By the time we finish setting both rooms back up, I'm grateful that Sam brought extra food.

We sit down on the couch with our food, and Sam turns on the TV. I don't even realize I've been staring at him until his eyes catch mine, playfulness showing in their chocolate brown depths. "What is it, Kat?" His tone is light.

"Thanks. For everything. It wasn't as bad as I expected, but I couldn't have done all of this without you. So, thanks."

"I'm happy to help. It didn't take as long as I thought it would. You're pretty strong for how scrawny you look." He playfully ruffles my hair, and I glower at him. He laughs and then goes back to finding a movie for us to watch. "*Indiana Jones* or *Avengers*?"

"You choose." He enamors me, and I can't imagine I'll be watching much of whatever he puts on.

Once we're finished eating our second dinner, I snuggle up to him on the couch, lying my head on his lap. Sam relaxes into the couch as he props his feet onto the coffee table and runs his hand through my hair. I hear a slight rustling and feel the weight of the blanket he puts over my body.

I'm startled awake and realize Sam is carrying me. "Shhh, it's ok. I'm just taking you to bed." I wrap my arm around his neck and lean into him more. Once in my room, he gently lays me down and pulls the covers over me.

I look up at him as he leans down and places a soft kiss on my forehead.

"Goodnight, Kat. I'll call you tomorrow."

I reach for his hand, stopping him from leaving. "Stay with me?"

Sam nods, removes his shirt and shorts, and climbs in next to me. We lie next to each other, and the silence feels suffocating.

Why does this feel awkward?

I move closer to him, pick up his arm, and lay my head on his chest, wrapping my arm around his middle. He relaxes into me and wraps his arm around my body, pulling me closer to him.

He kisses the top of my head. "Goodnight, Kat."

I kiss his chest. "Goodnight, Sammy."

Chapter 38

Sixteen Years Old

Sam holds his hand out to me. "Will you dance with me, Kat?"

I look at him, trying to make sure I heard him correctly. "You, you want to dance with me?"

Sam smiles his big, familiar smile, showing the dimple in his left cheek. "Yeah. I mean, if you want?"

"Ok." I stand and take his hand.

It's only a few steps from where I was sitting to the dance floor, where a lot of others are already dancing.

The song changes to a slow song, and I look up at Sam, trying not to show the worry on my face that maybe he doesn't want to slow dance. I'm secretly hoping he does, but I can't handle the embarrassment if he changes his mind.

I'm relieved when he puts his hands on my hips and starts slowly moving from side to side. I put my hands on his shoulders and follow along with his steps.

"You look pretty in your dress." Usually, Sam is so confident, but right now, he seems shy as he ducks his face a little and avoids my gaze.

I still can't believe he asked me to dance. I know he asked me to save a couple of dances for him when we were at my house. I just thought he was trying to be nice since Kevin couldn't come.

"Thanks, Sammy. And thanks for asking me to dance. I was starting to feel dumb just sitting there watching everyone."

I don't tell him this, but truthfully, I was starting to feel lonely. I'm not a popular kid, not like Sam and Ethan. I've never really had a boyfriend, and boys aren't exactly lining up down the street to ask me out.

My thoughts stop spiraling when Sam pulls me in a little closer, and my heart starts racing. With how close we are now, I have to move my arms so that they are draped around his shoulders instead of having my hands on them. He's so tall.

"I've wanted to ask you to dance all night and finally got the courage to do it." He gives me that shy smile again.

"Really?" I can't hold back the surprise in my tone.

"Really. I'm just glad you actually said yes." He's glad?

I've had a crush on Sam since the beginning of summer. It's one of the reasons why I insisted that Liv and I go to the beach with him and Ethan almost every day. I just wanted to lie on the beach and watch him. I thought for sure he had noticed me staring at him when he wasn't looking. I can't believe he thought I would say no to him asking me to dance.

The song ends, and a new, more upbeat song starts to play. "Do you want to keep dancing?" Sam seems unsure again.

"Yeah. Let's do it." I can't hold back my excitement as I beam up at him.

We dance for several more songs until I'm feeling a little sweaty and thirsty.

"Do you want to get a drink with me?"

"That's a great idea." Sam looks around, "Actually, why don't you hold those two seats over there for us, and I'll get us some drinks?"

"Sure." I wait for him and think about how great it felt when he touched me while we were dancing.

Every time his arm or hand brushed mine as we walked over to the chairs, I felt shivers. I imagine what it would be like if Sam liked me, too.

***

P resent Day

The next morning, I wake up alone. The space where Sam had slept is empty. My momentary disappointment is replaced when I hear the sound of dishes and smell food wafting in from the kitchen.

I woke up briefly at one point in the middle of the night and found that I was still wrapped up in Sam's embrace, my leg had shifted the rest of the way in between his thighs. The last time I slept that well was with Sam in Chicago.

It's funny to think back to that time and how much has changed between us since he slept in my bed in Columbia. I laugh at the memory. I was mad at him for forcing me to go to my parents' house for Thanksgiving. But the trip ended with Sam and me getting closer.

Stretching and pulling down my tank top, I get out of bed and make my way into the kitchen.

"You know, I was thinking." I wrap my arms around his middle and hug him from behind while he stirs what looks like eggs and vegetables in a pan on the stove. "I could get used to waking up to you cooking me breakfast."

He turns around and chuckles, "How did you sleep?"

"Good, you?"

"At first, it was hard to fall asleep. I kept thinking about this gorgeous woman in my arms." He winks at me and kisses my forehead. "But once I fell asleep, I slept really well. I made coffee." He gestures to the pot sitting on the counter.

"My hero." I clasp my hands together and wave them in front of me, batting my eyelashes.

Sam drops his gaze to the floor, and I brace myself for whatever he's going to say next. "I need to go back to my dad's house and help with a few house projects today. I was thinking, there's somewhere I want to take you." He looks back up at me. "Will you go out with me tonight?"

"You mean, on a *proper* date?" I wink at him.

He rolls his eyes. "Yes. A proper date, menace. I'll even pick you up."

The smile that crosses my face is immediate. "I would love to."

"It's a date then." He returns my smile.

Chapter 39

That evening, I'm dressed in warm clothing, per Sam's instructions, and sitting on my couch waiting for him to arrive. My knee is bouncing so much I'm afraid it'll come loose from the joint and start walking on its own.

When I feel like I can't take the nerves any longer, I hear the doorbell. Stopping to look at my reflection in the mirror by the door one last time, I open the door and greet Sam.

"Wait." Seeing the motorcycle jacket in Sam's hand makes me nervous. "You aren't thinking I'm going to—I don't think this is a good idea."

"Yes, I do, in fact, think you're going to get on my motorcycle with me." I feel the color drain from my face, and he adds, quietly, gently, "I'll keep you safe, Kat. I promise."

I can't take my eyes off the black motorcycle jacket he's holding out to me or the one he's wearing himself.

Finally lifting my eyes to his face, I see he's looking at my feet. "But you need to change your shoes. You can't ride with me in those slip-ons."

"Well, that's too bad because just this afternoon, I threw away all my other shoes. Darn, I was looking forward to riding with you." I shrug as if that is the end of the story.

"Nice try." He steps inside, hangs the jacket he was holding onto a hook by the door, takes his off and hangs it on the same hook, and drags me down the hall to my bedroom.

Sam gently pushes me down onto the bed and walks over to my closet, pulling out shoes he deems suitable. Walking over to my dresser, he asks, "Which drawer has your socks?" I hear his words, but I'm too stunned to process them.

Is he serious about riding a motorcycle? *Didn't he crash last time?*

"Kat?" His gentle voice breaks through my fog. "Which drawer are your socks in?"

"The top left." I watch as he opens the drawer, chooses a pair of socks for me, and shuts the drawer before walking back to where I'm still sitting. He kneels in front of me, and that action shocks me out of my stupor.

"Oh my God, I can put on my own shoes." He shrugs, handing me the socks, and sits on the bed next to me.

"Didn't like me kneeling in front of you?" His voice is playful and enticing.

I'm remembering our time in Chicago when he was on his knees in front of me, and my cheeks instantly flush. I can see his big smile from the corner of my eye.

"Sam, I—" It comes out way too breathy. Shaking my head to clear the lust forming, I try again. "I thought the last time you rode a motorcycle was when you had your accident." I frown at him, my eyebrows pulled together in concern.

"I rode it to my dad's house the night your parents gave it to me, and I've been riding it each time I've been home. I was definitely nervous the first couple of times, but it all came back to me." He looks at me with so much sincerity as he adds, "I wouldn't ask you to do this if I were hesitant at all. The weather looks great, and we aren't going too far. Trust me?"

He looks at me with so much hope shining in his eyes. "Yes. I trust you."

"Then let's go." He stands and holds his hand out to me. I slowly take it and let him pull me up.

Before we move, his lips are on mine. His kiss is gentle, but the way his hands grip my waist tells me he's holding back. He breaks away from me too soon. "Shit. I meant to wait until the end of the night before kissing you."

"I don't mind the little detour." I smile wickedly at him and bite my lip.

"Stop biting that lip, or we're never going to get out of here, and I have special plans for us." Sam tugs my lip from my teeth, grabs my hand, and walks towards the front door.

He lets go of my hand and puts his jacket back on, zipping it up and snapping the buttons at the top and bottom. Sam grabs the other jacket. "Turn around." His voice is gentle, the way one speaks to a frightened animal.

I do as he asks. He helps me put on the black motorcycle jacket, then spins me around and zips it up. He zips up the sleeves, making them tight against my wrists, and fastens the snaps on each one.

"Where did you get this?" Testing out the jacket, I find that it's snug, but in a way that still allows me to breathe. I feel the built-in protective pieces throughout.

"I bought it for you this afternoon. Along with the helmet and gloves I have for you downstairs."

"Wait. You bought these for me?"

"Kat, I used to love riding, and I can't imagine you being in my life and not having you ride with me. My backpack." He winks at me.

I don't remember him wearing a backpack when he came in, but I look around anyway.

"Missing something?"

"Your backpack. But I don't remember you coming in with one. Where did you set it down?"

He starts to laugh but quickly reins it in when I look at him quizzically. "No, little menace." Sam lightly tugs on my braid. "The passenger on a motorcycle is a backpack. And tonight, I'm very much looking forward to you being mine."

I'm still confused when Sam adds, "It's because you'll sit a little higher than me and hang on to me. Nice and snug against my back. Like a backpack." He waggles his eyebrows at me and then pulls me out of the condo and down to the street, where his motorcycle is.

I stare at the two helmets on the seat and wonder where he stored the one for me when he drove over here. He drops my hand again and picks up one of the helmets. He lifts the visor before helping me put it on.

"This should be a pretty close fit. You want it to be snug, and it shouldn't move when you shake your head."

He gestures for me to test it, so I shake my head, and the helmet stays in place.

"You shouldn't feel any pressure points, and you shouldn't feel like you're going to bite the inside of your cheek. Does it feel ok?"

"Yeah, it feels a little strange, but it's comfortable enough." He helps me fasten the chin strap before stepping back to examine me.

"Good." Sam hands me a pair of gloves, which I take and put on. He takes out his phone and snaps a quick picture of me, pockets his phone, and then reaches for his own helmet. "You look too cute not to take a pic." He winks at me before securing his helmet.

Once his helmet and his gloves are on, he straddles the motorcycle, gesturing for me to climb on behind him.

When he sees I'm looking a little confused, Sam points down to a small peg. "Step on this with your left foot and swing your right over. There's another peg there. You keep your feet on those the entire time, ok? Put your hands on my shoulders for balance as you swing your leg over."

I nod and climb on behind him.

"When I lean into a turn, you're gonna lean with me. Try to relax your body against mine, and don't be afraid to lean into me during the ride or when we stop. Try not to move too quickly."

A nod is my only response again. I'm too nervous about this to talk.

Sam reaches behind him and grabs ahold of each of my hands, bringing them around his waist. "Snug, like a backpack." He closes his visor, and I follow his action, closing mine, too. I feel the bike shift under us as he takes the weight of the bike onto his feet, and lifts the kickstand.

I tighten my grip around him while still allowing him room to breathe and feel a pleasant rumble in his chest. *Did he just groan?*

I'm terrified but also feel hot in all the places our bodies are touching. I turn my head and lean my helmeted head against his back.

"Is this uncomfortable for you?" The sound is muffled with the visor down. The helmet is so bulky that it feels weird to rest it on his back.

"It's the most comfortable I've ever felt." Sam pats my left hand with his before adding, "Now, hang on."

I tighten my grip as he starts the motorcycle. Sam's body shakes with laughter that I wish I could hear over the roar of the engine. He checks over his shoulder to make sure it's all clear and drives off.

The longer I'm behind him, the more my body starts to relax. I'm still holding onto him like my life depends on it, but I'm not as nervous. Each time he stops at a streetlight, he pats my hand or reassuringly rubs my knee. It takes about 20 minutes before I realize where we're going.

Ethan, Sam, Liv, and I used to come here a lot as teenagers. Liv and I usually sunbathed while Sam and Ethan surfed. Sometimes we would come with a group of other people and have parties along the beach.

If we stayed long enough, I would sit on my beach blanket, face away from the water, knees to my chest, and watch the sun set over the land. Even facing the water, I loved watching the sky change from blue to purple, pink, and orange before darkening to a deep blue and then black.

It was always one of my favorite views. Sometimes Sam and I would sit next to each other. We usually sat there in silence, absorbing the colors and the quiet.

The sunsets at Folly Beach aren't the same as the ones on the west coast, where the sun sets over the water, causing it to gleam. But I will forever love the view, no matter which coast I'm on.

Sam parks his motorcycle in a designated space and shuts off the engine, sliding the kickstand into place. Slowly, I extract myself from him and his bike. I stand there watching him dismount, his body movements smooth, as if this is such a natural part of him. He removes his helmet as I continue to stare at him.

Sam catches my stare and smiles his big, brilliant smile that shows off the dimple in his left cheek. "Need help getting that off?" He gestures towards the helmet still on my head.

I reach up for the chin strap but struggle to find the end of it.

Sam walks up to me. "Allow me." He reaches up and unfastens the chin strap, letting me pull the helmet off my head. He takes it from me and locks both helmets on what I realize are designated helmet holders. *Handy.*

My hand reaches for my braided hair, and I'm glad when it doesn't feel like it's a mess. Sam turns back to me and nods toward the beach, where I see a picnic blanket set up with a backpack in the center.

"You set this up and then came to get me?"

He looks at me with a guilty expression. "Actually, I asked a friend to set it up for us, so it wasn't sitting out here for an hour."

"Oh. Smart." I lean down and start to remove my shoes and socks. "I don't want to get sand in my shoes."

"Good point." He takes off his shoes and socks as well. Once our feet are bare, he takes my hand in his and leads us down to the picnic spot. It's still bright out, but we have about an hour before it'll be too dark to see anything.

When we reach the blanket, he gestures for me to sit down. Unzipping the motorcycle jacket, I take it off and set it aside. I might want it as it cools off.

Sam sits next to me and reaches into the backpack. He hands me a glass bottle of root beer. I twist off the top and take a sip as he pulls out containers of food, two plates, napkins, forks, and a couple of light blankets.

He opens one container of what looks like pasta salad, scooping some out with a serving spoon, and places some on each of our plates. Next, Sam pulls another container with sandwiches. He hands me a plate, but stops midway. "Kat?"

"This is incredible." My voice is thick. "You are incredible." He sets the plate on the blanket in front of me, reaches for my hand, and brings it to his lips.

"I'm glad you like it."

I'd always imagined going on a date with Sam. We often went to lunch and dinner together in college, but those times were nothing like this. This is romantic. A perfect setting. Something my mind could never imagine.

We quietly eat, the silence comfortable instead of awkward, and I laugh out loud at the memory of my not-date with Chris. How different these two men are and how different these experiences.

"Penny for your thoughts?"

"I was just thinking about my dinner with Chris." I know I've said the wrong thing when Sam frowns, so I hurry to explain. "No, I mean. It was awful. I never told you because I was embarrassed. But it was so incredibly uncomfortable."

The corners of his mouth lift into a wicked smile. "Awful, huh? What made it awful?"

I huff out a laugh. "Well, the biggest problem was that I realized I didn't want to be on a date with him while we were driving to the restaurant. I couldn't remember if we had said it was a date or if it was just friends hanging out. So, we were making small talk, and when we got there, it was just an uncomfortable silence."

I shake my head at the memory. His gaze remains fixed on me as he lowers himself on the blanket, propping onto one elbow.

"Sam, I couldn't even look at him; it was so awkward. Finally, he said something about it being weird, and he wasn't even really sure why he asked me out. We agreed that we would eat our pizza and he would take me home right after." I'm laughing now at the memory. "I was so relieved, and when we pulled up to the condo. He didn't even walk me to the door. Just basically said, 'Well, it was good seeing you again. Bye.'"

I look up at Sam, and his eyes are equally amused and upset. "He didn't even walk you to your door?" The words are seething. "What an asshole."

"It wasn't like that. I think we just both realized what a terrible mistake we made." I reach out and run my hand through his hair. "Besides, if things went well, you and I might not be sitting here on this incredibly thoughtful date."

He sits up, scoots closer to me and puts his arm around me. Pulling me into his side, Sam kisses my forehead. "He didn't know what was right in front of him."

We finish eating, watching the waves and the impending sunset. When the weather starts to cool, Sam gets up and wraps one of the blankets around my shoulders, setting the other blanket next to him.

He sits back down next to me, starts to put his arm around my shoulders, but I stop him before he can. He looks at me with narrowed eyes, but quickly smiles when he realizes I'm putting the blanket around him as well. "Thanks."

We watch the ocean and the changing colors of the sky in silence as the sun sets behind us. Deciding I want to watch the sunset while lying down, I start to move the repacked backpack off to the side and lie on my back, looking up at the sky.

Sam grabs both blankets and lays them on top of me, leaving half for him. He lies next to me, and I have to look at his handsome face: his strong jaw, his unbelievably long eyelashes, and his mouth-watering smile.

Even though this is our first proper date, there is no doubt in my mind that I'm in love with him. He's everything I've wanted for years, and I feel so lucky to be here with him.

He catches me staring at him and smiles again. "You're missing the view, Kitty Kat."

Why does that nickname always feel like he's saying more?

"I'm enjoying the view just fine." I smile back at him and shift to my side so I can look at him properly. He leans into me and places his lips on mine. I love his soft kisses, but this one is desperate—a promise of more.

I turn onto my back again to give him better access, and he lies half on me as he deepens the kiss, his hand running up my waist and stopping just under my breast. *I want him.*

"Sam, I want you," I moan into his mouth.

He pulls back and runs his hand through his hair. His eyes searching mine. "I want you, too, but I'm not going to take you here at the beach with all the sand and anyone who can walk by. You need to decide if we pack up and leave now so I can get you home and have my way with you, or finish watching this sunset?"

"Take me home," I whisper into his ear before kissing his neck.

He shivers at the contact and jumps into action. We fold the blankets, and Sam shoves them unceremoniously into the backpack. I pick up our jackets as he carries the backpack. Grabbing my free hand in his, he leads me back to his motorcycle.

We put on our shoes when we get to the sidewalk, and Sam helps me with my helmet again before putting his own on. I put the backpack on and climb onto the bike behind him like we've done this hundreds of times.

The 20 minutes back to my place are agonizing. I'm getting braver on Sam's motorcycle and even take one hand away from his waist and run my fingers down his leg. He shivers at the contact, and it takes everything in me not to run my fingers along his length, knowing I'll find him hard for me.

The third time I run my fingers along his thigh, he grabs my hand and wraps it around his waist again, holding it in place for a moment. I know it's his way of telling me to cut it out, so I behave and keep my hands on his stomach.

We finally make it back to my place, helmets in hand.

Sam spends the night devouring me like I'm his personal dessert buffet.

Chapter 40

I wake up the next morning with Sam's arms still wrapped around me. I don't think I've ever slept naked before, but I feel confident next to Sam. As I listen to his deep breathing, I allow my mind to drift to last night.

All of a sudden, I feel nervous. Here I am, lying naked in bed, Sam at my back, his arm around my waist, and last night he told me he loved me for the second time.

He was falling asleep as the soft, quiet words fell from his lips. I'm still not sure if he realized what he said. Again.

Why can't he just say it in a way that feels like he knows he's saying it?

But once again, I didn't say it back to him. I've loved Sam for so long that none of this seems real. I almost want to be cliché and pinch myself, but I hold back that urge.

Should I say it back? I know in every fiber of my being that I love Sam. But can I say it? It feels too vulnerable. *I have to tell him.* I need him to know that I feel the same way.

I still can't remember if I told Ethan I loved him during that last phone call, and I can't let this be another moment I question or regret.

Sam's arms tighten around me. He kisses my neck, and in a moment of bravery, I say, "Sam?" I peek at him over my shoulder.

"Hmm?" His eyes are closed, and he looks so comfortable. Content.

"Did you mean it?" Sam's eyes pop open as he moves up onto one arm, his other still draped over my waist. "You love me?"

He chuckles softly, "Yes. I love you, Kat. Always have. Always will." He lies back down next to me and stares at the ceiling, one arm under his head, the other between us.

My voice is quiet, unsteady, as I speak the words aloud, "I love you, too."

He looks at me in surprise and gives me a small, shy smile. "Yeah?"

"Yeah," I repeat.

That small smile cracks wide open.

Sam turns to his side, kisses my neck, and pulls me into his chest. My core heats as I feel his hard cock against my stomach.

Looking over at the clock on my dresser, I groan at the realization that I have to get ready for work. Catching the reason behind my groan, Sam plants a soft kiss on my lips.

"I wish today were Sunday so I could lie in bed with you all day." He groans before adding, "This is a busy week for me, and I'm not sure I'll have much time to woo you."

"Stay the night with me then. If the only time I can have with you this week is to sleep in your arms, it'll be enough."

"You sure? I don't want to overstay my welcome." He looks shy, like I might turn him away.

"Yes. Please stay. Bring some clothes so you don't have to leave early to go back to your dad's house and get ready."

"As you wish."

I playfully smack his arm. "Don't go all Westley on me, or we're both going to be very late today."

"Is that a promise, Buttercup?" His deep voice is seductive.

"I'm not going to let you seduce me right now, Harris." My tone is playfully sharp.

He squeezes my ass and kisses my neck. "You sure about that? I am *very* good at seducing." His hands continue exploring my body, and his mouth dips down to lightly bite my nipple.

"Sam... I... fuck... what was I saying?"

"Something about responsibilities, I think. But this beautiful body of yours is distracting me."

"I have a client meeting I can't be late for." I groan as his mouth sucks and nips at my nipple. "Please promise you'll come back tonight."

"I'll come back tonight," he breathes into my ear, causing shivers to run down my spine. He kisses me on that very sensitive skin just below my ear. My core tightens in anticipation of his lips on other parts.

I groan and get out of bed, making my way to the bathroom.

He calls after me, "Guess I'll have to work a little harder at my seduction next time."

I laugh as I close the door behind me.

By the time I'm out of the shower and dressed for work, Sam's made us coffee and oatmeal for breakfast. "I feel like I should have asked what you wanted for breakfast. You used to always eat oatmeal, but I've been making you eggs and pancakes." He runs his hand through his hair in the way he does to relieve his nerves.

I kiss his cheek and pick up the bowl of oatmeal as he hands me a mug of coffee. I can't hide the smile as I see he made my coffee just the way I like—lots of creamer. "I still eat oatmeal almost every morning. But mostly because I don't like cooking. I love your eggs and pancakes. Thank you, Sam, this was incredibly thoughtful of you."

His shoulders visibly drop as he leans against the counter, his bright eyes twinkling as he watches me walk over to the bar. "I love to cook, and I'm happy to make you breakfast every morning." My stomach flips at the thought of him making me breakfast every day. I could definitely get used to Sam being around *every morning*.

I set my breakfast in front of me and slide onto the stool. Looking up at him, I see he's still watching me. "You gonna eat? Or just stand there staring at me?" I raise my eyebrow in challenge.

"You are so breathtaking. I think I'll just stand here staring at you." Sam smiles smugly. My cheeks and neck flame as I look down to hide how my body reacts to his words.

"Such a smooth talker," I tease.

"Not smooth, just the truth." He picks up his food and joins me at the bar.

We finish eating and part ways, promising to see each other later that night.

Heading to work, my mind replays our conversation this morning. *I love you, Kat. Always have. Always will.*

I let his words sink into my soul and start to feel those old wounds, of feeling rejected by him, finally begin to heal.

Chapter 41

"So, I'm sure Ethan told you about this at some point, but my dad's firm puts on this sort of formal event to celebrate their clients. I think it's so they can all dress fancy, drink, and enjoy the sunshine."

"Yeah, I remember Ethan talking about how fun they are."

"Well, it's in three weeks, and I'm allowed to bring a plus one." I look down at my fingers, fidgeting. "I'm hoping you'll come with me?" I say it to the ground.

Sam steps forward, gently lifts my chin, and leans in close to whisper in my ear, "Are you asking me on a date, Kitty Kat?" Fuck, his breath on my neck does something to me every time.

"Ye... Yes." I gulp.

Sam stands up straight and takes a step backward. "Ok. Sounds fun." How does he go from making my knees quiver to nonchalance so quickly?

I recover from the whiplash and add, "It's black tie, so you'll need a tux."

"I can make that happen, but," Sam's voice turns molten, "what will you be wearing?" His gaze sears into me, and I feel my body heat.

Ignoring his innuendo, I say, "A dress of some sort. I'm going to Columbia this weekend to visit Liv, and she's going to take me dress shopping."

"Oh." His face drops. "You'll be gone this weekend?"

"Yeah. I should have told you earlier, but I didn't solidify plans until today."

I know we agreed I was his, but I still don't know how to navigate all of this. I don't want to upset him with these last-minute plans. "Columbia is bigger, so they have a lot more options for dresses than Charleston does."

He looks at me like he's reading the emotions as they flit across my face. "Kat, I'm not mad that you're going to Columbia. I've loved the time we've spent together. I feel like I just got you back, and I'm a little bummed that I won't see you." He cups my cheek with his palm and runs his thumb along my cheekbone. "I'm so happy you're going to spend time with Liv. I know you miss her."

Sam's mouth is on mine before I can react; my body melts into him. His easy affection with me always surprises me. I know it's because I'm still waiting for the other shoe to drop.

Sam steps away from me too soon and walks over to my bed, where he sits and removes his T-shirt before lying down. "Actually, some of my old friends have been bugging me about hanging out with them. This'll be the perfect time for that."

I stand rooted in place, just soaking him in, memorizing his features, the way he moves his body, the fact that he's so comfortable removing his shirt with me.

"Friends have been *bugging* you to hang out? Why haven't you spent time with them?"

"Have you seen yourself?" He says in disbelief. "Why the fuck would I want to hang out with a bunch of smelly dudes when I can have this smart, compassionate, and gorgeous woman in bed every night?" He smiles confidently at me.

I've been staring at him too long when he sits up watching me. I feel the flush of embarrassment on my cheeks as I walk over to the bed. "Oh my God, don't ignore your friends!" He laughs but doesn't say anything.

Sam's been sleeping over since that first night when he helped me move Ethan's things out. It's weird how we went from not seeing each other to sleeping together in Chicago to Sam moving back to Charleston and sleeping in my bed every night. It feels too fast and not fast enough.

We have a comfortable routine, and it's been nice to fall asleep in Sam's arms and to wake up with him lying next to me. We eat a quick breakfast in the morning, and then one of us, usually Sam, cooks dinner.

We eat our dinner and then cuddle on the couch. Sometimes we read books together, and at other times we watch movies. But we always end up making out and then head to the bedroom, where Sam ravages my body and makes me see stars.

Now that Sam is working for himself, he rents an office from one of those office share places. I know it isn't his ideal working space, but he seems happy with it for now.

When Sam left his large architecture firm in Chicago, a few of his clients followed him, and all of them have been sending referrals his way. He has plenty of work to keep him busy, but since he can set his hours and choose his projects, he's always able to spend time with family, and with me.

I'm deeply in love with this man, even if part of me still thinks he's just killing time with me until someone better comes around. And I'll be devastated—*heartbroken*—when he decides he's had enough of me.

The thought breaks my heart, it's all I can do to shield my expression from him. I turn onto my side, my back towards him.

Soon, I hear his breathing even out, and I know he's asleep. It takes me a while to settle my mind enough to fall asleep finally.

Chapter 42

Twenty-Seven Years Old

"Hey sis, how's it going?" Ethan sounds tired when he answers my call.

"You sound tired." I'm sitting at my desk, staring at my computer screen.

"Yeah. I didn't sleep well. I had a long day at the office, and I didn't work out, and ate like shit. But I know you didn't call me about my sleeping habits," he chuckles. "What's up?"

"How much trouble do you think I'll get in if I refer to the other side as sniveling pigs in my motion?" I look out the window and take in downtown Columbia.

He barks out a laugh. "You know if you have to ask, the answer is don't do it. But now I need to know the story."

"This guy is such a tool." I lean back in my chair. "Everything bad that ever happens to him is somehow my client's fault. I swear, Ethan, this guy could be walking down the street, and a fly could land in his mouth and somehow, he would argue my client had control of the fly." I blow out a breath. "It's exhausting arguing against all of this bullshit."

"Then don't." He says it like it's so simple.

"What do you mean, 'then don't'?" I fiddle with my hair.

"I mean, don't get into the weeds with every outlandish argument. Stick to the facts and move on from the rest."

"Yeah. I guess that could work." I say it slowly as I mull it over.

"It always works for me."

"Ok. Thanks. I know I just saw you two weeks ago, but I miss you."

"I miss you, too. Hey, how have things been at the office with Philip?"

"Well, I would be lying if I said I wasn't avoiding him. He hasn't messaged me or tried to talk to me, so I guess that's the best I can hope for right now."

"If only we could avoid the people we break up with forever," he laughs out in response. I know it's been a while since he's dated anyone seriously, and I'm about to push him on this when I hear loud noises coming from his end of the call.

"Whatever, nerd. I'd better get back to this motion. Text me later? I love you."

"Love you too, sis. Good luck, and I'll talk to you later."

***

P resent Day

I wake up Saturday morning to Sam's head between my thighs. "I have to get in as much of you as I can before you leave." His voice is rough with need.

"Fuck." I grab onto his hair as his mouth works my clit. He slips a finger inside of me and pumps in and out. It isn't long before he's adding another finger.

His mouth continues licking, sucking, and softly biting my clit as I'm writhing below him. "Sam. Please," I pant, begging him for more.

He curls his fingers in just the way I like it as my orgasm crests, my pussy clamping down on his fingers. He keeps working me until I come back down.

"I don't think I'll ever get enough of tasting you. Of feeling you lose control from my touch." He leans back onto his heels and smiles up at me, sucking my wetness from his fingers. "Now be a good girl and turn over. Get that pretty ass in the air for me," he growls as he moves to stand at the edge of the bed.

I obey him, knees on the edge of the bed, legs spread for him. I feel his cock slide along my slit. "Always so wet for me." His voice is gruff, and it sends shivers up my spine. Slowly, too slowly, I feel him enter me. He grabs my hips and pulls me to match his thrusts. "Fuck," he growls, "you always feel so good, Kitty Kat."

I feel good. No, *he* feels good.

I start to feel another orgasm building as he continues to thrust into me.

"Sam, please." I don't know if I can take much more of this.

"Tell me what you want."

"Faster. Harder." I can't form sentences when he's pounding into me like this. But I groan as he does exactly as I've asked him.

It only takes a few more thrusts before my body explodes into ecstasy, and I scream his name. He continues to grind into me, his grip on my hips bruising, before he finds his own release.

He leans over me, placing soft kisses along my spine, while we both catch our breath. Slowly, Sam pulls out of me, and I hiss at the loss.

"Come on, beautiful, let's go shower so you can leave me." He sounds sullen, but he's all big smiles. Moving out of our bed, I make my way towards the bathroom with him.

"It's only for today. I'll be back tomorrow."

Sam reaches toward the handle, turning on the water for the shower. "It'll be a cold night in bed without you." He turns toward me. "You don't mind if I sleep here tonight, do you? It's much better than my old room at my dad's house."

His question takes me off guard. He already has his own key. *Why does he think it wouldn't be ok to stay here while I'm gone?* "Of course, you can stay here. Do you feel like you can't?"

"No. I just know I've been spending a lot of time here, and I don't want to assume it's ok to stay when you aren't here." He turns back to the shower, adjusting the temperature. "I don't want to make assumptions."

"I appreciate that, but you don't have to ask. Of course, you can stay." I kiss his bare back right in between his shoulder blades and wrap my arms around him. He wraps his arms around mine in front of his body.

He turns around to face me and pulls me into him. My body tingles in all of the places he's touching me, and I melt into him.

"I love you."

"Mmmm. I love you, too," he whispers as he kisses the column of my neck.

Chapter 43

I made it to Columbia and feel giddy as I pull into the parking space at Liv and Talia's place. I walk up to the familiar front door and knock.

It feels strange to be on this side of the door, knocking, waiting to be let in. I also don't know if I can or should just walk in. While I'm waiting, I send Sam a quick message letting him know I've arrived.

> I made it to Columbia. Have fun with the guys.

I hope you have a great day. I can't wait to see what you choose.

> You'll be waiting a long time cause I'm not showing you until the day of the event.

Rude!

I love you.

> I love you, too.

I'm smiling at myself as Talia opens the door and pulls me into the house. "Why are you knocking?" she teases me.

"I didn't want to walk in on you and Liv—well, you know." I look awkwardly at anything but her. She laughs at my discomfort.

"We keep the door locked when those *activities* are taking place, Kat. You have nothing to worry about there."

"What a relief! But I think I'll continue to knock." I give her a half smile and make my way into the kitchen. "Mind if I get a glass of water?" I call over my shoulder.

"Of course not. Get whatever you want. Liv is almost ready and should be out in a minute. Are you ok out here? I need to finish up some work."

"You aren't shopping with us?"

"No. I have this project I need to finish."

"But it's Saturday! You can't play hooky?"

"Wish I could. But I'll meet you for dinner and drinks later."

I huff out an overdramatic breath, "Fine. Be responsible."

She laughs as she walks towards the bedrooms. I grab a glass of water and make my way back into the living room.

Everything looks just like I remember, except now there are obvious signs of Talia—a painting here, books there. I can't hold back my smile at how seamless Liv and Talia seem to be.

"God! Finally, you're here and ready to go! Do you know how long I've been waiting for you?" I look over to see Liv walking down the hallway. She's wearing dark skinny jeans and a cute top that hangs off one shoulder, exposing a tank top underneath.

"I'm so sorry you had to wait to start getting ready until I got here after my two-hour drive." The sarcasm drips from my words.

"Get the fuck over here and give me a hug, bitch!" I do as she asks. We hug briefly before she steps back. "Now, let me see you." She looks me up and down. "Yeah, Sam looks good on you." She winks at me. "I guess he does have a big cock, considering you look completely satisfied."

I gawk at her before my tongue catches up with my brain. "Oh my God. Can we not talk about Sam's, um, cock?" I crinkle my eyes at her.

"Um, excuse me, but you owe me lots of details. Like every single one of them. How big? Is he thick? DETAILS!"

"Liv, you don't even like cock... or men. Why do you want me to give you the details of Sam's," I swallow, "thickness?"

"Because I know you like men and especially like him. I need to know that he's keeping you happy." She gives me this innocent look and bats her eyelashes, her blue eyes twinkling. "I could tell you about my sex life if it makes you feel better."

"I'm not giving you details. You'll just have to live with the knowledge that I'm happy with Sam for as long as he'll have me."

Liv looks as if she's exhausted by me already. Shrugging, she loops her arm in mine as we walk towards the door. "Bye, babe!" she shouts to Talia, who responds in kind as we walk out the door.

***

Liv drives us to a popular shopping area where she insists we'll find "the perfect dress."

We walk into the first place, and I'm skeptical when I see nothing but wedding dresses. "Liv, I'm not getting married. I need a dress for a black-tie event."

She gives me a side eye. "For once in your life, just trust me. She keeps walking towards the back, and I cross my fingers that she knows what she's doing.

We walk through a doorway that opens into a large room with various dresses in a variety of colors and styles.

It looks like prom threw up in here. Liv heads straight for the racks and starts grabbing various dresses.

"Liv, you know I only need a single dress, right?"

She gives me a sidelong glance, and I laugh at her reaction. She rolls her eyes at me before responding, "You have to try out different styles to know what works best with your body. Once we have that down, then we can start looking at different colors and details. We did this for prom; why are you acting like you don't know how to choose a nice dress?"

"Maybe because prom was forever ago, and while you tried on a billion dresses, I saw one I liked and chose it. Then I spent the rest of our shopping day reading a book."

She looks at me with disgust, and I'm laughing again.

"God, I missed you, Liv."

She smiles at me, content. "I missed you, too. Now stop distracting me. We have work to do." I groan internally. This is going to be a long day. I feel it in my bones.

Liv thrusts so many dresses into the arms of the dress shop employee that I only have a second to give the shell-shocked employee an apologetic smile before Liv rushes me into the dressing room.

I lose track of how many dresses I try on before I want to give up and wear a potato sack.

Sorry, Dad, Olivia couldn't stop making me try on dresses, and I was about to end up in prison for murder.

He would understand, right?

I sit down in the dressing room, needing a break in between dresses, and message Sam, hoping he'll save me from this obnoxious fashion show.

Send. Help. Can't. Try. On. Another. Dress.

LOL

You could have stayed here in bed, but you chose to leave me…

I take it back!

Beam me up, Scotty!

If only it were that easy!

How about you give me a sneak peek?

Good try.

Find anything you like?

Not yet,

The guys are glaring at me, so I'd better put my phone away. You've got this! I love you.

Wait, I thought you were sending help to rescue me?

He doesn't respond, so I tuck my phone back into my purse and pull another dress off the hanger.

I don't even look at it as I put it on. I've tried on so many dresses at this point that I feel like a robot. I shuffle my feet as I make my way out of the dressing room.

"Oh my God, Kat. Look at yourself!" She's giddy as I step onto the platform in front of the mirrors that form a half circle so I can see myself from various angles.

I look into the mirrors and feel my heart jump. "Wow," I gasp. "This is gorgeous." My eyes move up and down the length of the dress as I move slightly to adjust the angles.

The cobalt-blue dress is floor-length. The neckline is straight and shows off just the right amount of cleavage while keeping the girls tucked in. The bodice is form-fitting but not so tight that I feel like I can't breathe.

It features a high waistline, which then drapes out and brushes the floor. It drags a bit, so I'll need to wear high heels. *Sam will like that.*

There's a long slit on one side that extends up a little higher than mid-thigh, providing ample airflow in hot weather. I move a bit side to side, testing the slit to make sure I'm not going to embarrass myself by showing too much. It's perfect because the dress overlaps a bit where the slit is.

I step off the platform and walk around the shop, watching the opening in the mirror. It definitely shows my leg in a very sexy way, but it's not so much that I worry about showing other parts.

"It's perfect," gushes Liv.

Stepping back up onto the platform, I can't stop staring at myself. The color somehow makes my green eyes stand out more and gives my skin a tan and flawless appearance. I look at my chestnut hair. It's longer than it's been in a long time and flows a little past my waist.

Pulling my hair over my shoulder, I admire the back of the dress, which is open, showing off my toned back. I bite my bottom lip as I contemplate what to do with my hair. I don't want to cover the back of the dress.

"I think you should wear it in a sort of half-up, half-down style so it sweeps over your shoulder but leaves your back exposed." Liv looks at me contemplatively. "Maybe an intricate braid so it stays in place." I love that she just reads my mind.

"That sounds lovely, but you know I'm terrible at things like that. I'm lucky I know how to put my makeup on." I give her a weary look.

"You should definitely have someone do your hair—and your makeup." She says the last part like she doesn't trust my abilities. That's fair. I guess.

"I don't know anyone I trust in Charleston."

"I do. I'll give her a heads-up and pass on her number to you. She'll be perfect." Liv's tone is soft, and I detect a hint of awe as she continues to look at me. "I've missed you, Kat. I know we talk all the time, but it isn't the same. I'm sad I won't be there with you to see you all dolled up."

I step off the platform and walk over to her, taking her hands in mine. "I'll send you so many pictures. I'll even send you pics while my hair and makeup are getting done. I'm going to send you so many that you'll feel like you're there with me. Always know that even if I'm not with you physically, I'm always with you. You're my best friend. You should have thought about this much sooner, because there is no getting rid of me." I smile big. "Thank you for helping me today."

"You mean thank you for dragging your ass here and making you find a dress that you look hot as hell in? You're welcome." She shimmies her shoulders a bit as she turns around. "Now we need to find some shoes."

I look around the place again. There are no shoes in sight.

"Oh, not here." Liv looks back at me as if I had spoken my thoughts aloud. "We have another stop to make." I groan at the thought.

Chapter 44

By the time we find the perfect shoes—silver stilettos with a delicate strap that goes around my ankle—I realize it's already time to meet Talia for dinner.

I don't know how Liv can shop for so long. I'm starving, and I'm getting hangry. We get into Liv's car and make our way to the restaurant.

"Ok, Miss Grumpy Pants, what's eating you?"

"Too much shopping. Can't function anymore. Need food."

"Aww, poor baby," she laughs. "Thanks for letting me do this. I know this isn't your thing, Kat. But it was so fun for me, and I loved spending the day with you."

"Aw, Liv, don't go getting all mushy on me." I push her arm teasingly and giggle. "I'm glad we got to spend the day together. We need to make plans to spend more weekends together. I can't go several months without seeing you in person again." I grab her hand and give it a little squeeze, which she returns.

We pull up to the restaurant, and Liv hands the keys over to the valet. It isn't a fancy place, but the parking is terrible.

"Talia is already inside, and she has a table for us."

"Bless that woman!" I look up to the sky in jest.

We find Talia and join her at the table.

"I'm just going to message Sam real quick."

"And how are things going with loverboy?" Talia gives me a knowing look.

"Very well, I think." I pull out my phone and focus on my message to Sam.

> I found a dress. And shoes. I think you'll like them.

Aw, you got me shoes? But, Kat, I don't wear high heels.

I snort at his message and look up to Liv and Talia staring at me. I wave them off.

> Shoes for me, silly boy.

Oh, thank god.

I'm glad you found something you like. I can't wait to see it.

Would it be weird if I told you I've missed you today? I know I just saw you this morning.

> I've missed you, too.

I swear I can still taste you and it's making me miss you more. Especially that sweet cunt of yours.

My face flushes and heat surges to my core as I reread his message. Liv and Talia are looking at me again, and I drop my eyes in embarrassment.

I put my phone away and look up at Liv and Talia, who are still staring at me with expectant gazes. "How long have you been staring at me?" I accuse.

Talia is quick to respond, "Long enough to know that whatever you were texting Sam caused you to blush."

"And long enough to know you are in deeeeep with that man." Liv raises an eyebrow at me.

"I think I am. I don't even know what to say, but I am in deep." I grimace as I look down at the menu in front of me.

"So why do you look terrified right now?"

"I'm not terrified," I'm quick to answer. *Am I terrified? Maybe. A little.* "It's just a lot to take in sometimes. I've been in love with him for so long, and to know he loves me, too? It feels like I'm on the precipice of something huge.

"Like I have to jump off of this massive cliff, and if I do, the bottom will either be the best thing I've ever done in my life, or it'll kill me."

I take a moment to compose my thoughts by taking a long drink of my water.

"Sam is everything I ever hoped he would be and more. And sometimes that scares me."

"What scares you about it?" Talia's voice is soft as she leans back in her seat.

"What if he doesn't feel the same way I do?" My knee involuntarily starts bouncing under the table, and I chew on my bottom lip.

"That's always the scariest part about falling in love." Liv looks at Talia as she speaks. "Jumping—knowing it will either break you or somehow make you whole." Talia smiles at Liv and dips her head in embarrassment. Liv turns her attention back to me. "But the turmoil leading to the jump? It's the worst kind of torture."

Liv raises Talia's hand and kisses the back. "You have to decide, Kat. Either you embrace the fear and jump, knowing the possibility is huge, or you continue living in fear, knowing greatness will never come to fruition."

"Sounds so poetic when you put it like that."

Talia's the one who responds, "Love is poetic. In the best and worst of ways."

I think about what they both said while we look over the menu and the server takes our orders. I'm still thinking about whether I'm brave enough to jump off the cliff while we eat and when we return to the condo.

I know how it feels to love Sam and watch him choose someone else.

I know what it feels like to love Sam and lose him. And that was all before I ever actually had him.

Now? I'm not sure I could survive the jump.

***

I'm lying in my old bed when I finally call Sam.

"Hey, beautiful, how was your day?" He sounds happy, and I detect the slight slurring of his words.

"Too much shopping." I chuckle. "But I had a good day. How about you?"

"It was great. We mostly played poker and drank all day."

"Just how much drinking did you do, Sammy?" I try to keep my tone teasing.

"Just enough to still remember my name," he laughs at his own joke.

I'm worried about him. "Are you home?" I sit up in bed unable to lie down until I know he's safe.

"Yeah, I ordered a ride. I'll have to go pick up my bike tomorrow morning. The problem is, you aren't here, and all I want to do is snuggle up to you so I can smell your lavender hair."

"Lavender hair?" *Oh my God, drunk Sam is excellent.*

"Yeah, my love. Your hair smells like lavender. I really like it."

I try to hold back my giggle. "What else do you want to do?" I just want to know what he'll say in his drunken state.

"I want to soak my cock with your pussy. I want to taste myself on your lips. I want to fuck you so hard you can't walk tomorrow." His voice, still drunk, goes husky with desire.

I want all those things, too. But my conversation with Liv and Talia comes rushing back, and I feel like I can't breathe. I want to jump, but what if Sam doesn't want the same thing?

"Kat? You still there?"

Realizing I haven't said anything for long enough, Sam must think the call dropped, so I quickly say, "All of that sounds great, Sam."

"Kat? What's wrong?" He suddenly sounds sober.

Trying to recover so he doesn't detect my insecurities, I quickly respond, "Nothing. I miss you, is all."

"I miss you, too." He doesn't sound convinced.

I'm not convinced either.

"What time will you be heading back tomorrow?"

"Liv and Talia want to get brunch, so I'll leave after that. Are you going to be there?"

"I'll be impatiently waiting for you at home." He yawns, and I realize how tired I feel.

"I guess it's time to get some sleep." I don't want to hang up, but I'm not sure I can stay on the phone with him either. My feelings are too tangled up, and I don't want him digging into them right now.

He must detect my off tone because when he responds, his words sound strained. "Yeah, ok. I hope you sleep well, Kat." He takes a brief pause before adding, "I love you." It comes out almost like a question.

"I love you, too, Sammy. Goodnight." My voice is too quiet.

"Goodnight." He sounds sad, and I hate that I've ruined his mood. I hang up before I can say anything more.

There's no stopping the tears that stream down my cheeks. The last several months have been riddled with so many high emotions, and I almost feel like I haven't processed anything.

I went from trying to avoid everyone to relying on Liv to get me through, then moving home and throwing myself into my new job, all while avoiding the fact that I'm living in my brother's condo because he's no longer there.

Then, when Sam moved back to Charleston, I threw myself into him. I know that with Sam, I'm scared he'll break my already broken heart.

I curl up under the blankets and allow myself to feel all the things I've been holding back.

The loss of Ethan is overwhelming, and I let the tears fall.

I let the pain soak into my bones and overtake me.

It isn't long before Liv quietly walks into my room and climbs under the blankets with me. She lies next to me, gently stroking my hair. She doesn't say anything, just lets me know she's here while I let the tears fall until there's nothing left.

Chapter 45

I'm not sure when I fell asleep, but I wake up to the sun shining through the blinds. I roll over to find the bed empty; Liv must have gone to her bed after I finally fell asleep.

I see my phone on the bed next to me; the battery is dead. Getting out of bed, I locate my phone charger and plug the cord in. Climbing back under the covers, I plug my phone in and lie there, staring at the dark screen until it turns on.

When it does, I see it's already 9:00 a.m. I haven't slept this late in years. I suppose all that crying left me exhausted. I check my messages app to say good morning to Sam, only to find a few messages he sent last night.

> Hey, I'm not sure what happened, but I feel like you're upset.

> Did I do something wrong?

> I'm here if you want to talk.

> Sleep well, my love.

I didn't mean to make him feel bad or to worry about me. I send him a quick message back.

I forgot to plug my phone in, and it died. I just woke up and didn't see your messages until now.

I'm not upset with you. I think I was just feeling overstimulated from all the shopping and socializing yesterday.

His response is almost instantaneous.

I hope you slept well. I can't wait to see you.

I can't wait to see you.

Are you sure you're ok?

Yeah. I'm sorry for worrying you. I love you.

I love you too. Have fun at brunch. Text me when you're heading this way, ok?

Trying to lighten the mood, I message back:

Yes, Mother Hen.

I laugh to myself and wait for his response.

You love it.

I do love it. And you.

See you in a few hours!

Liv walks in and stops when she sees me watching her. "Hey, I wasn't sure if you'd be awake, so I was just trying to quietly check on you."

"I just woke up a few minutes ago." Liv's expression is tight, concerned. "Thanks for last night, and sorry for basically freaking out."

"Don't ever apologize for that." Liv's words are soft, but she's using her no-bullshit tone. "Kat, you've been through hell the last several months, and it's ok to have ups and downs. No one expects you to be over it."

"I don't think I'll ever be over Ethan not being here." My voice cracks, and I furiously wipe at the tears streaming down my face. "Sometimes it feels ok, and other times—I'm not sure how I'm supposed to continue living like it doesn't matter. Like... like he didn't matter. Like *he* doesn't matter."

Liv sits down on the bed next to me and holds my hand. "I think that's the problem, babe. You aren't supposed to live like he doesn't matter, but you are supposed to *live*. Some days will be hard. Some hours, some minutes will feel like the world is crushing you. It's ok to take some time for yourself during those times. And I am *always* here to talk or just listen."

"I know, Liv. Thank you."

"No, I mean it. Even if you just want to call me while you cry. I'll sit on the phone with you, so you don't feel alone. I'll stay on the phone with you until you fall asleep, or while you go grocery shopping, or while you eat. And I'll drive to Charleston on the weekends, or you can come here if you feel like the condo is too suffocating. I'm here. Always."

"How did I get so lucky having you as a friend?" I smile at her through my tears.

"I'm not even sure. But you must have done something to make the reincarnation gods happy in your last life." She winks at me, and I laugh. "You ok, babe? Do you want to stay in, and we can make breakfast?"

I lean my head on her shoulder. "I'm ok. I think last night was just a poor combination of too much peopling and feeling overwhelmed about Ethan and Sam. I'd love to go to brunch if you and Talia are still up for it?"

"Definitely still up for it. But seriously, no pressure if you'd rather stay in."

"No, let's go." I start to get out of bed. "But I want a shower before we do anything else."

"Ok. Freshen up, and we'll leave when you're ready." Liv hugs me and kisses me on the cheek. "Everything's going to work out with Sam. Just remember to trust your heart, and don't let your head get in the way too much." I smile slightly at her words and watch her walk out.

***

I hurry to get ready for the day and pack up my car before we go to brunch at one of our favorite places. I'm feeling better as we say our goodbyes, and I head back to Charleston. I spend the two-hour drive listening to music and singing along to my favorite songs.

I make it back to Charleston around 2:30 p.m., and Sam is waiting for me. I spot the pink tulips and white calla lilies, my favorites, on the counter. Dropping my bags by the front door, I immediately walk into his arms, letting his warmth seep into me.

We stand there in each other's embrace for several minutes when Sam whispers in my ear, "Do you want to talk about what's bothering you?" His words are soft. He's not accusing, just concerned.

I lean back and look into his face. Sam's chocolate brown eyes are sad, distant, and he has small dark circles; I wonder if he didn't sleep well.

I take a deep breath before responding, "I guess I just have bad days still with Ethan. I miss him, and being back in Columbia made me realize how much has changed over the last several months. It was overwhelming last night."

He pulls me tight against him again and kisses my temple. "I've been worried." He kisses my temple again. "I've felt some distance from you. I know you're used to having Liv be the only person you go to. I don't want to push you to talk about things if you aren't ready. I just want you to know I am here, too. Whenever you want to talk. I'm here."

I bury my face into his chest and tighten my grip around his waist. My body wracks with the sobs I can't seem to contain. He runs his hand through my hair as his other hand tightens on my back.

I breathe in his cologne and let his pine and salty sea air scent calm me. "I know, Sam. I'm sorry I've been distant." I step away from him. Sam reaches up and gently swipes away the tears remaining on my cheeks.

He picks up the flowers on the counter and hands them to me. They are already in a simple, clear cylindrical vase. "They're beautiful," I lean into them and breathe in their scent, "and smell so good!" I take the few steps over to the coffee table and set the flowers in the center.

"I'm glad you like them." He walks over to my bags and picks them up with one hand. Walking towards me, he holds out his other hand, which I take, and Sam leads me into the bedroom we've been sharing.

Once inside the room, he places the bags on the floor, holding up the garment bag that carries my formal dress, and gives it a little shake. "You gonna give me a little fashion show in this dress you picked out?" He gives me a confident smile that causes my core to clench in anticipation. *I want that wicked mouth on me.*

"Nope." I smile innocently back. "You're gonna have to be patient because I'm not showing you until the night of the party."

He gives me a wounded look, and I laugh. "Hmmm. Well, I suppose I'll have to find something else for us to do before our dinner reservation." He walks over to the closet to hang up my dress.

"Dinner reservation?"

"Well, not a typical reservation. I hope you don't mind, but I have no plans on sharing you with anyone else tonight. I ordered food and scheduled it to be delivered at 5:30." Sam looks at me with some hesitancy before adding, "My plan was for you to give me a little fashion show, and then I planned to make good on my promise last night to fuck you until you couldn't walk tomorrow."

I stand there stunned at how easily this man takes me from bawling to overheating so quickly.

He shrugs and fakes exasperation, "I suppose I'm just going to have to skip the seeing you in a pretty dress part and start with dessert first." I feel the warmth spread through me at his words, and my core soaks in anticipation.

"Dessert?" It comes out breathless, almost a moan.

Sam doesn't say anything, just gives me a meaningful look. He walks to me, lifts me with ease, and slams his mouth to mine. I wrap my legs around him and deepen the kiss. He walks us over to our bed, breaking our kiss as he sets me down. I groan in protest, and he chuckles. He looks at me, asking for permission.

I reach for the button on Sam's jeans and begin tugging them down. Finally getting them undone, they drop to the floor, where he steps out of them. Sam tugs his T-shirt over his head and reaches for my shirt, pulling it over my head with ease. I stand up and pull my leggings down. I step out of them as Sam's gaze shifts to my bare bottom half.

"No panties?"

"Nope." I pop the p and move back onto the bed.

Sam removes his boxer briefs so quickly that he almost trips over them. I quickly hide my laugh at his blunder.

He climbs over me on the bed and takes his time with his dessert.

By the time dinner arrives, I'm exhausted. My body aches in the best of ways, and I'm confident my legs will be shaking if I try to walk on them right now.

At the sound of the doorbell, I start to get up, but Sam motions for me to stay. He tugs on a pair of grey sweatpants and walks out to greet the delivery person. He comes back in carrying the food and two trays that look like they were made for eating in bed.

"You weren't joking about ensuring I couldn't walk after, huh?" My voice is incredulous.

"I never joke about sex, Kitty Kat." The corners of his eyes crinkle as he gives me a mischievous smile that makes my body heat—ready for more.

Chapter 46

I've spent too much time in this chair getting my hair and makeup done. But looking at my reflection in the mirror? Worth it! My makeup is subtle enough that I still look like me, but my best features are enhanced. My hair is in an intricate braid that pulls my hair over one shoulder.

I get into my car and drive back to my place so I can get dressed. The condo is empty when I walk in. I'm not surprised, but it still feels unsettling. I've gotten so used to Sam being around when I'm home.

Sam wanted to make this feel like an official date, so he's getting ready at his dad's house and then picking me up when it's time to go.

I have about thirty minutes to finish getting ready before he's here. I blast pop music on the speakers to get me into the party mood. Once I have my dress on, I decide an impromptu dance session is necessary. I sway my hips to the music and sing along at the top of my voice.

I'm startled when I turn around and see Sam standing in the doorway of our room, watching me, his eyes are big as he drinks me in, his dimple making an appearance as he smiles widely. He makes me feel like the most beautiful woman in the world.

"Oh God! You scared me!" I clutch my hand to my chest as my heart rate slows back down.

Sam is wearing a black tux and a white button-down shirt that appears to have been made for him. His tux hugs his muscles in all the right places. His black bowtie makes him look debonair, and when my gaze shifts to his cobalt blue pocket square, I can't help but smile. Liv must have told him the color of my dress.

"You are absolutely stunning." His voice is thick and husky as he leans on the doorframe.

"Yeah? You look pretty amazing yourself." Sam in a tux? *Fuck me.* I pull my bottom lip in between my teeth and watch his gaze shift to my mouth.

Sam walks up to me slowly and stops when he's so close I'm forced to look up at him. He gently pulls my lip from my teeth. "I want to bite that lip." He bends down and barely brushes his lips against mine before taking two steps back.

I'm disappointed at his chaste kiss.

He must sense my thoughts because he answers my unasked question, "I want to do wicked things with that mouth of yours," he looks me up and down, slowly, "and the rest of you, for that matter, but," Sam sighs, "we have a party to get to, and what I have in mind will take more than just a few minutes and would ruin that hair and makeup you just paid for." He reaches his hand out to me. "Shall we?"

I've lost the ability to speak with his words, so I opt for nodding and taking his hand. We stop by the front door, where I left my high heels, and I put them on. I'm still several inches shorter than he is, even with the height from my shoes.

"Turn for me so I can get the full effect." He motions the action with his finger. A grin spreads across my face, and I oblige.

He stops me with gentle hands on my shoulders when my back is towards him. He moves in, and I feel his warm breath at the nape of my neck. He trails soft kisses down my spine, and I shiver at the touch.

"I don't know how I'm going to keep my hands off of you all night," he groans into my back as he trails kisses back up to my neck.

"Then don't." My voice is a challenge, and he groans in response.

"I think both of our dads would be very disappointed if I'm groping you all night in front of their clients and friends." He gently turns me so I'm facing him and once again holds out his hand for me, which I take in mine. He wraps his hand around mine, places my arm in his, and we walk outside.

When we get to his SUV, he opens my door with a little bow. "My lady."

"Ever the gentleman." I smile at him. He helps me in and kisses my hand before walking to the other side and getting into the driver's seat.

As soon as his seatbelt is fastened and he's started the vehicle, Sam places a hand on my leg and gives it a gentle squeeze. My brain short-circuits as his thumb draws slow circles on my thigh.

By the time we make it to the event location, my body is tingling from his touch, and it takes everything in me to refrain from demanding he take me back home. I remain sitting as he gets out, walks over to my door, and helps me out. He wraps my arm around his, leans over, and kisses the top of my head before leading us the rest of the way to the outdoor event.

I'm in awe at the size of this party. Around 30 large round tables line the vast dance floor, while several large white canopies are scattered around the perimeter of the event space. Long tables with appetizers and desserts, and makeshift bars are under each of the canopies.

String lights hang over the entire space, and I can't wait to see everything once the sun goes down. It's gorgeous, and if I didn't know any better, I would think we were attending a large wedding.

Sam's voice interrupts my thoughts as he leans down and quietly speaks, "They didn't hold back, did they?"

"I guess not. I can't imagine how much this costs, but," I look up at Sam, "it's beautiful."

He looks down at me, his smile lights up his eyes. "Yes, you are."

"Such a charmer," I tease. I look away and see Mom and Dad chatting with some people I don't recognize. I nod in their direction, "Well, should we go say hi?"

"Sure. You gotta make sure they see you're here." He winks at me, and we make our way over to them.

Mom sees me first; her face morphs into a huge smile as she puts her hand over her heart. "You look incredible, pretty girl." She shifts her attention to Sam, "Wow, you clean up nice!" She hugs him first. When she hugs me, Mom whispers, "Look at you two."

When she pulls away, I give her a look that I hope conveys "don't start." She just smiles in response.

Once Dad finishes his conversation, he turns his attention to us. "You both look great." He pulls me into a quick hug, "I'm glad you're here, Kat. Sam," Dad looks down at our interlaced fingers, "it's great to have you here with her."

What is going on with these two?

He gives Sam one of those bro hugs where they clasp hands and pat each other on the back with the other.

Dan walks up and gives Sam a knowing look. "Son, glad to see you. Kat, wow."

"Thanks. Now," I look at the glasses in our parents' hands, "I think I need a drink to make it through this." I grimace a little and look towards one of the bars. "Shall we?" I look up at Sam, who nods in agreement.

"Everything ok with your parents?" Sam says quietly as we walk away.

"You noticed that, too?" My eyes are big when I look up at him.

"Yeah. Are they freaked out by us dating?"

"They haven't said anything, but," based on what Mom whispered to me, "I think they're happy for us."

Sam gently lifts my hand and brings it to his lips.

We both get drinks and mingle until dinner is announced, right at 6:00 p.m. *Leave it to a bunch of lawyers to ensure everything is on schedule.* I chuckle at the thought and wave at nothing when Sam inquires.

Sam and I make our way around the tables until we find our names at one of them, indicating where we should sit. We aren't at the same table as either of our parents, and I'm grateful for that.

I recognize one client I've worked with a little at our table and make small talk as servers in white shirts and black slacks place plates on the table in front of each person.

Each guest was asked to indicate whether they wanted fish or steak as their entree when they sent in their RSVP. I chose the salmon and Sam the steak.

The chatter at the table continues as we all eat our meals. Our wine glasses are constantly replenished, and despite eating while drinking, I know if I have much more alcohol, I will quickly be tipsy.

I look over at Sam, who notices the water glass in my hand. He leans over to me and whispers in my ear, "You ok?"

"Yeah, just feeling a bit tipsy. The water should help."

By the time the multiple-course meal is finished, a live band plays a variety of slow and fast songs, and the dance floor slowly begins to fill up.

"Will you dance with me, Kat?" I'm not sure about dancing in these shoes, but Sam's face looks so earnest that there's no way I can turn him down.

"I would love to."

Chapter 47

S am leads us around the dance floor in rhythm to the slow dance the band is playing. He looks down at me and smiles so big I see the dimple in his left cheek.

He leans down and whispers in my ear, "This reminds me of homecoming the year you were supposed to go with Kevin."

"Yeah?"

"I was so nervous to ask you to dance with me. My palms were so sweaty I thought for sure you were going to notice." He looks at me, a little embarrassed. "I had to hype myself up to ask you. Then, when Ethan went off to dance with Kayla, I knew that was my moment. I thought I was going to trip over my feet the entire time."

"Really? You were so smooth. I was so worried you would hear my heart pounding in my chest. I thought you were so hot in your suit. I loved how your hair was a little messy from running your hands through it. I was so nervous I was going to step on your feet."

"That was one of the best nights of my life." He takes a deep breath. "Because of you." He smiles at me, and I can feel the love radiating off him.

"Mine too." I smile back.

"I was thinking," his fingers fidget along my spine as he speaks, "what if I moved in. You know, officially?"

I feel the shock hit my face before I can school my expression. I know he catches my body stiffening at his words.

"It's just, I'm there so much anyway, I thought—" Sam abruptly stops talking and looks away from me.

I'm feeling panicked at his words. Move in? Yeah, he's there all the time, and I want him to stay, but the thought of taking that next step makes me feel nauseous. "I—" *What if he decides to leave? What happens when he doesn't want me anymore?*

He takes a step away from me, and his voice is quiet when he speaks again. "Unless you want something different? Maybe I've been reading this all wrong, and you don't want me to be there as much? Or at all?"

His voice is flat. My tongue feels like lead in my mouth. But I finally whisper out, "I *do* want you there."

"I've just felt like you've been holding back from me. I'm so deeply in love with you, and sometimes it feels like you have one foot out the door. I can't figure out why." He looks at me, anguished.

"Sam, I..." I look into his eyes, searching for answers I won't find from him, but knowing he's right. I have been holding back. Protecting my heart from this man who broke it once before.

He takes another step back, dropping his hands from my waist and running one through his hair.

It's at this moment that I realize while I've been trying to protect my heart, I've been breaking his. I reach out for him and pull him back into me.

"Don't go."

"I don't want to leave. But I can't continue giving you everything I have and only get half of you in return." I'd do anything to remove the pain from him. "If I'm not what you want anymore, I need you to be honest with me. I need you to tell me what you want."

"I want you." My words are soft, barely above a whisper.

"Do you?" The skepticism in his tone matches his expression. "Why are you holding back?"

"I'm scared." The too-loud words are out before I can think to stop them.

I take his hand and pull him off the dance floor, finding a quiet place for us to sit at the edge of the party. I gesture for him to sit next to me; I'm relieved when he does.

"Sammy, I've spent my entire adult life comparing all of my partners to you." I take in a deep breath and blow it out. I look down at my fingers, fidgeting in my lap. "After I begged you to choose me instead of Claire, I just never got over it. I—" I look out at the dance floor and see all the happy faces. "I never got over *you*." I look up at Sam to find him watching me, his eyes are downturned in regret.

"I'm so sorry. I wish I could rewind and take it all back. I never meant to hurt you like that."

I grab his hand and gently stroke my thumb along his. "I know that now. You've shown me so much love these last few months."

"But?" I can feel the worry coming off him, like he's afraid he won't like the answer.

"But," I start slowly, "I'm terrified I won't recover if you break my heart again."

He looks like I've stabbed him in the chest, but he doesn't say anything.

"You're right. I've been holding back. Not because I'm not in love with you. Because I am. Sam," I gently cup his cheek with my palm and turn his face, so he is fully looking at me, "I'm so deeply in love with you. To the point that I already know I won't recover if you decide you want something or *someone* else."

I drop my hand from his cheek and look briefly at the dancing couples before returning my attention to him.

"So, I've been holding back to hang on to the last shreds of my heart. Trying to protect whatever parts aren't already yours because I'm terrified to lose you again."

He shifts next to me as his expression softens. "Kat, I'm not going anywhere. I don't want anyone but you. I've never wanted anyone but you." Sam looks down at the ground. "Even when I was dating Claire. I stupidly thought that being with her would somehow get you out of my every thought." He looks back up at me. "I've been yours long before Seattle.

"My entire heart has been yours since we were kids." Sam reaches for my hands and holds them in his. "Why do you think I stayed with you at that dance? It wasn't just because you were Ethan's sister. I saw you. I saw the look on your face when you realized Kevin wasn't coming. And it ruined me. I couldn't bear seeing you distraught."

I lean in and place a soft kiss on his lips, which he gently returns.

"Kat, it killed me when Ethan told me to stay away from you. My heart was shredded when you dated Kevin after that. It cracked again when you were so torn up after he broke up with you. And then, after I realized how much I hurt you with Claire? I haven't told you this, but I haven't had a serious relationship since I broke things off with her."

"Really? Why?" I don't hold back the shock in my tone.

He shrugs a little like he's going to sidestep the question, but then his expression quickly changes to what I can only describe as determination.

"I could have. I dated, but my heart already belonged to someone else." He looks at me with such gentleness, and I see the vulnerability on his face and in his rigid body. "It belonged to you."

Kat, I love you. Always have. Always will.

Tears sting in the corners of my eyes when Sam reaches up and softly cups my cheeks with his palms.

Hoping Liv and Talia were right, I jump off the cliff.

"I'm all yours, Sam. Every part of me is yours. I'm sorry I've been holding back from you. I promise I won't do that anymore."

He kisses my cheeks, my forehead, and then my mouth. His kiss starts gently and then turns into something more feral. Hungry.

I open my mouth for him, letting him deepen the kiss. Our tongues explore each other. Our kiss is an apology, a forgiveness, and a promise.

He pulls away too soon and looks around, embarrassed. I follow his gaze, remembering where we are. He leans his forehead against mine and looks into my eyes. He looks like he wants to devour me, and I want him to.

"If you keep looking at me like that, I'm going to have to find a place behind the bushes to take you," he growls.

"Is that a promise, Samuel Harris?" My tone is teasing, but I would let him if that's what he wants. I would let him do almost anything to me right now.

"Fuck, Kat." He runs his hand through his hair and then looks back to the crowd gathered on the dance floor. He stands up and holds his hand out to me. "Come on, I still need to dance with you. But when we get home, I'm going to ravage you while you wear that dress." His eyes twinkle with his barely restrained desire.

"You promise?" My voice is full of heat as I think of what's in store for me later.

He chuckles before responding, "I promise."

I take his hand and allow him to pull me up. He kisses my hand before he positions my arm, so it's wrapped around his as he guides us back to the dance floor.

"Sam?"

"Hmmm?"

"I want you to move in. Officially."

He steps back from me and looks into my eyes. "Are you sure? I don't want you to feel rushed."

"I'm sure. Please move in." He leans in and brushes his lips across my cheek.

Sam pulls me into him and guides us in a slow dance. I can't resist leaning my head on his shoulder.

He tenderly kisses the top of my head. "Ok. I'll move in."

I move closer to him, and we continue dancing.

"Sam?"

"Yes, Kat?"

"You still have furniture and stuff in storage, right?" I look up at him.

Sam looks down at me quizzically. "Yes?" It's more of a question than a statement.

"I've been thinking that I want to donate Ethan's furniture. Maybe start fresh. Could we use your things instead?"

"We could..." he draws out the words. "I was thinking we should pick some things out together. That way it isn't mine or yours but ours."

I smile at him. "I would love that."

"I love *you*."

"Promise?"

"Promise." He kisses my lips gently, and I open for him.

The scariest part was the jump. But knowing that Sam is jumping with me? I don't feel as scared.

***

*S*ix Years Old

"Hey, Kitty Kat." Sam walks outside. It's summer, and it's already warming up fast.

"Hi, Sammy." I look back down at my Barbies and continue playing with them.

"Can I play with you? Ethan isn't feeling well, and I'm tired of playing Mario."

"Sure! Do you want to be Ken?"

"Okay." Sam sits down across from me and grabs one of my Ken dolls.

I'm playing with Malibu Barbie because she's my favorite.

"Do you think Barbie and Ken will get married?"

"Probably." Sam shrugs as he responds.

"I think Barbie would be so pretty in a wedding dress. Should we throw them a wedding?"

"Sure. Do you have any fancy clothes for them? Ken should be wearing a nice suit if he's going to marry Barbie."

"Yeah. Let me find it."

I stand up and walk over to my pink and orange polka-dot case, where I keep my Barbie and Ken outfits. I find the wedding dress and the suit and walk back to where Sam sits. I hand him Ken's outfit and work on changing Barbie into her dress.

"Ok, Ken should stand over there, and then Barbie can walk down the aisle."

Sam moves Ken where I tell him, and then I make Barbie walk to where Sam makes Ken stand. "Ken, do you take this woman to be your wife?"

"I do," Sam speaks for Ken.

"Now you have to ask for Barbie."

"Barbie, do you take this man to be your husband?" Sam asks.

"I do," I speak for Barbie.

"Now do they kiss?"

"Duh." I move Barbie over to Ken and position her so he can kiss her. Sam makes Ken kiss Barbie and smacks his lips to make a kissing noise. I laugh at the sound.

"I don't know if I'll ever get married." My voice is small as I look down at Barbie.

"Why not, Kitty Kat?"

"Because I don't think my husband will want to play Barbies with me."

"I'll marry you, Kitty Kat, and we can play Barbies when Ethan is sick."

Chapter 48

One Year Later

I'm on the back of Sam's motorcycle with my arms wrapped around his waist. It's funny to think that just over a year ago, I was terrified to get on his bike.

He keeps trying to convince me to drive it, and I'm just not ready for that. Besides, I love the feeling of my thighs hugging his. I love snuggling into him as he drives.

If I were driving, I couldn't run my hands along his thighs or up and down his chest. Every time I do it, I feel him shiver in response.

I love how he reacts to my touch.

Tonight, we're going back to Folly Beach for another picnic. Sam and I frequently make the twenty-minute drive so we can sit on the beach and watch the sunset.

I feel a bit warm in my motorcycle jacket, but I snuggle into his back a little more and tighten my arms around him. I smile when I feel Sam's gloved hand run up and down my arm and briefly pat my gloved hands before returning to his handlebar.

Sam parks close to our favorite spot and turns off the engine. We both climb off and take off our helmets, jackets, and gloves. He locks the helmets to his bike, as he always does, and picks up the backpack from the floor, where I'd discarded it to take off my jacket, slinging it over his shoulder.

I hold out my hand to him, and he takes it, bringing it to his mouth and planting a soft kiss on the back before leading us onto the beach.

We're silent as we walk to our favorite spot—the perfect position to see the water and the sun as it falls behind the city.

My mind strays to our first proper date almost a year ago. I was extremely nervous about our relationship at the time. I was so afraid that Sam would break my heart again.

But now here we are a year later, and I couldn't be more in love with this gorgeous man.

Sam is everything I always dreamed he would be and more.

Every day, he shows me what it means to be loved, and I couldn't be more grateful for him.

"Penny for your thoughts?" Sam looks at me over his shoulder.

"I was just thinking about our first *proper* date and how scared I was to get on your bike." I beam up at him.

"Still scared?" He smirks, and I feel my knees go weak.

"No," I answer, quickly and honestly. "I trust you, and I love riding with you."

His smile is so big, his eyes crinkle. "Good. You know what? That was a great night."

"It ended even better than it started." I wink at him before settling into the blanket he pulled out of the backpack and laid down for us.

"Maybe we should have a repeat." His voice is husky, and it sends sparks into my core.

"Mmmm. I definitely think we should have a repeat. But first, I'm starving. What did you bring to eat?" I reach for the backpack, but he gets to it first.

"Turkey sandwiches, pasta salad, and some lemonade."

"Sounds great."

Sam pulls out some plates and serves the food, then hands me a plate and a bottle of lemonade.

"Thanks, love."

He leans over and kisses my cheek before taking a bite of his food.

We both eat in silence as we watch the waves crash into the sand. When we're finished eating, he tugs me over to him, wrapping his arm around my shoulders.

His body feels tense next to mine, and I'm about to ask him about it when he suddenly stands up. Holding his hand out to me, he looks down with an expression I can't quite place. "Walk with me?" His voice is deeper than usual.

My stomach is in knots and I'm regretting eating so much. But whatever this is, I need to embrace it. Steeling my nerves, I take Sam's hand and let him pull me up.

He starts to walk, but I pull him back into my arms. I get on my tiptoes and brush my lips against his. He kisses me back, wrapping one arm around my waist and gently gripping my neck with his other hand.

I run my tongue along his lips—a silent request for him to deepen our kiss. The way he responds to me helps calm my nerves.

I'm panting when he breaks our kiss. My eyes fixed on his, I see the fire in his gaze. I want him to take me back home, but he pulls me up to the water, where we walk along the beach a short distance from our picnic site.

The sun is setting as he stops along the water. He turns to face me. Still holding one of my hands in his, he reaches into his pocket and pulls something out before dropping to one knee.

I can't breathe.

This can't be happening.

"Sam—" it's little more than a whisper.

He has a small black box in his hand, and he's looking at me in a way that makes me feel like the most loved person in the universe. But I also detect the nerves he's trying to mask.

He clears his throat before speaking, "Kat, I've loved you for almost my entire life. You've been my friend. My confidant. My lover. There is no one else in this world that I want by my side.

My entire heart, my body, and my soul belong to you. I would be honored if I could call you mine for the rest of our lives."

He lets go of my hand and opens the box slowly, revealing a gold band with a square emerald in the center surrounded by small diamonds. *It's beautiful.*

My breath catches when recognition hits me, and I feel the sting of the tears forming in my eyes as I look down at him.

This man, who holds my entire heart in his hands, and the ring he's offering me.

Sam's voice is gentle and hopeful as he continues, "Katherine Emily Oaks, will you marry me?" I look into his hopeful chocolate brown eyes and see how nervous he is, as if he thinks I would ever say no to him. My heart feels like it'll burst at any minute.

I pull him up so he's standing in front of me. "Yes. A thousand times, yes," I gush. I watch as his features shift from nervous to elated.

He gently runs his thumb against my cheek and wipes away my silent tears before I can't take the distance anymore and roughly pull him into my arms.

Sam kisses the top of my head, my hair, my cheeks, and then finally my mouth.

He kisses me like a drowning man, and I'm his life raft—desire pools between my thighs.

He pulls away, and it takes everything in me to let him. Sam takes the ring out of the box and places it on my left ring finger.

I'm turning into a puddle when he pulls my hand up to his mouth and kisses the ring, and then kisses the back of my hand. "I love you so much, Kat."

"I love you." I look down at the ring, admiring it. "Sammy, your mom's ring is beautiful. Are you sure about this?" I look back at him, trying to gauge his response. "The ring, I mean?"

"Yes," he answers without hesitation. "She would have loved that it's you."

I wipe away the tear that trickles down his cheek. Placing my hands on either side of his face, I gently pull him down to me and kiss him, trying to send all of the love I have for this man to him through this kiss.

Epilogue

Three Years Later

Sam –

I haven't been able to sleep all night. Instead, I've been staring at my gorgeous wife and our adorable son.

He's perfect—ten fingers, ten toes, and a head full of blonde hair.

When the nurses offered to take him for the night, I insisted that he needed to sleep with me. So here I am, sitting on this god-awful hospital chair, with this perfect, tiny human on my chest.

Despite the uncomfortable seating options, I can't resist smiling at my baby boy.

A few weeks ago, I read that newborns like to be skin-to-skin. Kat laughed when I tugged my shirt off earlier, but he seemed pretty comfortable to me, so we spent almost the entire night with his tiny bare body against my naked chest—a blanket covering his back, so he doesn't get cold.

I finally put my shirt back on and put on his blue and white checkered sleeper onesie when the temperature in the room dropped.

I don't hold back my smile as I look over at Kat, fast asleep. Watching her bring our son into this world was the most fascinating and terrifying experience. I wanted to take her pain away. But she's strong. Never gives up.

And I still can't believe she's mine.

It took us a long time to reach this point. I know what my life was like without her, and it isn't something I want to experience ever again.

My son stirs in my arms; I want Kat to keep resting, so I stand up and walk out of the room, quietly closing the door behind me.

I walk the hallways with my perfect boy in my arms, memories of the last couple of years with Kat drifting through my mind.

We still live in the same condo, but I've spent the last couple of months turning the spare room into a nursery. I painted the walls green, and once the paint was dry and the fumes were aired out, Kat put up large dinosaur stickers on the walls as I assembled baby furniture and hung Ethan's skateboard on one wall.

I read that the paint fumes aren't good for pregnancy, so I wouldn't let her into the room until I knew enough time had passed. Kat was mad at me, especially toward the end. But there was no way I was putting her or our child at risk. I eased the tension with foot rubs and midnight ice cream runs.

I lean my head down and place a soft kiss on my son's tiny head, breathing in his baby scent. Choosing his name was one of the fastest agreements we've ever had.

I just wish his namesake were here.

Fuck, I miss him.

I never imagined walking down the aisle without my best friend, my brother, in many ways. I always pictured him standing by my side, waiting with me, encouraging me through it all.

It was hard on Kat, too.

A couple of days before the wedding, she had a major meltdown. She drove to Columbia without telling anyone. I kept calling her, but she wouldn't answer. Finally, Talia called to tell me Kat was safe and sleeping at their place.

Kat called me an hour later, apologizing for leaving like she did. I wasn't mad that she left. I know there are times she just needs her best friend. Losing Ethan has been one of the hardest things we've been through.

We got married a little over two years ago. Our friends thought we were crazy for wanting to get married only six months after I asked her to be my wife. But we had spent enough time apart that we didn't want to delay.

As an early wedding gift to Kat, I finally relented and showed her a picture of my *I'm a Slave 4 U* Britney Spears costume—I wore tiny shorts, a pushup bra, and even had a yellow rubber python around my neck. I don't think I've ever seen her laugh so hard.

I can still vividly picture that day—me standing at the end of the aisle waiting for her. I was so anxious. I wasn't worried about getting married. No, I was concerned that Kat might change her mind.

It feels ridiculous now to think back and remember being nervous. Of course, she wouldn't change her mind. I smile at the memory.

I stood there fidgeting with my tuxedo coat, waiting for her. I kept looking at my groomsmen standing next to me and felt the gaping hole left by Ethan's absence.

But I finally saw her, Kat's dad walking with her, and my heart stopped.

I've always thought Kat was beautiful. But seeing her in her wedding dress? Fuck. She took my breath away.

Her dress was simple, with lace on the top and a flowing skirt. Her hair was pulled back into a simple bun. She didn't wear a veil; instead, she had daisies intertwined in her hair. I didn't know she was going to do that, and when I saw her inclusion of my mom, it reminded me why I love Kat so much.

She slowly walked up the aisle towards me, and it took everything in me not to run to her, pick her up, and kiss her before the ceremony even started. But somehow, my feet stayed planted in place. My eyes never left her.

By the time we got to the reception hall, all I wanted to do was take my beautiful wife back to our hotel room. Instead, I stood in the reception line, greeting our guests, barely able to keep my eyes and hands off Kat.

I smile at the thought as I take baby Ethan's tiny hand in mine, bring it to my mouth, and place a light kiss on it.

When everyone was finished eating dinner, it was time for our first dance. I was so nervous having everyone's attention on me. "Just keep your eyes on mine, Sammy," Kat said quietly to me as we walked onto the dance floor.

"That won't be a problem, my love." I took one of Kat's hands in mine, placing the other on the small of her back.

I pulled her close to me and felt my body relax as she leaned into me, her head on my chest. "I love you more than words can describe," I whispered into her hair.

"I will always love you, Sammy. She smiled up at me. That smile was all it took for me to forget that we were dancing in front of hundreds of people.

It was just the two of us as the room melted away.

"Is there something I can get you, Mr. Harris?" A nurse interrupts my thoughts.

"No," I look down at Ethan in my arms and then back up to her, "we're just going for a walk while my wife sleeps. Thank you."

She nods to me in acknowledgment, and Ethan and I continue our slow walk.

With Ethan joining our little family, I couldn't be happier. I was nervous when Kat said she wanted to try for a baby.

Of course, I was ecstatic about the trying part. But the baby part? I was terrified. Still am.

I've always known Kat would be a great mom. She's compassionate and kind. She seems to always know what others need.

But me? Fuck, I'm terrified I won't live up to Kat's—really my—expectations of me. But I'll do anything to make her, and this perfect boy in my arms, happy.

Ethan starts fussing, and I know I can't delay any longer. "Ok, baby boy. Let's go find Mama so you can eat." I raise his tiny body up, kiss his head, and start walking in the opposite direction, back towards the room where we're staying.

The only time I've left Kat's side has been to take Ethan on walks so she can rest or to talk to the nurses if Kat or Ethan needed something.

Ethan's been in either my arms or Kat's since our parents left after visiting hours yesterday evening. I wouldn't have it any other way. Putting him down and leaving him by himself is unfathomable to me—even if he's in the same room. I know I'll have to do it eventually, but that can wait.

As I walk back into the room, I see that Kat is awake.

"Hey, where'd you go?" She still looks tired, and I wish I could do anything to let her get more sleep.

The nurses coming in all throughout the night made it tough for her to rest while Ethan slept, and then, of course, she was up when Ethan needed to eat. I was, too. If Kat was awake, I would be too. I don't want her to feel like she's in this by herself.

"Hey, my love. We just went for a walk so you could rest. Isn't that right, baby boy?" I say the last part to Ethan. "We were just coming back because little Ethan is getting hungry."

Kat holds her arms out to me so she can take our son.

"Let me change his diaper first, and then he'll be ready for you." I make my way over to the changing table and get to work.

"You know you don't have to change all of the diapers."

I smile down at Ethan. "You carried him for nine months, and I can't feed him; changing diapers is the least I can do, my love. Isn't that right, baby boy? Mama can't do all the work." I coo at Ethan.

Kat chuckles behind me, and I can't resist looking at her over my shoulder. She's lying back on the hospital bed with her eyes closed. I wish I could take her home so she can rest more easily. Hopefully, a few more hours until the doctor gets in.

We could stay at the hospital for a couple of days, but Kat asked to be released as soon as possible. I want to think it's that she just wants the comfort of her own space, but part of me worries that she's stressed out from the last time she was in a hospital—the night her brother, my best friend, died.

When Ethan is cleaned up, I walk slowly over to my stunning wife. I kiss my son's head before gently transferring him to Kat's waiting arms. She gets settled with him, and the sight of my beautiful wife and perfect son takes my breath away.

I didn't know I could love this woman more, but seeing her with our son? I don't doubt that my heart was the size of the Grinch's before this.

A few months ago, I told my dad how nervous I was about being a dad. *"I don't know how to share my heart with him when Kat owns it,"* I said to him.

"Son, it's hard to describe, but that little boy will own your heart, too. There's room for both of them."

I couldn't imagine it then, but he's right. I would do anything for this little guy and the woman holding him.

I gently sit on the edge of Kat's hospital bed, not wanting to be far from the two people who share my heart. Leaning over, I place a soft kiss on Kat's forehead.

She looks up at me, her green eyes crinkling at the corners from her big smile. "He's perfect, right? How did we make such a perfect baby?"

"My love, did you forget how we made him?" I laugh quietly. "I can remind you, if you need me to." I beam at her, waiting for her response.

Her shoulders rise up and down as she laughs silently. "Sorry, Harris, you'll have to wait several weeks before you can remind me." Kat winks at me before kissing Ethan's tiny hand.

I stand up, wanting to give Kat more room, and make my way back to the uncomfortable chair. I don't want to be far from them, so I pick it up and move it right next to the bed.

Sitting down, I take Kat's hand in mine and bring it to my lips. "All that means is that I have several weeks to think of how I'm going to make sure your legs are shaking by the time I'm through with you." I wink at her and watch as the blush rises on her cheeks.

The sight is breathtaking.

"God, I love you," she laughs out.

"I will always love you, Kat." I kiss her hand again and lean back in the chair, watching my beautiful wife and our son.

Acknowledgments

This story began as a series of random scenes that kept coming back to me. One day while riding in the car, I finally started writing them down. Once I began, Kat and Sam would not leave me alone until their story was complete.

I never would have reached this point without the immense support and love from so many incredible people. I am deeply thankful to everyone who listened to me talk continuously about Kat, Sam, Liv, and Ethan. I am eternally grateful to the people who read numerous versions of this story and offered suggestions to make it better.

Thank you to my husband. You pushed me, supported me, encouraged me, and listened to me incessantly through this entire process. I wouldn't have made it this far without you. You, most of all, made me believe in myself and showed me that it's okay to want more. Buckle up for the next one, babe! I love you. Always have. Always will.

To my alpha and beta readers, Cheris, Irina, Jamie, Sara, Elle, Marbles, and Amanda, you helped me make this story significantly better than where it started. Thank you for reading, reviewing, and offering endless guidance. I can't wait to continue sharing stories with you.

T, you are everything and more. I'm at a loss for words to express my gratitude. Your friendship has meant so much to me, and I'm so lucky you've been on my team! Please don't ever leave!

D, thank you for answering all of my random questions, helping me through some of my writing blocks, and encouraging me to keep going. I'm just sorry this isn't releasing on your birthday.

Thank you to all of my ARC readers, reviewers, and everyone who took a chance on an indie author. You all are incredible, and I will be forever grateful to you.

Finally, to my sister. There isn't a day that goes by that I don't think of you. There isn't a day that goes by that I don't wish I could pick up the phone and ask for your advice. Thank you for the years you gave me. I love you.

About the Author

Amelia C Rose lives in the Pacific Northwest with her spouse, their two boys, and three cats. When not devouring books or writing, Amelia enjoys getting outdoors, kayaking, camping, and hiking. Amelia's stories range from contemporary romance to dark fantasy/romantasy.

Follow Amelia:

IG: author.ameliarose

TikTok: author.ameliarose

Website: www.authorameliarose.com